That Existential Leap:

a crime story

That Existential Leap:

a crime story

Dolan Cummings

Winchester, UK
Washington, USA

First published by Zero Books, 2017
Zero Books is an imprint of John Hunt Publishing Ltd., Laurel House, Station Approach,
Alresford, Hants, SO24 9JH, UK
office1@jhpbooks.net
www.johnhuntpublishing.com
www.zero-books.net

For distributor details and how to order please visit the 'Ordering' section on our website.

ISBN: 978 1 78099 495 6
978 1 78099 503 8 (ebook)
Library of Congress Control Number: 2016955581

A CIP catalogue record for this book is available from the British Library.

Design: Stuart Davies

Printed and bound by CPI Group (UK) Ltd, Croydon, CR0 4YY, UK

CONTENTS

Prologue

He called me Koshka. Koshka, Ka-Koshka, krasievaya Koshka. It was a pet name – literally – the Russian for little cat. But it was the first name I really felt was mine, a name I could grow in. My given name had been Nisha. But when I started high school, my parents had given in to my childish dislike of my Indian name, and I had been allowed to choose an 'American' name. I chose Claudette. Claudette was to be my own invention. Not a shy, goofy little girl like Nisha, but a cool, sophisticated girl who would be popular and have a great boyfriend. Well, you won't be amazed to discover that it didn't work out like that. But it wasn't that Claudette was just Nisha by another name. No. Claudette took on a life of her own, and turned out to be even goofier than Nisha. Claudette was not exactly unpopular: worse, she was popular with the wrong kids, the dorky ones. And of course she didn't have a boyfriend.

I don't know how or why that happened, but in any case I was glad to come home to Nisha at the end of the school day. For all her faults, Nisha felt like me, and I came to think of her as the real me, and Claudette just some phantom at school. I continued this double existence till Siegfried kissed me on the lips, twice, pushed a stray curl behind my ear and whispered, krasievaya Koshka. *Beautiful* little cat.

I had been a fiercely sentimental child. As little Nisha, I had felt a strong attachment to home and could not bear the thought of change. My sentimentality had clung promiscuously not only to my parents, my older sister Arti and our home in New Jersey, but to everything in it. I had an extensive collection of stuffed animals, each with a name and even distinctive imaginary character traits that I would explain to any visitor who cared to indulge me. I had a horror of losing any of those toys – I could make my heart swell and my eyes fill with tears just by imagining

Pooky or Panda forlorn in a puddle somewhere. (Even then I sensed this was an unhealthy exercise.) I was equally attached, though, to household junk, especially the Indian bric-a-brac that littered the house, but even ordinary stuff. I remember crying once because a neighbor failed to return a serving dish with a picture of a horse on it that my mother had taken over with some home-made sweets.

I grew out of it, of course. Or rather I became more discriminating. Instead of reaching out to the world and forming more grown-up attachments, I retreated into myself, like the Russians fleeing Napoleon or the Germans. In adolescence, I came to think of our home as my parents' house, and of my parents as part of the world rather than an extension of myself. I was alone, but secure in myself. By the time both my parents were killed when I was fourteen, I was able to take it in my stride. My best friend Roxanne – that is, Claudette's best friend Roxanne – matured differently, broadening her interest in the world without ever becoming alienated from her family. Indeed, her new relationships seemed to evolve by analogy with her family ties, while imperceptibly performing the opposite function, and transforming those family ties into grown-up relationships. I had no such virtuous dynamic to shape my relationships. It was all or nothing. When Siegfried kissed me, he became my mother and father, my world, my everything.

A voice at the back of my head told me this was a bad thing, a very bad thing. But I disowned that voice as resolutely as I disowned my family. I hurled myself into a new life.

Presentiments of greatness

> *Providence has not created the human race entirely free or entirely enslaved. It is true that it has drawn a circle of fate round each and every man which he cannot escape; but, within its vast limits, man is powerful and free; so likewise are peoples.*

For almost a year before that kiss we observed one another in the reading room of the New York Public Library, and somehow developed an affinity, though we never spoke. Then one Saturday afternoon as I approached the library, I saw Siegfried coming down the main steps, wearing a grey business suit as he always did, and with a beating heart I dropped my books. He stooped to help me, and his eyes flashed into mine, again. 'It's you,' he said. I suppose I blushed. 'Let me buy you a cup of coffee,' he said, carping the diem. 'OK,' I said. I can't remember much of the ensuing conversation, except that one way or another we established our mutual admiration, and from then on we both knew that our destinies were intertwined.

I was reading *Crime and Punishment* in Russian at the time, or trying to; I was taking Russian at school, but the pages of my brand new Russian-English dictionary were far more worn than those of the novel itself. It was an auspicious co-incidence, Siegfried said: he loved that book. He explained that he had picked it up in a bookshop back home not long before he'd come to New York, knowing it was a famous book, but very little about the novel itself. After the first few pages he had realized that he had to read it. It was his idea, you see. He was Raskolnikov, an extraordinary young man who would disregard law and convention in order to achieve greatness. This revelation had been very annoying for him, of course – the discovery that his brilliant and unique idea had been part of the general culture for well over a century. Having read the whole thing, however,

Siegfried had felt somewhat better. Dostoevsky had been trying to pre-empt and contain him, but Siegfried would not be so easily contained; he would show the world a different ending.

I was terribly impressed by all this, though I had barely finished the first chapter. I confess that I bought a translation after our meeting; Siegfried had suggested we discuss the book when I finished it, and I didn't want to wait a year for our next meeting. In fact, it was one week later that I approached Siegfried in the reading room to announce that I was ready. 'Very good,' he said. 'Let's have Kaffee und Kuchen.' That's coffee and cakes, in German, which seemed the most natural thing in the world.

'K&K' became a regular thing with us. We met every week in a place Siegfried had found down in the village. It was winter and I enjoyed being with Siegfried in the warm, bright coffee shop when it was cold and dark outside. He would always have an espresso and a slice of ginger cake, while I experimented with extravagant concoctions of cream and pastry and chocolate and fruits and cinnamon and all sorts of things. 'It's a wonder I don't explode,' I used to say. We discussed books and ideas at great length, and Siegfried told me about himself with abandon, sharing his hopes and dreams as best he could articulate them. There was something reckless, almost embarrassing, about his candor, his uninhibited ambition, but the more Siegfried talked to me, the more confident he became. And I was more smitten with every mouthful.

Then I would accompany Siegfried on his heroic walks about Manhattan. For a time I tried to advise Siegfried about subway lines and buses, which he used only rarely and with little planning. But he laughed when I warned he could end up on the wrong side of the park, for example. 'But there's a fence!' I protested, when he insisted he could simply walk across the park at any point he fancied. 'Fences and gates are just suggestions,' he said, flexing his leaping arm. Siegfried thought nothing of walking seventy, eighty blocks or more, and regularly even strolled the whole length of the island, or wandered over to the boroughs on a whim. There was something Napoleonic in his bearing. Without even knowing it, he would lead armies of pedestrians against the traffic lights, making a mockery of the jaywalking law. He walked fast and was unused to company, so as well as having to skip-walk to keep up, I had problems negotiating the various obstacles that littered the sidewalk, not least other people. He would dart repeatedly into narrow corridors that opened up in the human traffic, forcing me to slip in behind him rather than walk at his side. And time after time he would fall off the curb into the street when I followed him round the wrong side of phone booths and other street furniture. In time, though, he came to think of me as an extension of himself, and I was able to benefit from his formidable sidewalk skills.

It was on one of these walks that I first saw another side of Siegfried, one that put flesh on the bones of his ambition. It was getting dark, and we found ourselves in a quiet area near the Bowery. Suddenly I was aware of someone following us, two men, in fact, with menacing gaits and big coats. I looked round once too often and one of the men shouted for us to stop. Siegfried looked at him, and then at me, untroubled, and we continued walking. Then there was the sound of the men hurtling towards us. I turned, afraid, but Siegfried's arm was already waiting for me, and he put me behind him, launching himself forward in the same movement.

I had noticed before that Siegfried was possessed of an unusual physique. Although he liked to describe himself as barrel-chested and bull-necked, I am happy to report that this was inaccurate. A casual observer might have described him as the 'lean and hungry' type. But there was more, something about the way he moved. Now it was clear: Siegfried was barely human. As he launched himself forward, his shoulders dropped and the nervous tension he usually carried was gone, replaced by a cool flexibility. Now this extraordinary man was loose and muscular, with all the menace of a tiger.

The fight, such as it was, was over quickly. One of the men seemed to have a weapon of some kind, but before he could use it, Siegfried had thrown him into the gutter. Having head-butted the second assailant, who went straight down and didn't move, Siegfried turned back to the one in the gutter, and kicked him in the head before he could get up. That was it. Our assailants lay still, unable or unwilling to get up, Siegfried took my arm and we continued walking. I was shaking, naturally enough, scared nearly as much by Siegfried's metamorphosis as by the thought of what might have happened without it. Then he kissed me for the first time. Just a brush on the cheek to reassure me, but it changed things between us.

Although I was in love with Siegfried, I had never thought of him sexually till then. That sounds strange, perhaps, but he didn't seem to invite sexual thoughts. He had always been funny with me, very interesting, affectionate, chivalrous, but not sexy. I know it was terribly old-fashioned of me to be sunk by his fighting prowess, but I really think it was the kiss that clinched it: it gave me a sense of his bigness, that he could be so brutal one minute and so tender the next. I thought that was wonderful. But he didn't kiss me properly for several more weeks. And in fact, my infatuation was never without doubts. I was conscious that Siegfried had very quickly become the most important person in my life, and frankly I almost resented it. I was afraid of losing myself, and unsure if he was really worth the risk.

The fact is that Siegfried lacked charisma. Back home there had been occasions when he would be talking to a group of people and gradually they each lost interest and stopped paying attention. He would keep talking while looking around for an interested face, but sometimes he would end up talking to himself. Well I suppose I was the face he had been looking for all along: I welcomed his thoughts and made them my own. There was one time when he explained existentialism to me by holding my hand and putting on a French accent. I couldn't stop laughing, but I understood something I'd been struggling with forever. And all this made Siegfried very happy. It made me happy too, despite my uncertainty.

What I saw in Siegfried is hard to describe because it wasn't anything very obvious beyond his being clever and serious, but it had to do with the way he made me feel about myself. He gave the overwhelming impression of a great historical figure in his youth, and it was terribly exciting to be close to him. And undoubtedly my belief in Siegfried helped to dispel his lingering sense of embarrassment at his awkward existence in the world. He needed someone to see beyond his present, to discern his future. It was only by seeing what he was about to be that one could understand the real Siegfried. I could see it, or rather feel it, but I was reluctant to commit on the strength of a feeling.

Our relationship was necessarily of the present anyway, with all the difficulties that entails. We found ourselves playing characters from films, half-consciously acting out whole scenes from Siegfried's favorite film *Badlands*, for example, while we waited for reality to kick in. Nonetheless, both of us benefited immensely from our time together. I suppose that for the first time in his life, Siegfried did not feel lonely. Not that his loneliness had ever been a conventional thing. It wasn't that he had felt empty or bored; quite the opposite in fact. He had felt himself to be limited somehow by his own identity. Siegfried saw in me fertile soil for the thoughts spilling from his own troubled mind.

That first proper kiss came after a visit to the opera. We saw *Der Rosenkavalier*, and once again I saw a new side of Siegfried. During the bittersweet trio towards the end of the opera, strong, bold tears streamed down his face, and I began to cry myself, more in response to Siegfried than to the opera itself. This emotional side of Siegfried was something of a revelation, and yet it was somehow in keeping with the rest of his character. The missing link perhaps. Afterwards we wandered to the park. 'Do you want to go and look at that fountain?' Siegfried asked. We stood at the fountain, and when I turned my face from the fountain to Siegfried, he was already looking at me. 'Koshka, Ka-Koshka, krasievaya Koshka.'

We went to Siegfried's apartment, and I was impressed by the Spartan décor. In the living room he had a long couch and not much else. In the bedroom a futon and more of the same. He held me close for a long time, till eventually I whispered 'just do it', only later remembering that this was the Nike slogan. For his part, Siegfried would later compare the event to the famous chord from *Tristan and Isolde*. When it was over Siegfried held me close again and smiled wearily. I wriggled under him and pulled his head into my chest, offering comfort to my great and troubled hero. He brushed his face against my body, but the waking Siegfried could never properly relax in my presence. At the moment that he fell asleep, the full weight of his body sank into mine like all the cares of the world.

I had been living with my older sister since the death of our parents, and now I effectively moved in with Siegfried. Apart from occasionally getting on at me about college applications, Arti was pretty laid-back, and had confidence in my ability to look after myself. I was the clever one, she said. So as long as I called her every few days and reassured her that I was doing well at school, I could do as I pleased.

During this time I often had the feeling that Siegfried and I were acting a sequence in a movie, one of those compilations of scenes; the lovers laughing in a café, the lovers strolling in the park, the lovers letting their hands touch so awkwardly, all set to music to drown out the dialogue. Because the dialogue is so intimate that it's unfilmable; silly and trivial to an outsider. It made me wonder what would happen next: in a film, something bad would happen. I wondered what could possibly go wrong… In real life, though, things don't revolve around love affairs.

Other stuff happened.

Siegfried had been collecting interesting crime stories from newspapers and the internet: mafia stuff particularly interested him, but also anything that seemed unusually audacious or somehow colorful, as he put it. He had a number of stories in the last category, and he soon noticed that several of them had been written by the same reporter. There was little else to connect them other than that peculiar, perverse, almost baroque quality that attracted Siegfried, and it struck him as encouraging that someone else should share his interest. The reporter's name was Amy Wong.

Then Siegfried stopped for cigars one Sunday evening at a gas station in Queens, and found himself in the midst of a robbery. He later recounted this to me in detail. After making his purchase he had been distracted by a headline and picked up the newspaper, and apparently he was not noticed by the motorcycle-helmeted thug who charged into the store. He lowered the paper and watched as this ungracious criminal brandished a sawed-off shotgun in the face of the young clerk and demanded all the money in the register.

As the clerk moved to open the register, the robber saw him toss something under the counter. He pushed the young man against the wall with the point of his gun and reached over to find the object. After thrashing around with his arm for a few seconds the robber produced a small cardboard box and placed it triumphantly on the counter. The clerk began to grind his teeth furiously and his face grew as red as his hair. The box contained dozens of little plastic capsules packed with money. The raider whooped with delight and stuffed the capsules into his jacket. Then he invited the clerk to keep the small change in the register, and made to leave.

The red-faced young man cracked. In a rage, he began hurling candy bars at the stunned gunman. Cigarettes, batteries, anything that came to hand was sent flying at the robber. And as the robber lifted his weapon, Siegfried decided it was time to act. He launched himself at the gunman with only his newspaper for a shield. Naturally, Siegfried overpowered his opponent. The shotgun fell from his hands and skidded noisily across the floor-tiles, and the robber escaped as Siegfried rushed to secure it. The young clerk meanwhile, having launched himself over the counter in pursuit of his assailant, had tripped over the debris that now littered the floor. He lay there cursing furiously as Siegfried picked up a few capsules that the robber had spilled.

'I'm guessing these are supposed to be in a safe,' he told the kid. The kid sat up in resignation. 'This was gonna be my last day on the job,' he confessed. What a bummer! To have your own, quiet little heist ruined by an armed robber. And now, instead of disappearing with a small fortune, the kid was left to explain to his boss why he had spent a whole weekend dropping money into a cardboard box under the counter instead of down the plastic tube into the safe. Or to disappear with no money, risking arrest and imprisonment for someone else's crime. Siegfried was moved by the kid's predicament. He looked around the store: it was old and kind of beat up, not part of a big chain. 'Does the closed-circuit TV work?' he asked the kid.

'Nope.'

'Well that's something.'

And there were no other witnesses. Siegfried looked outside into the peaceful, near deserted evening. A station wagon pulled into the empty forecourt. 'OK, kid, get behind the counter and act normal. The situation is fixable.'

It was reported the following day that disaster had been narrowly averted during the night when thieves used home-made dynamite to blow open the safe in a Queens gas station. Fortunately fire fighters had been called, and the resulting fire had been extinguished before the fuel tanks could be ignited. The gas station was owned by a Russian family, and speculation quickly began that the bombing was mafia related. Much wilder speculation surrounded the question of what had been in the safe. A police investigation was continuing.

The most detailed and interesting report on the incident was by Amy Wong. She pointed out the flaws in the various theories of what had happened, and suggested that this was something uncanny and peculiar, not like other crimes. This was the work of someone, she surmised, who saw every tangled shoelace as a Gordian knot. Siegfried was delighted with that. I was less sure.

One night not long after the gas station incident, Siegfried and I both awoke suddenly. A bad dream. We moved closer, taking comfort from the fact that we had shared the same dream. So close, so in love that our unconscious thoughts collided. So close that we were almost the same person. Then dread overcame me. What if we really were the same person? What if we shared the same dreams because Siegfried existed only in my imagination? I awoke in a cold sweat to find Siegfried still there, there in the flesh. And I pressed myself gratefully against the wonderful, wonderful flesh.

The lad never meant it

Who is this Siegfried, this mysterious figure who so transfixed our narrator, and who seems at this stage in her story to promise so much he cannot possibly fulfil? It's bound to end badly, no? Well, in any case, he belongs no less to another story, but one from which he is absent. That indeed is the source of his mystery in this other story, which it falls to me to tell, though I am just as absent from it. Unlike the little American, I am not a character in this story, or in any other. My perspective is that of an outsider, an eavesdropper, even, albeit one of unnatural perspicacity. More of that later, but now to our story, which continues from where Siegfried left off across the Atlantic in Glasgow – no mean city – Siegfried's home.

Home. Indeed, Siegfried was missed by a kind of family, though not his own. His friends, two brothers, John Paul and Tommy Gizzi, noticed his absence and were perturbed by it. The two had also a rather older brother, Steph, who was a police sergeant, and important for our purposes because he connects Siegfried with a certain other character we'll encounter in a moment. A few weeks after Siegfried's disappearance, having ascertained that Siegfried had left his job, but having no way of contacting his actual family, John Paul and Tommy asked Steph to look into it. Nobody had filed a missing person report, and Siegfried had not been imprisoned or hospitalised. He did have a police record, though, from a bar fight the three friends had got into shortly before he left.

Siegfried had been interviewed at the time by DS (now DI) Alexander, who happened to be Steph's best friend. Alexander might be considered an older, more law-abiding version of Siegfried. Think of him as yin to Siegfried's yang, if you can bear to consider that all humanity is contained in two different versions of sullen Scottish manhood. Steph asked Alexander if he remembered the case. He did, vaguely. Steph told him that Siegfried was a friend of his brothers', and was missing. Alexander had always found the Gizzi brothers amusing.

'Did I know him? Was he at our school?'

'No. Some proddy school, same one as Jamsie, I suppose. He was his pal.'

Alexander had a vague memory of Jamsie. 'He's the guy who used to get hash for your brothers, isn't he?'

'Did he? I don't remember.'

'That's why you're not a detective,' Alexander said, not for the first time. 'Anyway, I've not heard of him since he had his run in with the Fullerton boys. I think I'd remembered a name like Siegfried. Ask the drugs squad.'

'I suppose, but I don't think he was into that. Jamsie's more of a chancer than a proper doper – him and Siegfried used to talk about doing banks, apparently. Not serious, or at least Jamsie wasn't. But Tommy reckons this guy might actually have done something.'

'Ask the drugs squad.'

Sergeant Gizzi duly consulted the drugs squad, and they couldn't help either. John Paul wanted to file a missing person report, but since he didn't know Siegfried's family to check with them if they knew where he was, his brother told him it would be a bit daft. Siegfried was cagey about that sort of thing, John Paul explained, realising that really Siegfried had been an occasional drinking buddy rather than a close friend, and suddenly feeling a bit daft right enough.

'Well, I'm sure he'll show up,' said Steph.

'Aye.'

He didn't show up, but Siegfried began to play on DI Alexander's mind. Alexander had been impressed at the time that this guy had battered the Fullertons, over some slight in a bar as he remembered, and got away with it. One of the witnesses, admittedly a young girl, had described him as 'tigerlike.' Now,

Alexander could run after a suspect and look after himself if things got physical, but his movements lacked grace. He could certainly not have been described as tigerlike. He blamed a cruciate ligament injury he'd suffered playing football at the age of eighteen.

Here's a funny thing: despite his middle-class background and cerebral character, Alexander had nearly become a professional footballer. On his debut game for the Airdrie first team, he collided with a clumsy Partick Thistle defender who 'left his foot in': it was an ugly injury. It came at that vital moment, just as Alexander's career was about to take off, and he never got back into it. Still, 'the lad never meant it,' as they say; 'it wasn't a malicious challenge.' Actually, it *was* a malicious challenge, but malice is a trivial thing.

The lad never meant it. A few months after enquiring about Siegfried, Steph used this expression about Darren Currie, the sixteen-year-old toe-basher Alexander was about to charge with murder. Granted, attempting to slash someone's face is somewhat less trivial than attempting to scythe down an opposing footballer. But the disproportionate outcome had been the same: in attempting to slash his face, this stupid wee bastard had cut a boy's throat and killed him. He never meant that.

When Alexander went into the interview room, Currie's expression hovered in a familiar fashion between gallus defiance and snottery collapse. Five minutes later, it had made up its mind, and Alexander handed the kid a hanky. Darren was a typical wee ned: malicious in a casual sense, but not a bad person. Apart from the murder. A thing like that can really screw things up for a person. Alexander read the charge and explained Currie would have to make a statement describing what had happened; his lawyer would help him with that.

A little later Alexander returned and picked up the kid's statement. 'Are you happy with this now?' he said with one eye on the lawyer, who nodded wearily. 'I never meant it,' said Currie tearfully.

'You swung an eight-inch blade at a boy's head. Did it not occur to you that might be a wee bit dangerous?' Suddenly that seemed a mean thing to have said. 'Look, give us your autograph, and then you can get some sleep.' Alexander exchanged glances with the boy's lawyer. 'Initial here, and here. Good lad.'

Steph was waiting in the corridor for Alexander. 'Hurry up,' he said. 'The lads are waiting in the pub for us.'

'I told you I'm not going,' said Alexander, irritated. For some reason, Steph was convinced that Alexander would join a lads' night out at some ridiculous lap-dancing place, despite Alexander's persistent assurances to the contrary. The outing had been Steph's idea, and everybody else had fallen in behind him, leaving Alexander looking like some kind of feminist. Not that the others were especially laddish. Even Stuart Munro went, and as Alexander and Steph were fond of saying, that guy's idea of canteen culture was having a yoghurt for lunch. Probably that's why Steph was in denial about Alexander's refusal to go along. Without Alexander's collusion, the enterprise was unavoidably fake.

When denial didn't work, Steph tried appealing angrily to Alexander's sense of camaraderie, but Alexander just growled at him. As far as Steph was concerned then, he was a selfish bastard. 'Aye, OK,' Alexander said, and went home to his wife.

'You know I hate all that shite,' he said when she asked why he was home so early; she had been convinced by Steph that he would be stumbling home in the wee small hours. Well didn't she know him at all? What kind of wife encourages her husband to go to a strip club anyway? She gave him one of those smiles that made him love her and hate her at the same time, perhaps because it suggested similar feelings on her part.

Ambivalence again, like the little American's. Women never seem to know their own minds, do they? Or maybe that's just human beings. The mixed feelings between Alexander and his wife were not, I think, the same as Koshka's existential ambivalence about the mysterious Siegfried. Alexander's wife was a grown-up woman, and her doubts more chronic than acute – or so it seemed to her at the time. There is also a young woman in our story, though, who might or might not be persuaded to view Alexander with the same wide-eyed urgency with which Koshka viewed Siegfried. Before we meet her, let me explain something about Alexander.

Steph and Alexander had gone to school together – St Stephen's, a private Catholic school, an unusual academy for any 'polis,' let alone two. Steph was a Catholic, Italian family and all that. Alexander was one of a few kids from Protestant families, but by the age of twelve he was a better Catholic than anyone in the place. Sin, guilt, confession: he loved all that stuff, couldn't get enough of it. But it wasn't religious scruples any more than feminist ones that kept him away from the lads' night out. Alexander had gone through a personal Reformation and embraced Protestantism at the age of fifteen – a cultural as much as religious rebellion that had also involved adopting Rangers Football Club, which had horrified his teachers and peers even more – and made the easy transition to atheism by the time he left school. Since then, he had never had the sense that his feelings had anything to do with anything or anyone other than himself. Three years studying theology in Cambridge, though an unusually rewarding consolation for the loss of a football career, had done nothing to disabuse him of the sense that he invented those feelings out of nothing.

When Alexander met him for lunch the day after the lap-dancing thing, Steph had forgotten his displeasure at Alexander's refusal to join the gang, and resumed his usual cheery demeanour. Steph is a tubby, jolly sort of person, Alexander often noted to himself; you know the type. Although he was a uniform and Alexander was a high-flying detective, they met regularly in the canteen to eat egg and chips and exchange racist jokes. (They couldn't talk about football on account of Steph's still erroneous affiliation.) After a brief report on the previous night's debauchery – including a particularly embarrassing story about Stuart Munro trying to get change from a lap dancer – they talked about the Currie case. The primary witness was Leanne McGlone, Currie's girlfriend. Alexander had gone to see her at home that morning, but she'd left early for school, so he had called the school, which turned out to Alexander's great surprise to be St Stephen's, and arranged to interview her there in the afternoon. 'Watch out for Father Barry,' Steph warned him. 'He'll have you back in the box before you can say, "No Pope of Rome!"'

That was very funny, but Alexander was more interested in telling Steph about Leanne's older sister Adele, whom he'd met in the morning. He had a story of the sort on which his friendship with Steph thrived. Leanne's family were show people, gypsies, and they lived at the caravan park in Partick. That was good already, but Adele was something else. She was fantastically good looking for a start, even at a quarter to eight in the morning, and she swore like a trooper. Alexander told Steph how she had subjected him to an intense five-minute oration of remarkable if obscene articulacy, during which he had been allowed to say nothing.

It is sadly beyond my powers, and anyway it would be an affront to decency, to reproduce this monologue here; Alexander himself could only remember a few choice phrases for Steph, but certain points emerged that would prove to be of some import. Adele had conceded that Darren Currie was a stupid wee bastard, but insisted that it was his pal Joe Brown who should really be in jail. Darren was totally in awe of the guy, who was one of those sad-bastard twenty-year-olds who surrounded himself with schoolkids to make himself feel big. Adele suspected that Brown had been somehow responsible for whatever Darren did. Her tone only softened when she spoke of Leanne. Towards the end of her oration, Adele had said, 'She's not going to have to testify.' It was a statement rather than a question or a plea, but this had struck Alexander at the time merely as a peculiarity of Adele's speech.

Steph confirmed that Joe Brown was a known associate of Currie's, though there was nothing to connect him with the murder. He'd heard of Adele, too, though only through the sort of uncreditable gossip that always surrounded good-looking women of her social class. The association of show people with 'rides' was particularly unfortunate, he noted.

Alexander met Leanne over tea that afternoon in a little office away from prying eyes, except those of his old adversary Father Barry, who was actually a laidback old soul who had played a major role, some of it unwitting, in Alexander's spiritual and intellectual development. Leanne was a scholarship girl studying Latin, French and music: her obvious brightness bridged the social chasm between the caravan park, not to mention Darren Currie, and St Stephen's. That was one mystery solved. The next question on Alexander's mind had been how he was going to get Leanne to testify against her boyfriend. Looking at her now, he wanted to know why she had been going out with him in the first place. He asked her instead whether she would like a biscuit. She wouldn't. He decided that he wouldn't have one either. Father Barry picked up a custard cream and went next door to take care of a few bits and pieces, he said.

'Right,' Leanne said decisively.

'Right,' said Alexander. Then he realised that his spiel was redundant. She was about to say something. He tried to look receptive.

'It wasn't Darren that killed the guy. It was Joe Brown. I saw it all.'

'But you've already told the police it was Darren…'

'I know, I know, but that wasn't true. That was what Joe told me to say.'

'And he told Darren to say that too, to confess to murder…?'

Alexander looked at the girl incredulously.

'Yes.' She looked nervously resigned to the next question. 'I don't know why I went along with it.'

Alexander gave her a look.

'That's not important anymore. I'll testify against Joe, and so will Darren if you tell him I am.'

The reason for the pair's initial lie *was* important, of course. If the case against Currie collapsed, this weakened the case against Brown from the start. You cannot just flip a case around and expect the new defendant's lawyer not to notice. Alexander didn't doubt that Currie would withdraw his confession. He believed Leanne about the whole thing right away; her story had that peculiar quality, truthfulness, and suddenly he knew that Darren hadn't killed the kid. It was obvious. And of course Adele's opinion backed this up. But truthfulness was a precarious foundation for a case in court. Without material corroboration, the whole thing would look like a belated conspiracy to pin the blame falsely on Brown.

All this only confirmed Alexander's dislike of confessions. Confess to a priest and you're rewarded with absolution; confess to a polis and you're rewarded with a prison sentence. In either case, confessions are nearly always given in bad faith. Alexander's confessants typically gave him a list of extenuating circumstances and looked at him as if he would give them ten Hail Marys and send them on their way. They never meant the crime; why should they mean the confession? A totally false confession was not so exotic, either, and this wasn't the first that Alexander had had to deal with. Some, like this one, were based on intimidation; others a genuine desire to protect the guilty. In common with insincere confessions, these were attempts to short-circuit the system, to fake a resolution in order to put a stop to things. To Alexander it was insulting, like being thrown a bone. He preferred to keep going till he had the truth for himself, till he understood the crime.

Some people believe that to understand a crime is to forgive it. Alexander knew very well this is nonsense. Quite the reverse: a crime that defies understanding defies condemnation. The criminal justice system is not designed for dealing with mad people or bad people. It is for reasonable people, good people who do bad things. Most criminals believe in the law they are breaking. Thieves believe theft is wrong; murderers believe murder is wrong; even rapists believe rape is wrong. The best they can do is to come up with a rationalisation for their own particular crimes, or have their lawyers do it for them. Alexander wanted to know what had happened and why, and he wanted the criminal to know and to understand that he was not an exception; he was wrong – and to know that Alexander knew it too. That was resolution, and that was what he would now seek with Joe Brown.

Visiting the boys' toilet on his way out of St Stephen's, Alexander looked at the graffiti on the wall above the urinal – 'Celtic Rule,' 'Rangers are shit.' He was about to make some amendments when he spotted another scrawl – 'Leanne McGlone is a slut.' He wanted to hit someone. That was his first reaction: to find the little shit who had written this and hit him hard. It was a disgraceful thing to say about a girl. Why would somebody write something like that?

After this initial wave of revulsion, he calmed down. It was natural that these boys should resent her. Leanne was a beautiful girl, and had spurned her classmates in favour of a wee ned from Partick, and a Protestant at that. Just for a second, Alexander was glad that Currie was a Protestant. It was him and the wee ned against these little papes. Jesus – the crap that goes through your head. Having rationalised the graffiti, he wondered why he had reacted the way he had in the first place. For all he knew the girl *was* a slut. But he felt ashamed of that thought. It was an ungentlemanly thought. He had no reason to see her as anything but a sweet and innocent child. And he'd already noted that she was beautiful… Fine, then – he'd been offended because he fancied her. He could live with that. He looked in the mirror as he washed his hands. (He didn't usually wash his hands after using a urinal.) You think too much, he said to himself. But as he was leaving the room he looked again at the wall: 'Leanne McGlone is a slut.' And yes, he felt a certain thrill. Are you happy now?

Alexander found Joe Brown dead on the floor of his mother's kitchenette. He had been stabbed seven times in the chest and stomach. Alexander suspected Adele McGlone immediately. The forensic surgeon later confirmed, 'This guy stabs like a girl.' Further, it seemed that in his death throes, Brown had repeated, in his own blood on the kitchen floor, the characterisation of Leanne found on the wall of the toilets at St Stephen's.

Adele was missing right enough. After the preliminary search of the caravans and interviews with her family, Alexander went to see Leanne at school again. 'I know she did it, Leanne. She told me she hated him before she did it, and now she's disappeared. It's not exactly the perfect crime…'

Nothing. She looked a little teary.

'Leanne, we found her fingerprints on the knife.'

Now she started giggling. Great giggly tears rolled down her cheeks. 'You liar! She wore gloves *and* disposed of the murder weapon carefully. She told me!' Alexander would have liked to think he had pulled off a smart trick, but he hadn't. Leanne was delighted as much as outraged by his brass neck, and she couldn't resist pulling him up. 'You won't catch her anyway. *Abiit, excessit, evasit, erupit!*' She was hysterical with laughter now. So charmingly hysterical that Alexander had to bite his lip to keep from joining in.

It transpired that Adele had been Brown's girlfriend not long ago, but he'd mistreated her. For her part, Leanne had resented his dominance over Currie; Darren's mother, she called him. Leanne was cagey about the details, but it seemed that with Currie out of the way, Brown had been sniffing around her. That was Adele's motive, or at least the trigger, and it also explained his valediction. The rest was more intriguing. Adele had told Leanne she had a boyfriend in America. She had decided to start a new life with him under an assumed name.

Flight records confirmed that Adele had left Prestwick for New York only hours after Brown's murder. She had known that Leanne would be compelled to tell the police everything she knew, so she had made it easy by telling her nothing of any use. The gist of Leanne's story seemed to be that Adele's boyfriend was Batman – a mysterious hero who had swept into her life by battering some lowlifes. She had no idea where he lived or even what his name was. All Alexander could do was notify the appropriate agencies and keep Leanne under surveillance for a while. Of course, Brown's own murder complicated his trial somewhat. The case against Currie was dismissed, but the Procurator Fiscal was not about to try Brown posthumously, and so for the time being things were out of Alexander's hands.

As for Leanne McGlone, her life was ahead of her. And what was she thinking? That's a mystery to me as much as it was to Alexander. I can't take you inside *her* head. Rather than speculating about such things, I'll hand you back for now to her American counterpart.

Staring into space

What is a man,
If his chief good and market of his time
Be but to sleep and feed? A beast; no more.

I half wake about eight or nine, roll over and push my face into my bedclothes. Sleep. Maybe I repeat the procedure two or three times over the morning. Early afternoon I sit up in bed. No school, no job, no place to go. Just two enormously abstract objects: life and the space to live it in.

Before meeting Siegfried I had assumed I would graduate high school and go on to university. But in Siegfried's company such assumptions disintegrated. My life was not simply ahead of me, but instead somehow in the air. I – or perhaps more accurately Claudette – had applied to several good universities, but when the moment came, I found myself unable to summon the enthusiasm to follow through. Siegfried's example suggested other possibilities, wonderfully imprecise possibilities.

I curl up and take a deep breath of bed-air, and for a second I relive the dream I've just been having. I am too much awake now to get more than a fleeting sense of it though, and so I roll onto my back and stare at the ceiling to retrace my thoughts. But now I'm troubled by the thought that perhaps the dream I have in mind is not recent at all, but one that I dreamed some time ago. It is a kind of déjà vu, but one I have vued many times déjà? Thought and dreams, I muse, exist in a constant present where nothing ever changes. Finally I decide that the dream, whenever I first encountered it, is not so interesting anyway, so I stretch out on my front and exhale.

It did occur to me that my attitude was adolescent – even that Siegfried was somewhat adolescent – that the grown-up thing to do would be to go to school like other people, to work hard and accept that sometimes life was less exciting than we might hope. But I was suspicious of such self-conscious grown-upness. Grown-up might be a description of someone's behavior, but to make it a reason for doing something seemed, well, childish. Maybe if my parents had still been alive, they'd have pressured me into going to school, and then I could have done the grown-up thing while clinging to my adolescent reluctance, striking a pose of resistance with a slacker attitude and cynical take on the whole enterprise. Among my schoolfriends I had observed both self-conscious grown-upness and such adolescent grudging compliance. I resolved rather to be grown-up about my adolescence. Like Siegfried, I would obey my inner voice and take responsibility for the consequences. If only it were as simple as obeying; right now it felt more like guessing.

My uncertainty about myself made me think of the hours that my friend Trudi and I had spent in front of the mirror at the age of nine or ten, practicing laughing and smiling, and how I had never got good at it like Trudi had. That stuff had make me aware of manners, how some people obviously took care of the way they comported themselves, and others seemed not to. And how some people seemed to take care to look as if they didn't. Trudi was always happy to play the girl, and I knew other girls who rebelled against girlishness. But I was always terribly ambivalent: I didn't want to be a girly girl like Trudi but neither did I want to 'be myself' in the labored way that other people played themselves. I was obsessed with this problem, but it wasn't an obsession that had any direction.

My head rests on the pillow in such a way that I can hear-feel the vibrations of my pulse. Casually I pick up the beat, tensing and untensing various muscles in a private horizontal dance as I grapple with the decision, or fail to. Now there is music that must be coming from upstairs: insistent snare drums with an electronic tone that gets narrower and narrower. I'm not moving my body anymore and it occurs to me that I'm experiencing rather than listening to the music. I feel drugged but also somehow freer to think, like a Buddhist monk or whatever, and I am even afraid to move in case I shake off the trance. I ignore an itch on the side of my face as the music funnels itself into a single narcotic high-pitched tone and I am detached completely from my situation.

Before I can reach enlightenment, my stupor is interrupted by the sound of the front door opening. Siegfried. I try to get up, not wishing to seem lazy. I sit up very slowly, and fumble to extricate myself from the duvet. I have crawled halfway across the floor before I realize that I'm still dreaming. Then I have to fight hard to wake up properly, finally coming to still face-down with my body stretched out rigidly and my arms folded beneath me. I sit up and throw aside the duvet just as Siegfried comes into the room. I look up guiltily through tousled hair and mumble that I had a headache.

Siegfried sat down beside me and put his arm around me and kissed the back of my neck. 'Is that better?'

'Not really,' I might have said, though it did feel nice. 'Where have you been, and what am I supposed to do when you're off doing whatever it is you do? My life revolves around you now, and I don't know what any of it means. Sometimes I think you're just crazy, and it's getting a little bit scary. What is with this whole Raskolnikov thing? What are we doing?' But I didn't say any of those things. Instead I smiled girlishly and put my arms around Siegfried, and that felt nice too.

We went out for K&K, then, but my uncertainty came with us. Uncertainty about myself, about Siegfried, about what exactly my role was to be in our thing together. In this sense, my position was the clearest expression of the incompleteness of Siegfried's own ambition. His bold and heroic rejection of the world had not yet matured into a concrete alternative that could accommodate anyone else. And I had very little reason to trust that it would. And so?

I would have been afraid of losing myself, except that I didn't know who I was anyway. I wanted Siegfried to tell me, but he couldn't. Over coffee, I asked him what he did when he was out without me. He shrugged. There was no secret. He wandered around looking for opportunities, but he wasn't very good at it yet. He still went to the library, to museums. Sometimes he played a sort of game, sneaking into office buildings and seeing how far he could get without being challenged, and then talking his way out of trouble, pretending to be someone else. He'd even tried a few cons he'd read about, and made a bit of new money – several thousand dollars in the past couple of weeks, in fact – but that too was just a game, and he found it embarrassing to talk about. It wasn't what he wanted, wasn't in the spirit of what he'd talked to me about before – all the heroic stuff that had made me fall in love with him. He apologized and asked me to be patient. He was sure that if he just kept looking about him, something would come up.

And what was I to do in the meantime? I had an idea all by myself. Pending new developments, I decided to write down the stuff he'd told me, and to make him fill in the gaps so I had the whole story. I began with a title, 'Siegfried: an existential crime story,' and resolved to spend my days composing the story of Siegfried's adventure so far as well as I could.

Later that night Siegfried and I sat at home listening to music. I drifted off on the sofa, and when I awoke Siegfried was standing at the window, staring more at the glass than at the city that lay beyond it. Smoking. Still listening to Wagner. The air was thick with cigar smoke and violins. Swirling, hanging. And Siegfried amid it all. Heroic, unhinged. It was Wagner's *Siegfried*, the music I mean. I wondered what Siegfried was thinking about. When he turned around and looked at me, I pretended still to be asleep.

As I began to write the story of how Siegfried had got to where we were, something did begin to happen around and about us. In fact, it seemed to me that the beginnings of a new narrative were cohering subtly in front of us, like images in an inkblot test.

The first figure to appear was the young man Siegfried had helped in the gas station. Siegfried recognized him at the library as we were leaving after spending a morning there together. The young man blushed awkwardly when he recognized Siegfried on the stairs, and physically hesitated, allowing Siegfried time to overcome his own customary awkwardness and greet him. He introduced me as his girlfriend, only to realize he didn't know the young man's name, nor the young man his. Having remedied that, Siegfried avoided potential embarrassment by simply explaining to me that he had met Ernest in the course of his adventures. Ernest seemed pleased with that, and after further pleasantries, Siegfried asked if he had plans for the evening. He didn't, and so we agreed to meet for drinks. It turned out to be the first of several evenings we would spend together in the weeks that followed.

Ernest hailed, of all places, from Glasgow, Kentucky. He was a law student, whose job in the gas station continued to pay for his studies, now that he had abandoned his plan to give up both for a new life. But he was still interested in the idea of another life, a grander, more adventurous life. Like Siegfried, Ernest was quiet and apparently shy until called on to talk about something important. No good at small talk but always ready to make a speech. I was jealous, of course, both of his sense of purpose and of Siegfried's admiration for it.

It turned out that Ernest's abortive heist at the gas station had been more or less directly inspired by *Crime and Punishment*, a coincidence with the air of inevitability. The episode now caused him some embarrassment, but while he had resumed his routine of work and study, like Siegfried, he would not let that deter him from pursuing his greater ambition. He later gave me a copy of a paper he had written while planning the heist, his own equivalent of Raskolnikov's journal article on the 'special right' of extraordinary men. Ernest had not submitted the paper for publication or shown it to any of his professors. It was not addressed to the academy, he said. He had not known to whom it was addressed. But in it, he articulated things I had been feeling for a long time, the same kinds of thoughts that had brought Siegfried to New York. His treatise was not limited to criminal law: Ernest argued for the superiority of spirit and good faith over rules and injunctions in every sphere, criminal law included. It was indeed less an academic paper than a manifesto for heroic defiance, and I wondered what an NYPD detective might have made of it had Ernest been arrested for the gas-station heist.

Over the course of one evening, Ernest unwittingly convinced me once and for all not to go to university. He spoke fondly of one of his professors and he was clearly in love with the law, but what he had to say about the everyday reality of college life was much less encouraging. It wasn't, I think, the prospect of hard work that put me off. Living with Siegfried was enough to convince me that inspiration needed *application* to be realized. He had perspired enough to show the greater aptness of that less happy rhyme: perhaps the true advantage of a university is that students are given something to apply themselves to, and don't have to sweat the big stuff like Siegfried. But to what end? Ernest said he felt only a fleeting affinity with his fellow students; certainly he had never shown his paper to them. They would have thought him insane, not because of its content, but simply because it would earn him no credit and would not further his academic career. With one or two exceptions, Ernest's fellow students were studying law because they wanted to be lawyers, or more precisely because they wanted good jobs. Going to school for them was a means to a means. And application without inspiration is supplication. More school was exactly what I didn't need.

I devoted my days to writing, then, but found this was harder than I'd supposed. Too much like work. I'd never had a job, but I was reminded of how much I had disliked schoolwork, despite apparently being good at it. My Indian parents succeeded in raising a fully American daughter without thinking through what this meant: thanks to their self-sacrifice and diligence, I inherited not a trace of their immigrant work ethic. Schoolwork was always a chore connected only remotely and intermittently to my own hopes and aspirations, which, come to think of it, were remote and intermittent all by themselves. Thus, the habits I had developed in the course of my life till now lent themselves perfectly to my present situation, and provided no ready means to transcend it. Still, my mind was made up, and I persisted, however woefully.

The young person's guide to doing something in a week goes like this. Monday you don't do anything; you have all week after all. Tuesday you do half an hour's work, and congratulate yourself for getting ahead of the game. Wednesday you take off to recover. On Thursday, there is no avoiding some hard work: obviously it's too late to do the thing properly, so you have to figure out some way to postpone it, or scale it down to something that can be done tomorrow. But Friday is practically the weekend, so it's just going to have to wait till next week.

I know what you're thinking: that's an outrageous stereotype. In fact, our young people today are as hard-working and motivated as ever. And yes, OK, maybe that's true and I'm sure I would say as much if the stereotype were rehearsed by some sanctimonious civics instructor harping on about the Gilded Age or the Greatest Generation or whatever. But I'm talking about my own generation – or a substantial part of it – about my school friends, about myself. I think I'm entitled to some self-criticism here. Because try as I might, lying in bed at noon staring at the ceiling, I can't seem to help living the stereotype. Call it laziness or call it existential crisis, I can't seem to get started.

My decision to write rather than going to school gave me an inkling of self-confidence, but gradually I realized that the future narrative ahead of me was not simply there to be perceived; what

I could see ahead of me depended on what I did, or did not do. As long as I merely waited for Siegfried to 'do something,' the inkblot would keep reverting to a shapeless blob. Instead, I had to use my imagination, which is a lot less fun than it sounds.

So here I sit in the library where we met, still staring into space, still waiting. Sometimes in the library I imagine rails hanging from the ceiling, that I might swing from, perhaps onto imaginary platforms or chutes on which I could slide through holes in the wall into other worlds. That's not an allegory; I never had the sense of being transported to other worlds by books, never really got that idea. Quite the reverse. Books are all too real, difficult, insistently rather than romantically 'other.'

I find myself fiddling with my new silk scarf, adjusting its position on my shoulders. I have recently developed a passing interest in fashion, in how clothes can change the way a person looks, and even taken to experimenting with my own style. I've always liked dressing up. But it troubles me that it seems fictional: 'dressing up' as whom? Clothes are for being seen in, but seen doing what? Shopping for more clothes? Being a 'sex object,' or a business person? I don't want to be those things. And yet dressing to 'be oneself' raises the awkward question of who one is.

I don't know about you, but I was beginning to bore myself, and so I plunged myself into Siegfried's story. Siegfried dressed conservatively; his younger self would have disapproved. The teenage Siegfried had vowed he would never work in an office as he had indeed gone on to do, never wear a suit as he still did for no obvious reason. He would sk8 4ever and listen to indie rock forever. He had been aware, of course, that such teenage thinking was a cliché, that people said those things in adolescence and then went on to live conventional lives. But he was determined that his own rebellion would be different, go to the heart of the matter, change the world. His realization in young adulthood that he had not done that, that he had misconceived what it meant, was perhaps what started Siegfried on his journey to New York. This adolescent rebel would not grow up without taking the world with him.

Siegfried: an existential crime story, by KK Koshka

Part one: dissatisfaction

A man's thoughts are vanity, sir.
They come unasked and gang away withoot a dismissal and he canna help them.

Siegfried sat on the top deck of a bus somewhere in Glasgow, *Paradise Lost* open in his hand. *The mind is its own place, and in itself, can make a Heaven of Hell, a Hell of Heaven.* But he was distracted, thinking about something stupid he had said at the office, when it occurred to him that he could embezzle money from work and not have to work anymore. He could be a criminal. Still, the thought merely nestled in a corner of his mind, while he went on worrying about his faux pas; needlessly torturing himself, in fact, over something his colleagues had surely forgotten. He did this sort of thing all the time. It was an article of faith for Siegfried at that time that the constant sense of embarrassment he felt was a condition of his youth, and not of life in general. At his better moments, he felt as though he were looking back on himself from the future, from a time when his blundering thoughts and actions would make sense as part of the development of his character. What he didn't know then was that his impending resolution would come not in spite of his distraction, but as a function of it.

People used to say that Siegfried wasn't quite human, whatever that means. He often seemed to be sleepwalking, and people would snap their fingers at him in an effort to wake him up. But he was driven by something inside, and he regarded external reality, that is *immediate* reality, as a distraction, a series of obstacles. In common parlance he was aloof, distant, a dreamer with his head in the clouds. Away with the fairies. Otherwise he might have been diagnosed as an over-intellectualizer, a pathological narcissist or a dangerously schizoid personality. Naturally, he didn't much care. Nonetheless, he couldn't stop thinking about himself. He had to justify every word and every gesture for himself after the fact: it was unbearable. And it was the realization that he must not allow himself to be contained by reality that kept tearing him away from self-examination. Simply analyzing himself made him part of the external world looking in, rather than the subject of his own world, whatever that might mean.

'You can't be yourself on your own,' Siegfried liked to say. It was this conviction that had driven him against his own nature to seek company during his final months in Glasgow, not just by opening his stupid mouth at work, but even by spending time with childhood friends who somehow had never really gone away. It didn't work. He didn't like himself in company. Which is to say that he didn't like what other people saw of him. *O, wad some Power the giftie gie us, to see oursels as ithers see us!* Siegfried saw too much. The problem was that in cold, objective terms, Siegfried was not great. He wanted to be judged on his future greatness, and not on his present mediocrity. How could he fail to be mediocre in the suffocating present?

Siegfried had nobody to talk to. It was not a simple problem: lots of people would have been happy to 'listen,' even sympathetically. But Siegfried's thoughts weren't addressed to anybody he knew. Occasionally he did think of something he wanted to say to John Paul or Tommy or whoever, and he would happily carry a phrase or two in his head until he saw them again. Usually these were thoughts about soccer, an interest he had developed only recently, and which therefore had an artificial quality that was of course not lost on him. To his own surprise, he had in fact persuaded his equally unsporty friends to join him in supporting Glasgow Rangers, despite the fact that two of them were from a long line of supporters of the rival team. But the thoughts that really bothered him were at once too personal and too abstract for his friends. Only Jamsie might understand, and he had recently gone off to teach English in Japan. Siegfried often imagined talking to Jamsie.

In the real world, he made do with John Paul, who was in fact well qualified to be Siegfried's partner in crime should he have wanted one. He was intelligent, almost naturally deviant, and unusually confident in his rejection of respectable society. He came from an Italian family that owned a string of chip shops, and he liked on occasion to affect the manners of a young mafioso. In fact, he worked part-time for a community arts project. He was less thoughtful than Siegfried, which he considered to be a virtue. Somehow the two young men got on very well. In fact, John Paul and Siegfried were the joint masterminds of an unconvincing universe. John Paul didn't know that, of course. But it was a constant source of anxiety for Siegfried.

More than once – before his realisation that his job offered a more practical possibility – Siegfried had tried to suggest collaborating on an audacious robbery. This usually happened when he became exasperated by his friends' lottery fantasies, which seemed far more ridiculous to him, but however serious he felt himself to be, it always came out sounding like a joke. He was sure it was not. They wanted large sums of money, and the most direct way to acquire such sums was theft. They were intelligent, resourceful, fit young men, more than capable of planning and executing a bank job or something similar. Why not?

If it had ever occurred to one of Siegfried's friends to insist that robbery is wrong, that might have been interesting. But their conversations never got on to such lofty territory. Instead, on those few occasions when they thought Siegfried might not be joking, his friends – usually it was Tommy – would wearily explain that such ideas were silly, unrealistic. That was just Siegfried's point, though: he refused to accept 'realistic,' a crassly self-justifying adjective as far as he was concerned. It meant only, 'this is not the sort of thing people like us, people in our situation, do.' To think like that was to condemn oneself to being the same sort of person, in the same situation, in perpetuity. Siegfried wanted to create his own reality, and in order to do that he had to disregard what appeared to be realistic. Or as he often ended up putting it in frustration: 'Fuck reality. Fuck it!'

Fuck it indeed, but until Siegfried acted on his conviction he was left having stupid arguments. As long as Siegfried had no credible programme of action, his ideas were just embarrassing. And the more he talked about it, the worse he felt: it was like carrying around a stinking lump of bullshit. So for a while he learned to keep it to himself, a private dream. But Siegfried could still smell the stench even if no-one else could, so these occasional arguments were inevitable. Siegfried had to justify himself to himself, and the only way to do it convincingly was to expose himself to others. To expose himself and then to struggle to maintain credibility. It wasn't easy, but Siegfried was never completely humiliated. Hard as his position was, Siegfried could not lose the argument. He could not lose the argument because he was right.

There are so many things that one doesn't do in life simply because they are not done. The narrow and predictable biography of the average human being is really quite disturbing. What is more disturbing perhaps is that this is no secret. Everybody who has ever bothered to think about it can see that there are infinite possibilities in life, and yet still they plow that same furrow, or at least choose their furrows from the same field, so to speak. Siegfried wouldn't have objected if they were talking about a good field, but really it isn't a good field at all. The deliberate choice of a dull and miserable life seemed to Siegfried to be inexcusable, and yet it was the norm, the reality.

Of course there is such a thing as reality. But it was always obvious to Siegfried that reality imposes itself on the individual at more than one level. There are the laws of physics and there are the laws of social engagement. The latter are no less 'real,' but they are considerably more open to negotiation. Moreover, this aspect of reality in turn presents itself on different levels. It's easy enough to break the petty conventions, and that's not unusual. There are plenty of wacky eccentrics around to prove that. Then there is the law, enforcing what you might call moral reality, and of course those unnatural rules are generally there for good reason. Siegfried was not opposed to civilization, by any means. Nonetheless, as long as one's purpose is civilized, breaking the odd law can give an individual a lot of space. And not just bad laws, but even perfectly good laws. (One may choose to murder a particular person for a particular reason, but that in no way diminishes one's belief that, generally speaking, people should not kill one another.) Moreover, it is easier to commit murder than to steal a large sum of money without at least threatening to kill, because there are physical measures to prevent the latter. The law itself, however morally compelling, has more in common with a lock on a bathroom door than a lock on a safe: it's a reminder not to cross an imaginary line, rather than a physical barrier. A gentle kick is enough to break it. Which is to say you *can* break these rules, as long as you're able to negotiate the consequences. This was why Siegfried was so fascinated by crime.

On one occasion before Jamsie had left for Japan, John Paul, perhaps in an indulgent mood, had suggested drugs smuggling would be a better bet than armed robbery. John Paul knew about drugs; it was part of his job. In fact he had been into heroin himself before that. It was something he kept quiet, but not because his employers would have objected: former addicts were prized in the field for their moral authority. The problem was that John Paul had never got addicted. Like anything else, in fact, he had not been able to stick at the heroin for more than a few months. His 'works' now lay in a shoebox under his bed along with his old Tae Kwon Do kit and a collection of broken art materials, the forlorn detritus of six-week enthusiasms. So for half an hour, the friends had discussed drugs smuggling – weighing up the most promising types of drugs, sources, routes and channels of distribution – none of them, not even Siegfried, taking it remotely seriously.

Even in jest, though, Siegfried had found something exhilarating in the fact that they were talking this way. After all there was no reason why they should not have been serious. Only Tommy refused to join in: he was terrified that their pretended criminality would shatter the masquerade of reality. For his own part, Siegfried revelled in the illusion of free conspiracy, while deep down he knew that John Paul and Jamsie were not with him at all. They were less uptight versions of Tommy, playing along with Siegfried just to annoy him, and never taking it remotely seriously. If anything, their sense of what was realistic was even stronger than Tommy's, and that was what gave them the confidence to joke about it. In stubborn reality, Siegfried was on his own.

Then on the bus, this little thought.

Part two: quickening

> *Freedom and power, and above all, power! Over all trembling creation and all the ant-heap!*

The very evening following the one when Siegfried's first real, and very private, criminal plan had come to him, he reluctantly went along to a party with his friends. One secret reason – semi-secret even to himself at the time, but perhaps indeed the only reason – he had agreed to go was that he expected Nicole would be there. Nicole was a girl who had apparently told someone who told someone that she wanted to go out with Siegfried. Or maybe it was just 'get off with' rather than go out. 'Whatever,' he had told whoever it was at the time: the difference was academic because Siegfried had no intention of doing anything about it. Had he felt otherwise, however, he was unsure what doing something about it might have involved. Siegfried was too self-conscious to go with the flow even in everyday conversation. He felt that he would have been surrendering himself. When someone asked 'how are you?' Siegfried could never just say 'fine,' like everyone else. Instead he would say 'swell' or 'super,' something stupid just to avoid saying 'fine.' Dating was always going to be a problem.

As he approached the party, Siegfried was stunned to see Jamsie, who was supposed to be in Japan, loitering on the corner. 'What the fuck are you doing here?!'

Having established that Jamsie had been deported from Japan for bureaucratic reasons, they exchanged peasantries – 'Splendid.' 'Smashing.' – and Jamsie announced that he'd been waiting on the corner for Siegfried's 'girlfriend,' but now guessed she was probably at the party already. So the two young men proceeded together without Siegfried's girlfriend.

'What girlfriend?' Siegfried asked on the way up the stairs; this response was supposed to be wearily nonchalant, but it came just a second too late to avoid revealing intrigue. Jamsie winked, and Siegfried told him to fuck off.

Once inside the party, Jamsie was joined by Tommy in the ritual teasing of Siegfried on this subject. He was 'on a promise,' they said, and yet they knew he was so sad he would run away. It bothered him that 'sad' is considered an insult. Is 'happy' a compliment? It transpired that the girl in question was not Nicole but Chantal, whom Siegfried dimly knew and tried not to notice standing across the room in a dress that made her hard not to notice. He had no idea whether there was any basis to this new rumour, but actually, he was a bit disturbed by the casual way in which the last contender had been swept aside. Jamsie revealed that Nicole had given up on Siegfried and was going out or getting off with someone else. ('The faithless bitch!') Siegfried had had enough of being the centre of the wrong kind of attention, so he wandered off, leaving Jamsie and Tommy to talk about whatever they talked about when he wasn't there.

Siegfried looked around the room. He didn't like the people and the way they were dressed, or the music, or anything about the party. Before he could leave, John Paul appeared with his girlfriend, and insisted Siegfried tell her about a fight they'd been involved in a few weeks earlier. Of course Siegfried had his reservations about the whole 'semi-articulate sidekick sings the praises of (brazenly self-conscious) vain hard-man' thing, but the incident had been weighing on his mind anyway. So he mumbled a series of incomprehensible phrases punctuated by gratuitous obscenities and occasional approving glances at John Paul while he went over the thing in his head.

It had been, as John Paul said, a classic bar brawl; too classic, in fact, to avoid an aura of inauthenticity. Fights don't need a reason. Everybody knows that. But doesn't that assume something else? A kind of implicit, ambient alienation perhaps. One that ordinarily requires no explanation. But ordinarily refers to other people. Siegfried did nothing without explanation.

Nothing without justification. There was nothing ambient about his alienation.

John Paul seemed pleased with Siegfried's rendering of the tale, but his girlfriend got bored and wandered off. Just the two of them then. John Paul moved closer. 'Have you talked to Chantal yet?' he asked, like a father checking his son has done his homework. Siegfried shrugged. John Paul shook his head. Siegfried had tried to explain things to John Paul before, how men who sleep with lots of women are really poofs. 'That's an interesting theory,' John Paul had said, both indulgingly and dismissively, like he did. It worried Siegfried that his words of wisdom often failed to ring true. On this subject he had given up trying, indefinitely suspended the argument. But within that argument lay the germ of Siegfried's greatness.

He left the party alone then, with the feeling of dissatisfaction weighing on him heavier than ever. He hated everyone he knew. It occurred to him that if he could somehow have met himself he would have hated him too. There was nothing of Siegfried in him, in the person experienced by other people, or at least nothing of substance. And yet if this person had died there and then, the real Siegfried would have died with him. The thought terrified Siegfried. He resolved then to be his own man at all costs. Fuck 'em all, he said out loud as he reached the foot of the stairs.

Siegfried never saw himself in other people. He never even took anybody to be his contemporary; everyone seemed either older or younger than himself, even people he knew to be his own age. He had disliked the way the people at the party had been dressed, the music they listened to, but there was no other style with which he identified. His own cheap business suits and his preference for classical music had been an attempt to affect a default, but this would have struck him as absurdly pretentious if anyone else had done it. Anything that could be pinned down, labelled, used for advertising purposes, was beneath contempt. The otherness of others was their particularity. The point of being a self is that one is nobody in particular. One's self is the default, the universal norm; it is for others to have character, distinction, amusing quirks of personality. Such were Siegfried's thoughts as he walked home.

When he got to the River Clyde, he paused on the bridge to look down at the black water. He felt in his pocket and removed a used train ticket. He'd been to Loch Lomond that morning, alone. It had been a whim, part of his campaign of moodiness. He made the ticket into a little boat, dropped it on the river and watched it sail west under his feet. Then he looked up. It was a clear night with countless stars visible: a sight which is supposed to humble its beholder. Instead, as ever, Siegfried became dizzily megalomaniacal. His bitter relationship with reality forgotten, he casually resumed composition of his own world.

Resuming his walk home, he soon realised that he needed to pee, so he walked up a side street and into a shady lane. When he finished he noticed the sound of people shuffling around further down the lane, a fight perhaps. He zipped up and walked silently towards the noise. A few yards on he saw three figures in a doorway: a girl backed up against the door, and two men. One of them seemed to be kissing her neck and groping her breasts roughly, while the other had his hand up her skirt. She didn't seem to be struggling, but that just made the spectacle even more hideous. Siegfried bolted forwards and threw a punch at one of the men, catching the side of his head. The other turned to face him and Siegfried kicked him in the groin. The man squealed. The first man punched Siegfried in the stomach, so Siegfried hit him again in the face, drawing blood this time. The other man was down, the girl looking on enigmatically. Siegfried took a step back. The one with the bloody face kicked out at him without much effect and then retreated, swearing. The other staggered after him, leaving Siegfried with the enigmatic girl. 'You'd better come with me,' he said, nodding his head in the opposite direction to the one taken by her companions/assailants. She hesitated for a few seconds and then followed Siegfried.

'You can sleep on the sofa,' He told her when they got back to his flat, but she had already found Siegfried's bedroom and was lying on the bed bouncing seductively. And pouting. 'OK,' he said. 'I'll sleep on the sofa. ...Uh, what's your name?'

'Adele.' He turned to leave the room, accidentally crashing his head into the edge of the door as he did.

'Didn't that hurt?' she asked, looking concerned.

'Yeah.'

'Well, why didn't you shout or something?'

'Do you think it would help?'

'Jesus,' she said. 'You must be a riot in bed.'

'I doubt it.'

She gave him a disapproving look.

'Would you like to come to New York?' he asked her.

'OK.'

He left for work early the next morning. Siegfried's job was in an insurance firm's life department. He was responsible for the payment of claims. And though it had felt real to him for less than twenty-four hours, the sting had been obvious from the start. If no premiums were paid on a policy for thirteen months, it was put into a sort of limbo. It floated in cyberspace you might say, until a policyholder appeared to make a claim. If this didn't happen then eventually, and somewhat mysteriously, the money reverted to the firm. Ordinarily it would have been a big gamble for an employee to rip this money off. It would have been easy enough to invent a claimant and pay out the money, but if the actual policyholder had shown up after the event, the guilty administrator would have been exposed immediately. In fact a couple of guys at another firm had been convicted and jailed for just such a misfortune a year before. But Siegfried was prepared to free himself of this risk by simply disappearing. He spent most of the day shuffling policies on the computer to make an electronic smokescreen to cloud his departure. He booked tickets for the first plane in the morning.

When he arrived back at the flat, Adele was lying on the floor watching *The Godfather*. He had the trilogy on video, part of a small collection of films he watched over and over. 'I quit my job,' Siegfried said. 'How d'you say "I quit my job" in Spanish?' She didn't know, and nor did she recognize the line from *Badlands*, so he had to tell her, 'Somethin' mi trabajo.' He sat down. 'We're leaving in the morning, OK?' She shrugged an affirmative.

But she didn't get it. Adele was a looker and admirably compliant, but their accidental acquaintance was no basis for anything else. Siegfried felt he'd simply not be able to make her understand him. He decided to leave without her. She would have to stay behind, like John Paul and the others. This added to his sense of failure, but he realized that he would have to make the leap alone. This final resolution made everything easier. Siegfried got up early and wrote Adele a note telling her she was welcome to his video collection. He assumed that she had a home to go back to. He had never asked. He washed and left.

As the plane lifted into the stratosphere he closed his eyes and grinned broadly. The little voice in his head that had been laughing at his foolishness was now silent. The little voice that had told him to be realistic, to grow up, was no more. The little voice that had been reading from the authorized script (put the money back, learn to have fun, get a girlfriend, be happy) was gone forever. We are not little men, he said to himself. We are big men.

Destiny and distraction

How exciting! With the preceding, our American narrator has truly matured into an author: it would not surprise me at all if she'd made half that story up herself. No matter. I shall resume the story of the big man in Glasgow, a story whose narrator demurs to talk about himself.

Shortly after the Currie case, Alexander worked a child murder that now came to court a year later. He had worked the case consummately, despite, he considered, rather than because of the fact that the murder had been committed on the night his own child Morgan was born. Any horror or rage he had felt had been submerged in the cold intellectual flow of procedure. Methodologically at least, Alexander was not a maverick. Admittedly, though, he had a certain flair in court. Having performed his day job so well, the detective's fine amateur-dramatic turn in the witness box was enough to extinguish the killer's last hope of evading the truth, and left the defence advocate tearing up his own script.

Fresh from this theatrical battle, Alexander marched triumphantly into the station with DS Chalmers, who had also testified. The desk sergeant, Mackenzie, already knew all about the result. 'Job done, Alexander,' he grinned. 'Job done?' said Chalmers. 'He fucking buried the cunt!' He paused, realising there were civilians waiting at the desk. Alexander grinned indulgently, guiding his herald to the security door, and Mackenzie buzzed them in. More uniforms greeted them inside, patting Alexander on the back. 'Good on ye, big man.' 'Some man, some man.' The big detective had never been one of the lads, but the lads respected someone who could put down a child killer; that was what detectives were for. There was speculation that Alexander would be put in charge of the 'vampire case,' another and especially disturbing high-profile child-murder investigation, which was currently going nowhere.

Mackenzie's head appeared again in the corridor. There was someone waiting for Alexander, an old woman called McGlone. He was suddenly intrigued. He and Chalmers entered the interview room to find an old woman sat with two shopping bags, propped on either side of her on the table, each adorned with a grinning cartoon face. Her own face was wizened and apparently toothless, and there was the trace of a beard. She looked up, and seemed pleased to see Alexander. 'Good morning, Super Inspector Alexander. My granddaughter Leanne said I should ask fir you.'

'I see. But it's just plain old Detective Inspector,' he corrected.

She ignored him.

Alexander exchanged glances with Chalmers. 'What can I do for you?'

The old woman reached into her bag and retrieved a video cassette. 'Evidence,' she said.

'Evidence of what?'

'You'll see.'

Alexander rolled his eyes, but Chalmers was still excited from the trial. 'There's a video player next door.' The old woman smiled expectantly.

It was CCTV footage, dated a year and a half earlier, showing an alley, from what seemed to be the back entrance of a shop. Alexander looked at the old woman. 'It's at the right bit,' she said. 'Wait a minute… There, look!' Three figures appeared: two men and a woman. As they came closer it was obvious that they were young, teenagers. One of the men pushed the woman against the wall. Adele, Brown, Currie. A fourth figure appeared, a young man in a suit. He stood, taking in the scene till he was noticed by Currie, who was standing back a little from the action and alerted Brown. There were words, and then Siegfried (for it was he) launched himself at Brown in what could only be described as a tigerlike manoeuvre. Brown was felled and Currie made a half-hearted lunge that was easily repelled by Siegfried. There was further scuffling and then Brown and Currie withdrew with more words. Siegfried gesticulated to Adele and they exited in the other direction.

'Where did you get this?' Alexander demanded, detecting a glimmer of familiarity as Chalmers wound the tape back to get a better look at Siegfried. Alexander's first thought was that this was an attempted rape, and unbidden, his detective brain began weighing up the difficulties of making a case against a dead assailant with no complaint from the victim. (Was the fact that the victim had subsequently murdered the assailant a help or a hindrance?) Before he had given up on this vain challenge he realised the attempted rape was probably not the point. 'And why are you showing it to me?'

'That one,' Mrs McGlone said, tapping her finger on the screen where Siegfried's image was now frozen. 'He *bewitched* my Adele. If she killed that stupid boy he deserved it, but it was this yin that put her up to it.'

'Wait,' said Alexander, ignoring the old woman's peculiar turn of phrase as his realisation of what the pictures showed spliced with his recognition of the man in the suit. 'This is the boyfriend in America?'

'I'm sure of it.'

'Adele's mysterious boyfriend is Siegfried,' said Alexander to himself. 'Take this up to Fat Boab and get stills of this guy,' he told Chalmers. Now he turned to Mrs McGlone to ask why she hadn't shown him this before, and demand that she tell him everything she knew about Siegfried. She must have known that Alexander would use anything she gave him to pursue Adele for the murder of Brown, but it seemed her desire to find her granddaughter was stronger than any wish to protect her from the police, and perhaps she really did believe Adele would be found guiltless. I've said already that Alexander was no maverick, however, so you'll understand that her answer was less than satisfactory: 'I only know what the spirits tell me.'

He rolled his eyes again. 'Did the spirits give you the tape?'

'No. I found that in Adele's room. *This morning*. Not my fault your lot never found it.' She gave him a look.

'Where did *she* get it?' Alexander demanded. Mrs McGlone shrugged. 'That I don't know, but I know there was something about the way that man moves. That's how I consulted the spirits, and they told me he's a devil. Unnatural.'

'Right. I don't suppose they gave you an address too?'

Alexander had a vision of going to New York to track down the mysterious Siegfried, but he quickly decided this was not realistic. Strathclyde Police detectives did not get to jet around the world in pursuit of suspects, not at least with so little to go on. Instead, he would have to prepare a stack of paperwork to send to the relevant agencies. It would be a drag, and in due course, the airline would confirm that a Siegfried had flown to the US shortly after the Adele incident, and they had no record of his returning.

Alexander went to the shop the CCTV footage had come from, a petrol station in fact. It was recently refurbished. There had been a fire in the office just over a year ago, caused by a freak accident, the manager said. He'd never heard of Adele, or so he insisted. Alexander didn't believe him, but had nothing else to go on; whatever story was lurking here would have to remain a mystery. One line of enquiry remained, though. Alexander could at least see if Steph's brothers had heard anything in the year and a half since Siegfried had disappeared.

Steph explained that since Siegfried's departure, John Paul had left his job in community work to pursue a new career as a film-maker – in fact, he wanted to make a documentary about Siegfried. This alarmed Alexander, as he had no desire for his investigation to be part of a film. More intriguingly, John Paul had resolved to go to New York in search of Siegfried. Unlike Alexander, he had the freedom to do that, and Alexander felt a pang of envy. It was he who needed Siegfried on official business. That phrase caused him to pause, however. Alexander often found himself analysing his own thoughts much as he might scrutinise a statement made by a suspect. Official business? It was not a phrase he used. He was deluding himself, then. His curiosity about Siegfried was as much personal as it was professional.

But it was the detective in him who asked Steph how John Paul intended to find Siegfried in New York. Apparently he had nothing to go on. 'Maybe I can help,' suggested Alexander, though whether this was the detective in him or some other part of him, he wasn't sure. 'Here's a free tip. Your wee brothers and their pals are Rangers fans, right?' Steph rolled his eyes in the affirmative, and Alexander continued. 'New York is Tim City. But there might be one or two bars where they show Rangers games. If Siegfried is keeping up, he'll be there. That's where I would go.'

Steph passed the tip on to John Paul, who, it turned out, was sufficiently committed to his film that he was keen to meet Alexander for more, even if Siegfried was of interest to the police. He was sure that he had nothing to give away anyway, and thought he might benefit from police information. Alexander did have something to give away, and he knew it was his personal curiosity that took him to a pub in the West End to meet John Paul a few nights before his departure. Tommy was there too.

It was busy, and they had to stand in a corner with their pints. Alexander was much older than Siegfried's friends, and felt slightly awkward. He asked John Paul what his film was actually about. Tommy grinned, while John Paul mumbled defensively. The basic treatment was that Siegfried was an outsider who had rebelled against society, but John Paul's material was a bit thin. So far he had Jamsie reminiscing about a fight, and Siegfried's interest in armed robbery (John Paul laughed apologetically when he mentioned this, and assured Alexander that this had always been symbolic). The rest would have to come from the

New York trip: John Paul was convinced he would find Siegfried doing something extraordinary. Failing that, Tommy pointed out, it could be one of those documentaries about the director searching for something he never finds, but John Paul just scowled at this.

'Did he not say anything unusual when you interviewed him about that fight?' he asked Alexander, and quickly followed this with a request for an interview on camera. Alexander said it was against policy, which he supposed it might well be. 'Did you know Siegfried's girlfriend?' he asked, to change the subject. The brothers laughed. Then John Paul looked concerned, 'Are you serious?'

'Yes,' said Alexander. 'What's the joke?'

'Siegfried never had a girlfriend that we knew of. He's… shy.'

'Are you saying he's gay?'

'No…'

'Not actively, at least,' Tommy said.

'He's not gay,' said John Paul, irritated, 'but he's never had a girlfriend that I know of. Did someone say he did?'

'No,' lied Alexander, 'but young guys generally do, don't they?'

John Paul smiled. 'That is just the sort of assumption Siegfried would object to.'

Interlude: the comedy of Eros

You don't fall in love with 'the girl on the bus.' It just isn't done. Maybe you look at her chest, maybe you chat her up even. But to fall deeply and silently in love with a stranger who just happens to be a regular on the same bus: that would just be sad. And there is nothing worse than being sad, right?

Steph was never sad. He never took the bus either. Steph's and Alexander's schoolboy friendship had been consolidated during the time the two had spent in uniform together as police recruits. Steph's indestructible cheeriness seemed to complement Alexander's own dour demeanour. Alexander used to call him the laughing policeman, and in return Steph called Alexander 'Taggart,' after the dour TV detective, which only served to flatter his considerable ambition. Steph's ambition was rather more modest, as is generally the case with happy people.

Back then, Steph was always telling Alexander about this girl he was after. He insisted on spilling out his heart in the pub every night, despite Alexander's obvious lack of interest. (Maybe Steph mistook his silently pained expression for that of a 'good listener.') Anyway, the girl was called Laura, and she looked just like the young Lauren Bacall, Steph insisted. Which kept Alexander slightly interested. Steph was smitten, but he was worried that she thought of him as a friend rather than a potential lover. This struck Alexander as peculiar, since he had never had a female friend and could not imagine how such a state of affairs might come about. It didn't matter though: Steph wasn't after Alexander's advice. He just enjoyed flaunting his anguish.

Alexander preferred to keep his anguish to himself. To mull it over on the bus. And, yes, love did make him sad. It is not just that an unfulfilled desire made him sad. He found love itself very hard to live with. He couldn't eat properly. He couldn't sleep properly. He talked nonsense to himself. The girl on the bus looked just like the young Lauren Bacall. Three or four times a week Alexander would see her on the 66. The rest of the time he'd see her in his head.

Laura was a nurse, which gave Steph hope: cops and nurses, he told Alexander, make ideal partners. Lauren didn't look like a nurse to Alexander, though. She had a distant quality that jarred with his impression of nurses as earthy, practical women. On their bus journeys she watched the window as if it were a cinema screen, only occasionally returning his gaze and causing him to stare at the floor. Despite her unnursely demeanour though, Alexander had a hunch that his Lauren was indeed Steph's Laura. It was the sort of thing that happened to him. He thought about the situation for a while, and then he suggested to Steph that Laura was probably out of his league.

It was Alexander's honest opinion, and since the alternative was getting into some protracted *Cyrano de Bergerac*-type nonsense, he thought it best to smother Steph's interest forthwith. Happily, Steph seemed to share this analysis of the situation. He had obviously suspected from the start that he was onto a loser, and so he resolved to be satisfied with Laura's friendship. She was such a nice and down-to-earth person, he said, that he would hate to risk losing her as a friend. This down-to-earth business left Alexander wondering what Steph saw in *him* as a friend, and frankly doubting the sincerity of his sentiments. People find comfort in the strangest ways.

It troubled Alexander for another reason, too. He just couldn't see Lauren in Steph's description of Laura, and he began to wonder if he had made a mistake. No, Steph said, Laura did not have a twin. And so Alexander studied his beloved on the bus, looking for traces of uniform, a name badge, an upside-down watch, sensible shoes. None of the above was in evidence. Lauren dressed unusually well for a young woman; she was stylish rather than trendy. Chic. And mysterious. He watched her face for as long as he dared and it gave nothing away. All he could say was that Lauren looked like a troubled drifter, a femme fatale. The sort of woman who would fall for the smart, laconic detective Alexander was not yet but was about to be. Of course he thought about following her off the bus to find out more, but he would have felt stupid doing that. Time after time then, he sat close enough to touch, unable to touch. As far as he could see, his only hope of reaching her was through Steph. And then only if *Lauren* really were *Laura*.

In desperation, Alexander considered making a move for Lauren on his own, striking up a conversation on the bus and charming her into loving him. But how? Why would she even have liked him? If she had liked him, frankly he would have thought less of her. It wasn't that Alexander suffered from low self-esteem, just that he hated what other people saw of him. He was just a polis in clunky polis boots. Entirely unlovable. If, despite everything, Lauren was Steph's friend, then at least Steph could read her a rough draft of the real Alexander, teach her to appreciate his deeper, darker qualities. As long as she and Alexander were just strangers on the bus though, he was entirely without hope. And entirely miserable.

For this reason he was unable to drop completely the hope that Lauren really was Laura, so when Steph asked him to help him with an old sofa he was giving Laura for her new flat, his heart spun uncontrollably. Alexander told Steph it would be nice to meet his friend, but this uncharacteristic sociability was a thin cloak for his own undying hope. As the two men heaved the sofa up six flights of stairs, the clashing aftershave fumes were quite overwhelming.

'Hi there,' said a voice from above. Alexander turned his head to see *Lauren* at the top of the stairs. He dropped his end of the sofa, causing poor Steph to tumble down several steps under its weight. Laura laughed. 'I thought you policemen were supposed to be strong!' She gave Alexander a teasing look. He blushed and picked up the sofa, smiling apologetically at Steph. 'I know your face from somewhere,' Laura said as she opened the storm door to make room for the sofa.

Ten minutes later the three were installed on the sofa in front of the television, drinking tea and talking about the weather. Which made Alexander think. Instinctively, he had denied ever having seen Laura's face before, except of course in *To Have and Have Not*. She had been quite charmed by the comparison with Miss Bacall, which Steph had evidently never shared with her. This revelation, along with the unexpectedly domestic ambience that had quickly resumed, gave Alexander an insight into the mysterious 'friendship' between his friend and the object of his desire. Quite simply, Steph was useless with women. It was hard not to be amused. Alexander managed to contain his delight in a slight smirk though, before turning his attention to Laura.

She was dressed in a knee-length skirt and a cashmere sweater: perhaps a little more Doris Day than Lauren Bacall, but a world away from the down-to-earth nurse described by Steph. A less-is-more application of mascara brought out something cool and urbane in Laura's expression. Alexander detected a new element in his feelings for her: it was lust. All this was making unreasonable demands of his tea, so he suggested they go out for a drink. The motion was passed unanimously. On the way out, Laura tapped Alexander on the arm. 'I know where I've seen you: it's on the bus. You're the guy who's always staring at the floor.' He said something forgettably stupid in response. She smiled in a way that combined how-are-we-this-morning? with you-know-how-to-whistle-don'tcha? to devastating effect. He took a deep breath.

It was raining outside, and while Steph huddled under Laura's umbrella Alexander walked manfully in the rain. Several times he exchanged glances with Laura, quietly thrilled that he no longer had to look away when their eyes met (or, more accurately, he no longer *felt* that he had to look away). He could tell that Laura was warming to him, and by the time he arrived at a suitable bar they were practically an item. It really was that fast, which was most disconcerting. Still, they all managed to act as if nothing had happened. Over drinks, Steph facilitated the customary exchange of personal information between Laura and Alexander. It transpired that Laura had been a ballet dancer in her teens and was currently taking a part-time course in choreography along with the nursing. In contrast, Steph explained, Alexander was an incorrigible workaholic. He was destined to become the youngest DI in the history of the force, Steph said, but his maverick ways would make him a thorn in the side of the establishment. Alexander smiled, but was strangely disturbed; it struck him that Steph had summed up his character a little *too* easily. Alexander was perhaps not as deep and dark as he had thought.

As he struggled to come to terms with what was happening then, to adjust to the fact that he was now in love with a real person, to face the sudden possibility of actual happiness, Alexander's usual quick wit and ready repartee deserted him. An awkward silence descended.

'Tell us that joke about the one-armed twin,' Steph suggested. 'I've still not heard it.'

He had heard Alexander telling the one-armed twin story to the sergeant that morning, and evidently had decided that he was missing out on something. Alexander looked nervously at Laura before beginning.

'It's a true story, an anecdote rather than a joke, right. I'm telling you this now because it's not that funny and I don't want you to get your hopes up. OK, there's these twin brothers who both work in the same supermarket. One of them has two arms but the other one has one arm missing, right? Or was it left? Let's say left, right? He used to have both arms but now only the right one's left…' Laura giggled gratifyingly.

'Is this the joke?' Steph interrupted.

'No, this is padding. I told you, this story needs all the help it can get. So one twin has two arms and he's the manager, and the other twin…'

'Just how unfunny are we talking about?' Steph interrupted again.

'Remember *The Two Ronnies*? Ronnie Corbett on the armchair…'

'I'll get a round,' Steph upped and left, leaving Laura and Alexander alone.

Alexander continued valiantly with the anecdote – which really isn't funny, I promise you – and when Steph returned a few minutes later Laura was wiping tears of laughter from her face with a stylish silk scarf. They were both deliriously happy.

The next day at work Steph bit the bullet. 'I think Laura likes you.'

'I guess,' Alexander said.

'I thought you two might get on,' Steph continued. And as Alexander realised what had happened, he almost felt guilty. Steph had taken this mysterious friendship to the extreme by putting Laura's happiness before his own. Naturally though, the self-sacrifice only made him happier. He developed an intolerable warm glow. And as for the happy couple… well, you can guess the rest.

I said before that Alexander didn't dislike himself before he met Laura, but having settled into a relationship with Laura, he didn't like himself at all. Instead of writing Laura into his own noir script, he was dragged into some horrible BBC sitcom about a cop and a nurse. Laura was nursing him into someone he didn't want to be. In her company, he felt big and stupid, a loveable plonker. Only a few weeks after that night in the rain, Alexander realised that his love was dead. But he began to see something new in Laura. Something that suggested the relationship might be worth pursuing after all. Not the promise of happiness that he had never really wanted anyway, but something far more in keeping with his personality, and indeed his ambition. As the love that had become lust turned finally to resentment, it hit him. Laura would make an excellent wife.

The dancing queen and the Devil

After his meeting with Siegfried's friends, Alexander bought a haggis supper and ate it as he walked home. It was late and he was hungry, but when he caught sight of Laura a hundred yards up the street, he almost ditched his supper in the nearest bin. He didn't like to be seen eating in the street by people he knew, especially something as undignified as a haggis supper. But he didn't ditch it. Laura was his wife, after all, not someone he was supposed to be self-conscious around. He couldn't eat it, though. As soon as Laura caught sight of him, he wiped his lips on his cuff and let his haggis-supper arm drop casually to his side. He greeted Laura with as much dignity as he could summon, but you know what she had to go and do.

'Give us a chip,' she said. Not, of course, because she was hungry. 'Pinching a chip' was a ritual of familiarity. Alexander held out the arm with the greasy package at the end of it, and Laura pulled out a medium-sized chip. She raised it to her lips and blew on it. Then she took a bite, leaving the rest of the chip hovering about her face. She licked her lips and blew again before taking another bite. She winked at him. In the beginning Alexander had been charmed by several aspects of Laura's behaviour that subsequently turned out to be very annoying. But this. This was the sort of thing he had always hated about her.

His decision to marry Laura had been less cynical than it might seem, though. Alexander was so steeped in detective lore that the idea of an unhappy marriage was almost romantic to him. For now, then, he was content to tolerate Laura, to tolerate that fact that she could only tolerate him because she still thought maybe there was someone else in him trying to get out.

Laura was on her way into hospital for the night shift. 'Well, the baby's at my mother's. There's casserole in the fridge if you get hungry later,' she said, nodding at his haggis supper and knowing that a woman's cooking was one aspect of married life he'd never got used to. She continued to cook for him, even if dinner on the table was the last thing he expected from their marriage. Neither of them knew what the first thing was.

'Aye, OK.'

His meeting with Siegfried's friends had unsettled Alexander, and he was in the mood to mope. His haggis supper finished, he carefully deposited the wrappers in a bin and stopped again at the off-licence on the corner of their tenement. As he drank, sitting at the kitchen table, he thought about Siegfried and Adele McGlone. And Leanne, who occupied a place in his thoughts out of proportion to their brief acquaintance some time ago. And before long he wasn't really thinking at all. He told himself that he was very unhappy, and then he felt guilty for feeling unhappy. He thought of the baby, his little Morgan, and suddenly he was angry that she wasn't there. He resented Laura's control over the child: she relished the role of the put-upon supermum, taking responsibility for 'the wean' (always a temporary singular, he suspected, in Laura's mind), while her feckless husband spent his time 'at the office' or 'out with the lads.'

Like that lap-dancing thing. Alexander had only last week refused again to accompany Steph and the others to a strip place, just as he had done last year, and yet Laura had once again fully expected him to go. No doubt she had enjoyed telling her workmates about how that bloody husband of hers was off with the lads to the lap dancing! That was the kind of relationship she fondly if perversely imagined for them. The truth, which revealed Alexander's true character, would not have made a good coffee-break story. This reflection made him think again about how much he hated strip clubs, how much he hated all that shite. Fucking filth, he said out loud. Then he tried to explain his objections with more nuance, as if afraid someone might have overheard him – Heaven forbid! – and mistaken him for an old-fashioned religious moralist. But he wasn't making any sense, so he soon gave up and sang a little song instead. And another, and another, till the bottle was empty. He put it in his jacket pocket, to be disposed of in the morning, and went to bed.

The following morning Alexander was given the 'vampire case' as predicted, but more than that: he was offered a new job running a special unit, which came with promotion to DCI. It was a major achievement for a man of his age, confirmation that his was as close as police work afforded to a brilliant career. Some man, Alexander, some man. The unit was being set up in response to a number of apparently cult-related crimes, including the child murder. He would have a psychological profiler and two detectives under him, and access to social workers and various specialists.

Somewhere at the back of Alexander's mind, though, lurked a bad feeling. Already there was a worrying ambiguity about the unit. Alexander's immediate superiors explained it as an exercise in demystification. The police were under pressure from Scottish CultWatch, an NGO that was stirring things up in the media, warning that several sinister cults were recruiting steadily, and were capable of unspeakable crimes. Alexander was seen as the man to bring the situation under control, and to do it boringly. He'd not come across any kind of cult activity in the course of actual criminal investigations, and suspected it was little more than a moral panic. He would bring the handful of disturbing cases that had got the media excited safely into the vernacular of police work, putting an end to talk of slayings and ritual and evil. But there were others in the top brass who took the cult threat more seriously, and believed it would be necessary to monitor the activities of suspicious groups and individuals rather than merely working cases as they arose.

For the time being, Alexander was in charge, and would treat all cases, starting with the 'vampire case,' as ordinary cases involving ordinary criminals, however disturbed they might be. But he was conscious that what Scottish CultWatch were pushing for was something quite different, and premised on a darker understanding of such crimes. For them, cults were a sinister force at work in the world, dangerously irrational, and not amenable to ordinary policing; their crimes were not ordinary crimes. It was only late in the day that Alexander discovered much to his consternation that his unit was to be called the Occult Crimes Unit.

Laura had just got the baby off to sleep in their room when Alexander got home, and she was trying on a new dress. 'Nice,' he said, smiling approvingly. 'Well, you can get used to this kind of number, now that we're moving up in the world.' She winked. He frowned. 'Oh, don't be cross,' she said. 'You didn't think you could keep it a secret, did you? Steph was at the hospital this morning. I can't believe *you* didn't call me right away!'

He sat on the bed to take off his shoes. 'Aye, well to be honest I'm tempted not to take it,' he said, annoyed that he had been robbed of his moment of triumph. She stopped what she was doing, and held her body in an overstated display of shock that could have been designed to annoy him. In any case it did. 'What?' he said, with even less charm than he had intended.

'We've talked about this,' she said.

'Have we? I mustn't have been listening,' he said, with even more unintended hostility.

'We've been praying for this promotion. It's everything we've wanted,' she said, with a melodramatic flourish that would have made them both laugh if they hadn't been in the state they were. 'What's the matter with you? Where's your ambition for Christ's sake?'

This was a reference to an argument they'd had before, a real argument, not like this one. Alexander considered himself very ambitious, but his ambition wasn't about rank or salary grade. In fact, he found it impossible to explain to Lady Macbeth what it was that he aspired to, so he knew he couldn't win the argument. He duly ignored her continuing appeals, and walked over to the crib. He gently picked up the sleeping Morgan and kissed her head.

'Listen to me!' Laura snatched the baby from him, waking her. Morgan began to bawl. 'Look what you've done now!' Laura accused, bouncing the baby in vain.

'She wants her Daddy,' Alexander said, and took Morgan back. She hushed. He looked at Laura, triumphant. Now Laura began to cry, silently, furiously. Alexander softened, but it was too late: she stormed out of the room.

'Christ,' Alexander said to Morgan. 'Of course Daddy's taking the job. Silly Mummy.'

What Alexander didn't explain to his infant was that he was determined to put his new unit out of business by demonstrating the diverse banality of its cases. He gathered the team early on the first morning. One of his detectives, DS Chris McGrain, was from the computer-crime unit; much of their work would involve the internet in one way or another. The other was relatively new, and had specifically requested the unit; DC Karen Smith. The psychological profiler was an old hand whom Alexander knew and respected; in fact DI Theresa Knox PhD, etc, was known as the best in Scotland, and was a star on the international conference circuit. A woman of reason.

They were given eight unsolved cases. Two of these involved the disturbing of graves: in one case a body had been stolen and replaced with that of a goat, and in the other the intruders had been interrupted and run off. Other cases involved suspicious theft from churches and cultish vandalism. These were serious cases, for all their kookiness. But the priority case, and the real impetus for the creation of the unit, was of course the 'vampire case.' Alexander had been involved in the early stages of the case, as indeed had most of the department, and he knew all the particulars. Things were getting desperate now; that's why Alexander was to take over from his more senior colleagues. But there were no witnesses, no suspects, no theory. The only thing to go on was the apparently occult character of the murder, and the media were going wacko on it; they had made the link with the grave disturbances, and a host of less serious but more bizarre occurrences.

The six-year-old victim had been 'exsanguinated,' a new word for Alexander: her blood had been almost completely removed. The blood had been taken from the carotid artery with a metal implement, and presumably some kind of suction device; there was nothing to suggest the use of fangs. There were no other marks on the body at all: exsanguination was the cause of death. Both McGrain and Knox had been on the case almost since the discovery of the body. Between them they had identified and eliminated a score of suspects. Collectively, the police had turned over every dangerous paedophile and every black-T-shirted weirdo in the west of Scotland and much of the world beyond.

Despite his anxiety about the presentation of the unit, his only real regret as he got to work was not having resolved the Brown cases. He felt bad that he had failed Brown's victim, disappointed that he had no reason to pursue Siegfried, and unreasonably distraught that he had no reason to see Leanne McGlone. This last regret was eased all too briefly when he ran into Leanne in the street not long after starting the new job. He threw his half-eaten pie onto a binbag outside a shop when he saw her coming, and tried to look composed.

'How are you, Miss McGlone?' She had stopped rather than simply saying hello as Alexander had expected.

'Smashing. …Did I see you at the ice rink the other day?'

It was an interesting question. He hadn't been there on official business, so in a sense, he reasoned, he hadn't been there at all. That wouldn't do, though. 'Yes, maybe you did. I had to see the manager about something.' That was a lie of course, and he sensed that she knew it.

'Are you having any luck finding my sister?' she asked cheekily.

Her sister? Alexander had almost forgotten about Adele, and realised with some relief that Leanne probably thought he'd been secretly watching her in pursuit of the New York fugitives. 'Oh. I'm not on that case anymore. It's out of my hands.'

'Right,' she said, her humouring tone confirming his theory. She didn't believe him. She looked as if wanted to say something else. He didn't want her to go. They stood in silence for longer than is normal.

CCTV footage, being less thoughtful than Alexander in its presentation of reality, would have revealed that he had indeed been at the ice rink, not talking to the manager, but watching Leanne. There had been about twenty kids skating on the rink, but he had spotted Leanne straight away – her short, blonde hair and her rainbow scarf and that smile. She was with a friend, a little dark-skinned girl, and they were holding hands as they danced about, laughing as they stumbled and slipped. Abba's 'Dancing Queen' was playing on the PA, and they were loving it, these young girls for whom 'cheesiness' was a recent and exciting discovery. But even as she stumbled Leanne was graceful. She was having the time of her life, and all Alexander could do was watch.

She was still standing there. 'It must be hard for you. Did they offer you counselling?' Alexander said in desperation. Leanne scowled. She had been enjoying talking to the detective – or standing with him – as an equal, as a person, not a customer. And she most certainly did not want counselling. He felt like an idiot, and as she politely took her leave, he was quite mortified.

He threw himself into his new job, though thoughts of Leanne lingered stubbornly in his mind. Soon after the unit's inaugural meeting, Alexander found himself in a pub in Partick with DS Chalmers, after very tame leaving drinks for a retiring desk sergeant. Both were avoiding their wives and thus remained together after the others had gone home. Chalmers asked about the case, though everyone knew it was going badly. Alexander said the situation was getting desperate, and he might have to resort to desperate measures. Then he made a joke: he might have to go to the caravan park and consult Granny McGlone, see if the spirits would help. Chalmers chuckled, and then Alexander watched him carefully as he ran with the idea. 'Can't do any harm, can it? And I'll tell you what, if there is such things as witches, she's it!' Alexander smiled and nodded in assent, and then Chalmers looked more serious. 'I'm surprised she's not been hauled in anyway. Have you not been interrogating all those people?' Alexander smiled inwardly at Chalmers' confusion of his investigation of people involved in occult internet groups, mentally unstable people who might have gone over the edge, with the search for *actual* witches. 'Tell you what, though. It's a shame that Adele fucked off. If she was still on the scene I'd come with you!' Alexander shifted nervously. Chalmers was close to his real motive, Adele's little sister.

It was enough, Alexander decided. If it seemed reasonable to Chalmers, he reckoned that circumstances being what they were, he could justify a visit to the fortune teller. He would take DC Smith, and hope to God there turned out to be something in the idea.

'Have you found him yet?' demanded the old woman. It took Alexander a second to realise that she meant Siegfried, not the killer. He explained that he was here about something else, all the while looking about him for signs of Leanne. Smith interrupted, and managed to flatter the old woman into offering them tea. They knew that people came to her with their problems, Smith said, and they hoped that she might have heard something the police had missed. She did the conspiratorial tone so well that Alexander felt insulted, but it seemed to be working. 'That poor wee girl,' Mrs McGlone said several times. Smith asked if she knew of anyone who meddled with the spirits in dangerous ways. That was a bit clumsy, and the old woman was put out, but Smith persisted cleverly, asking Mrs McGlone to explain the significance of the tarot card (not really) found on the child.

As the witch blethered on, Leanne arrived home, to Alexander's jubilation. (It was teatime, not altogether an accident.) She seemed pleased to see him too, but also wary. She perhaps expected news of Adele. Alexander took her aside and explained the purpose of their visit, and Leanne looked horrified. 'Can I talk to you in private for a minute?' he asked, gesturing to the door. They stepped out.

'Don't worry. We're just hoping your gran can give us a lead.'

'She's just a daft old woman. What's she gonnae know about a fucking murder?'

He was touched by her agitation. 'It's not what she might know; it's who. We're not looking for Count Dracula; we're looking for some sad wee bastard who's into tarot and entrails. The kind of loser who'd visit a gypsy fortune-teller at the fair.'

Leanne laughed, reassured away from some awful but unarticulated premonition. 'If you say so. So is she being any use, then?' She peered through the window.

'I don't know. My colleague has a better rapport with your gran than me.'

'I bet she does. Is that your girlfriend?' She smiled flirtatiously.

'No. I don't... How's Darren?'

'He's fine. Staying out of trouble.' Not, 'Darren, that silly wee boy? I'm not seeing him any more,' then.

Detectives are expected to ask questions, and they can sometimes get away with asking questions that don't strictly have anything to do with a case. Even so, Alexander hesitated before asking, 'Do you love him?'

She blushed. 'Yes... I don't know. I don't think love is... binary.'

Alexander smiled involuntarily and she smiled back, embarrassed. It was an awkward moment, but strangely exhilarating. Just as he meant to go back into the caravan he asked, 'Does he love you?'

She shrugged.

At this point Alexander really should have stopped, but the Devil wouldn't let him.

'I love you,' he said.

She didn't say anything. Maybe he hadn't said anything either. Thank God for that.

They went back into the caravan and Alexander exchanged looks with DC Smith. It didn't look good. The detectives mumbled their thanks and left. Smith was gutted that the interview had come to nothing, having convinced herself that Mrs McGlone would know something or someone who could help. Unlike Alexander, she believed that 'the occult' was a distinct world, and that its denizens would know each other. Never mind that Mrs McGlone was just a superstitious fairground fortune-teller, and the killer was almost certainly an isolated psychopath, and according to DI Knox a male graduate in his late twenties with delusions of grandeur, hardly the sort to patronise a crazy old witch like Mrs McGlone. He tried to explain this to DC Smith until she asked the inevitable question: why had they wasted time talking to her then? He shut up.

Had he told Leanne that he loved her? He thought of the times he had said the same thing to Laura. He didn't know how many times, but he knew that it coincided exactly with the number of times she'd asked him to say it. He simply didn't know if it meant anything. Anyway, she only asked out of a sense of duty. He thought of Leanne saying, 'Tell me you love me.' It was ridiculous. Such desperation on her part was inconceivable; the very thought was embarrassing, not even attractive.

Oddly enough, that desperation was the one thing he still liked about Laura. He found it strangely attractive, just as he admired those physical traits that betrayed her age: the faint wrinkles about her eyes, the slight looseness of her flesh. He found an erotic charge in her stretchmarks, and in the 'cellulite' she tried so hard to conceal. (Call me an old-fashioned feminist if you will, but has any red-blooded man ever been put off a woman by stretchmarks and cellulite?) It was so unnecessary, that uncertainty, but she wore it well. Laura had an air of dignified pathos that he found hard not to love. If only she would have shut up he might have loved her properly. He knew Laura felt she had failed herself in not pursuing her interest in choreography, and the reason she was always teasing Alexander about his having gone to private school was that she worried he thought she wasn't good enough for him.

He didn't think that at all, but then he didn't have to; yes, he let her think it for him. You see, these weren't idle thoughts that came to Alexander in the bath. As is so often the way with human beings, he formed his thoughts out loud in the midst of a conversation. With Laura. She threw him out.

I know what you're thinking: you'd be delighted if anyone said such honest and yet romantic things to you. But women are fickle. I'm joking. Frankly, I don't know much about women, but I do know Laura wasn't stupid, and she didn't throw Alexander out just because her feelings were hurt. It was because she knew where Alexander's feelings were going even if he didn't; and she was graciously doing his dirty work for him. He had never actually decided to love her, and without that commitment, his fondness for her, however genuine, was no good to anyone. Laura released the unwilling Alexander from her script, forcing him at last to take responsibility for himself.

Alexander brooded. He didn't love Leanne, of course. It was ridiculous. She was only a kid, and he had only met her a few times. But she was like no-one else he had met: so alive, so very young and alive and so determined to live. She gave 'life' a meaning beyond existence, but it was something he could not articulate, something felt only in her presence. He wanted her; he loved her. He thought of Leanne and he thought of Laura, and it seemed 'binary' to him. He didn't love Laura. It was a terrible way to feel about his wife, a woman he had married in good faith.

But then the good faith had always been hers, not his. He had been sleepwalking until now. Laura's reference to choreography made him think of Leanne slipping and tumbling across the ice. It had never occurred to him to feel disappointed that Laura had not pursued her dream. He thought again of Leanne. When he thought of her like this his heart lit up. Lit up?! 'I'm so stupid,' he told himself. 'Still, it's just a crush,' he went on. 'A horrible crush': that had a sensible ring to it. He spent his first evening away from home drinking with Steph, and let him do the talking.

After a night in Steph's spare room he was mercifully distracted from his self-absorption by a development in the case. Karen's imaginary tarot card had been mentioned on an occult blog that was logging developments in the case. Granny McGlone was in touch with someone after all. Alexander sat with DS McGrain as he traced the website. McGrain's arms were thin, like computer cables carrying nerve data to his hands rather than machine parts with a purpose of their own, but Alexander enjoyed watching him at work, expertly marshalling various computer applications to his own ends, *their* own ends. Before long, McGrain traced the web address to someone who was a good match for the psychological profile, but this guy had already been interviewed and alibied. Even so, it was a lead worth following, especially as there were no others. Alexander took McGrain to pick the guy up, while Karen went to keep Mrs McGlone under surveillance. The blogger was an IT support nerd at Glasgow University and he looked the part, which is to say that he looked like McGrain. Alexander didn't mention that to McGrain.

They took him to the station to get his blood pumping a bit and give him time to exhaust his protests about the Big Brother police state rifling through his private data. Alexander was often charmed, in fact, by his arrestees' touching faith in the rule of law, or more specifically in the sanctity of their own rights. He had never hit a suspect, and would never falsify evidence or otherwise compromise the law, but they didn't know that, and he sometimes felt an urge to remind them that they were in his power. He never did, though.

Alexander didn't mention Mrs McGlone till he and McGrain had their man in the interview room. He'd asked for a Coke rather than tea or coffee; the last person Alexander had served a Coke had been Darren Currie. The old woman's name had a gratifyingly dramatic effect on the nerd: the bubbles went up his nose. Then he demanded a lawyer. Alexander and McGrain exchanged looks, daring each other to hope this was something. The nerd had learned enough from cop shows on TV to keep his mouth shut till his lawyer arrived, so the detectives resigned themselves to a wait, reasoning that the alibi was a good thing: it meant there was someone else for him to give up rather than confessing himself.

The duty solicitor emerged from their consultation after half an hour and requested a word with Alexander. Long story short, his client had been conducting his own investigation into the murder, which he believed was one of many signs of impending Armageddon. He had spoken to Mrs McGlone after seeing the detectives visit her, and she had told him about the tarot card then. (The solicitor reminded Alexander that 'observing' the police conduct their business was not a crime; Alexander made a mental note to check that.) Though his client had done nothing wrong and had nothing to fear, he was now willing to share some information which might be of use.

When the detectives returned with the solicitor to the interview room, they were not well-disposed towards their amateur counterpart; the thought of having been followed was unnerving, especially for Alexander (McGrain didn't get out so much, so didn't have to worry about being followed). For his part, the nerd was equally put out by the knowledge that the police had been through his email, though he had the satisfaction of knowing they'd been unable to crack his encryption system. If they had, they'd have found the lead he was about to give them, and left him out of it. He had received four emails from someone claiming to be the killer. If he'd believed him, he might have told the police straight away. He didn't believe him, because his facts were muddled, but he thought the emails might lead him to something, and that the police would only get in the way. He thought they might lead somewhere because in them this avowed killer made references to Armageddon, in verse. In reality, this was useless: the poet had already been investigated and dismissed as a deluded nutter. Alexander sent the IT man on his way, then, with a warning that if he saw him following the police in future, he would be inclined to feel interfered with rather than simply observed.

Square one. But square one is never really square one a second time, because time itself is bleeding away. The chances of success diminish with every hour, let alone days and weeks. And Alexander had nothing. The pressure should have been unbearable, but Leanne continued to punctuate his thoughts. An imaginary Leanne would understand, commiserate, reassure. He couldn't think of anything without thinking of her; his bosses, the media, the public barely figured in his imagination. Meetings, missives and memoranda drifted through his consciousness; he had learned long ago to filter these things out when he had an important case, to think about nothing but the case itself. But this case gave him nothing to think about. He had only the desire to impress Leanne.

He allowed himself an hour on one of the grave disturbances, an exercise, like a chess problem. The transcript of an interview with a suspect congealed in his mind with the physical evidence to form a conviction that had escaped the detectives who had worked the case. It was obvious how to proceed; the case was all but solved. He imagined explaining this to Leanne, taking pride in his cleverness. (It was vanity, but vanity that served a purpose.) Absent Leanne, he made do with DC Smith, and let her take over while he returned to brooding, supposedly about the murder. Karen grinned with childlike enthusiasm as she saw what he had seen, and almost skipped off to organise the arrests.

Alexander went home to the bedsit he had taken temporarily – a man has to eat. As usual when cooking for himself he made too much food and wolfed it down too fast. Mince and potatoes; Scottish soul food. But Alexander ate like an animal. He thought, almost guiltily, that Leanne would disapprove, supposing that she ate different kinds of food, salad or something. Nectar and ambrosia. He wondered if it mattered. Even with Laura, food had always been a compromise: she had enjoyed 'experimenting.' Her favourite food had been *tapas* or anything like that. In restaurants she had always been the one to suggest just ordering 'loads of starters' and sharing those. Alexander would growl, preferring a plate of his own, mounted with food he could count on.

Instead of having an early night as planned, Alexander went back to the ice rink; there was an ice disco. She was dancing with a boy this time, not Currie, her eyes boldly flashing into his for seconds at a time, excitement overcoming embarrassment in a rush of adrenalin. The music was similar to the indie pop Alexander had been into at her age. But he had never shared his music with a girl, never felt the soaring melodies merge with his own surging hormones, never experienced the flimsy but undeniable joy of young love. He never would. Never mind. It wasn't young love that he wanted. It was Leanne.

He returned to his bedsit and continued moping. At times, he called it love. If there is such a thing as unrequited love, surely this was it. In his moments of doubt, he doubted not his own feelings, but the very idea of unrequited love. Then he thought about Laura and he doubted love altogether. He made himself miserable and for consolation, he turned again to thoughts of Leanne. He knew that she liked him. She had laughed at his jokes, she had given him flirtatious looks. That in itself was some consolation, but he wondered if she knew he was serious. Had it even crossed her mind that they could be together, make love, marry? Did she know that he had such thoughts? What would she make of that? Maybe she would laugh at him, maybe she would be shocked, horrified. It occurred to him that he could 'do a Siegfried,' just disappear to America, only taking Leanne with him. It was an unrealistic fantasy for him, but what's realistic to a sixteen-year-old girl?

Of course, Alexander had not completely shaken off the voice of realism, which did more than tell him what was unrealistic. It told him he was having a premature midlife crisis. In fact, it told him he was only pretending to have a premature midlife crisis: really he was just indulging himself. It told him to stop being such a sentimental fool, and to get back with Laura for the sake of Morgan. The rest of him sneered at that: 'for the sake of the kids' – you bourgeois, conventional drone! The voice was only emboldened by such sneering, taking it as evidence that the whole Leanne thing was an adolescent throwback. Yes, you are responsible for Morgan, actually. Grow up.

That was true, but since Alexander genuinely loved Morgan and was committed to looking after her, such an appeal to duty only made the voice unattractively pompous. And there was no way he was going back to Laura, even if she would have him. He was resolute about that. If he were going to be realistic, he would have to find another way to go about it, meet a woman of his own age, or at least a respectable age. There were millions of divorced men in the world who didn't fall in love with schoolgirls. He would have to be one of them. But he didn't want to be one of them.

A voice from somewhere, one that sounded suspiciously like Steph's, suggested just 'shagging' Leanne, and leaving it at that. It was risky, but just about plausible. She might even consider an older man to be an educational experience. The thought disgusted Alexander. He didn't want to be an educational experience; he didn't want to initiate Leanne into the adult world of carnal pleasure, just for the benefit of some scrawny kid she'd end up with later. He wanted to love her forever.

All the other voices laughed at that, even the ones that were generally sympathetic. It wasn't the sentiment; it was the words, the laughable words. Then another voice rose above the cacophony. Bold, calm, firm. 'Take her, Alexander. Tell her your story. Show her your world. She has no idea. You have to show her.' He began to ask himself what this meant – what story, what world? – but the voice wasn't in Alexander's head. He could hear it, physically. He turned around in his armchair and looked into the shadows behind him. It was the Devil.

Siegfried: an existential crime story, by KK Koshka

Part three: the trouble with New York

> *But he who is unable to live in society, or who has no need because he is sufficient for himself, must be either a beast or a god; he is no part of a state.*

Siegfried arrived in New York in the middle of the day without a particular plan. Instead he had a vague ambition with no precedent that he was aware of. Unlike Vito Corleone, he had nowhere to go, no community to bed into, no script to follow. Nobody to take care of. Nothing to live up to. Having cleared passport control and customs after arousing some suspicion – he had literally brought no baggage – he was hit by a kind of vertigo and hovered aimlessly at the exit. In desperation, he went to the toilet, and after evacuating his bowels he frantically destroyed his passport. Then with a renewed sense of purpose – no more than a sense, though – he went outside and got into a taxi. 'Little Italy,' after all, was the first thing to come into his head.

It was while sitting in a coffee place somewhere near Hester Street that Siegfried was struck by the awesome magnitude of the task ahead of him. He had made the leap, parted with Reality, and now he had to work things out for himself. He had no idea what that meant. A lesser man might have fallen back on tourism, taking comfort in the attractions of the city and avoiding the issue. Or perhaps gone to see a movie. Siegfried took a sip of his powerful espresso and frowned manfully.

He thought of asking the waiter if the Honored Society were looking for people with computer experience. Then he imagined what Tommy would have thought of that idea and laughed out loud, attracting a disapproving glance from said waiter. He was suddenly acutely conscious that organized crime was more embedded in exclusive ties and allegiances than the commercial world he had fled. Siegfried was anonymous, nobody. The café was not as he had imagined, less Italian, more generically American and modern, and yet somehow it seemed more authentic for being imperfectly so. Siegfried resolved to go for a walk. He wandered through Chinatown (which now occupied many of the streets he had learned from movies comprised Little Italy) reeling only slightly and not showing it at all.

He had always known, he supposed, that it would be like this. It was not enough simply to show up at a place truly to be there, because to *be* there implied reasons, expectations, of others as well as oneself. If he felt alienated from his surroundings it was because he was an alien. He had chosen New York very deliberately, and yet without having to think about it, because of what it symbolized. Freedom, a new start. A new life, hope. But such things could never be the qualities of a city itself; they were for its citizens, however newly arrived. Siegfried was no more a citizen of New York than a backpacker is a citizen of Thailand. It was not his legal status that kept him 'out,' but neither was the barrier cultural. Simply, he had no business in New York.

Siegfried's sudden disturbance was not merely mental. He lost his stride, stumbled, slowed down, stopped. He was free. Free. The feeling that had come to him in the café returned with terrifying force. Here he was in New York. Free. A wonderful New York street scene: sidewalk bustle, yellow cabs, the sound of distant sirens over the ever-present traffic noise, and cut! Cut to what?

It occurred to Siegfried that in the vernacular 'street' meant the opposite of what he was experiencing. Whatever else it might mean, it meant roots, ties, friendships and affinities. Something from which one could work one's way up, or fight one's way out, but not something accessible to outsiders. The street, in its literal sense, is no place to begin. For outsiders, the street is merely the

AB line, the location of transit. To inhabit the street without an A and a B, or at the very least a B, is to disappear, to be nobody. Siegfried wanted to sit down on the curb, but could not, would not, concede his predicament.

He walked on, faster, resolving to take care of the little things: something to eat, a place to stay. These were concerns shared by bums and tourists, but Siegfried was determined that his the similarity between himself and either was as coincidental as the similarity between the two. The Brooklyn Bridge appeared and he crossed it. He kept walking, like everybody else in the street, drifters of all kinds and locals alike. But he was unlike any of them. His destination was not in any tourist guide, was unknown to the most streetwise New Yorker, bum or otherwise.

With this thought he stepped into a bar. He took a stool with neither the studied familiarity of a regular nor the poorly concealed hesitation of a visitor, and ordered a beer just like that. The bar was gratifyingly like the New York bars he knew from TV: dark, a little bit sleazy, with all the activity around the bar itself, all eyes on the TVs mounted above it. The illusion those eyes shared, though, was not on TV but all about them. The social world, unscrutinized, taken as given, so unconvincingly given. And here Siegfried was, occupying the set, an extra perhaps, and yet refusing to follow directions, an unscripted desperado.

In objective terms, though unknown to those around him, he was a mere embezzler, undiscovered as far as he knew, and true enough, as he had told the immigration official at JFK, a tourist. He had at least destroyed his passport. If his enterprise was not necessarily crazy, he was determined to make it so. To exploit his freedom fully to his own unarticulated end. Otherwise, he was free, all right, free to drink in the day, like a bum or a tourist, again. Business was healthy for the time of day. To bums and tourists add alcoholics, or, more charitably, shift workers. There was no end to the things that Siegfried was not.

He was free from the script. But asserting that freedom was

not easy, because the script was flexible enough to accommodate all manner of improvisation. Had he produced a gun and shot up the bar in a fury of self-expression, the incident would have been written up as just another instance of craziness, the action of a deranged bum who would turn out to be a tourist, but no less of a bum for that. Whatever he did – here, now – Siegfried blended in all too easily, and he was all too aware of it. That feeling that had struck him in the café and again in the street came again. He frowned and stroked the condensation on the side of his beer bottle and had an idea. If he was going to be read one way or another, he could at least exert some control over people's misperceptions, pending the realization of his new self.

He had done one practical thing before leaving Glasgow, opening a bank account in an assumed name for his embezzled fortune, and taking out credit cards. So he had a head start. For the purposes of financial transactions, and most pressingly his accommodation for tonight, he was Art Vandeley. Story number one, then: Art Vandeley was a tourist, an architect from North Dakota if anyone asked – he thought it better to keep it domestic, and Siegfried's rather slight Scottish accent was sufficiently indiscernible that he thought nobody would mind if he didn't sound particularly North Dakotan.

What else? Siegfried had noticed a newsstand outside: he slipped from his stool and went out for a *New York Times*, returning with an adolescent lightness of heart too, but that didn't last. He found the job section and scanned it in search of ideas about who he might be. This is much less fun that it might sound: Siegfried didn't want to be any of these people, and suddenly this seemed a stupid idea. He could pretend to be an accountant, a museum curator, a chef, a submarine commander for that matter, but what was the point? So he could tell people in bars?

No, in reality he was either a tourist or a bum, a person of no consequence. If the former identity was convenient for the acquisition of goods and services, it occurred to Siegfried that the latter would be the better option should he come into contact with the police for any reason, and he liked the idea of conveying this impression with little more than a change of bearing, a sudden slouch or limp. He would be like Sherlock Holmes. Siegfried left a tip on the bar and wandered back towards Manhattan. He had been tired and disheartened by his efforts to place himself in conventional terms. All he could hope to do was to exploit the preconceptions of others, to slot himself into already-existing categories. These would insulate him to some extent, but the exercise was essentially the opposite of what he wanted to achieve. He wanted to create a new category, one that would allow him to be himself.

Siegfried remembered taking French at school. Their teacher had told the class never to write or say anything they hadn't already read or heard in French. Sensible advice; you can't just make stuff up. But Siegfried had been disturbed by this injunction, and wanted to know what happened when he had an original idea. 'We'll cross that bridge when we come to it,' his teacher had said, and everyone had laughed. Well here he was: standing on the Manhattan Bridge as it happened, frozen by uncertainty above the water line. And he could not describe what he was trying to do in any combination of phrases he had seen in print. He doubted, however, that it was completely original. Nothing comes of nothing, as whoever it was had said. It occurred to Siegfried that he was not well-read. And suddenly his destination was obvious.

He proceeded with something approaching real purpose over the bridge and through streets that seemed more laden with meaning than before. Having reconciled himself with the whole tourist thing, he was able to buy a guide book from a kiosk, and by the time he hit Fifth Avenue and began to head uptown, his once uncertain gait had become a march: to the New York Public Library. On arriving, however, he found himself facing a very similar problem to the one for which he had come for a solution. He had no curriculum to follow, no qualification to study for, not even a specific question to answer. So where to start?

One obvious idea was to start with ancient Greek philosophy and work forwards from there, but Siegfried's lazy streak was supported here by common sense. Surely there was a better way. Siegfried was not well-read, but neither was he completely uneducated. He did have scraps of knowledge gleaned from between the lines of his studies. A subscription to an offbeat Marxist magazine, sold to him by an alluring female on the streets of Glasgow, had equipped him with a serviceable political outlook involving a societal crisis that seemed now to parallel his own. He resolved to start with that sort of thing, then, and take it from there. He summoned up a stack of philosophical and sociological readers, with a rough idea now of what he was looking for.

He spent several weeks in the library, sleeping in a nearby hotel and passing a couple of hours before bed each evening wandering the streets and familiarizing himself with the city. The reading was not easy, and it was only that same feeling of vertigo that kept him at it, but he knew that in allowing himself this particular obsessive diversion from his existential plight, he was at least improving his chances of overcoming it. After those first weeks, though, he came up for air, conscious apart from anything else that the hotel was eating into his funds at an unnecessary rate. He found an apartment in the East Village, which required only a small amount of fraud to secure. He was well-presented and polite; it wasn't that hard to win people's confidence in the small measure required to conduct business. He also began to take an interest in the cultural life of New York, visiting galleries and attending concerts and plays, not as a tourist but as a man of the city.

One morning as Siegfried was dressing he noticed a spider on his bedroom ceiling. As a child he had been afraid of 'beasties' and would kill them in a panic, but with age he had softened and so he fetched a glass and some paper. Why do we insist on removing such creatures anyway? He didn't know, but it seemed to him a measure of domestic civilization. As he trapped the spider, he considered the ethics of the enterprise. He was keeping the spider alive, which was surely a good thing. But now he would take it to the window, four storeys up, and toss it into the wind. Would it actually survive? If it did, would it be leaving behind a hungry family of baby spiders? Would it be able to make a new life for itself? What was the point of spider life anyway? Siegfried didn't know the answer to any of these questions. He held the glass close to his face and wondered instead what kind of spider it was. Of course he didn't know that either, but at least the question didn't remind him uncomfortably of his own situation. He took the spider to the window and shook it out. There was no wind, and it spiraled slowly downwards. 'Bonne chance, mon ami!' Siegfried shouted after it, and then resumed his morning routine.

Make a new life. Siegfried would have breakfast, go to the library, read, stopping to use the toilet, have lunch, perhaps a coffee or a small cigar at some stage. Then he would go for a walk, see a film, attend a concert. He would most likely, it was true, notice women at various stages throughout the day. The human animal is supposed to have an irresistible desire to procreate, but as you already know, Siegfried had always resisted this idea, omitted it from his own conception of what it is to be human. It made no sense, or it made too much sense: its obviousness was an insult. He harbored thoughts along those lines, but he could not articulate them, could not make them his own. As for *love,* he had no idea. He suspected this was something he was never going to figure out in the abstract. But he would notice women, he knew, at various stages throughout the day. Then he might go for a drink, sit in a bar and watch the screen. He liked ice hockey, for what that was worth; he didn't know. Maybe he would go to a game in fact. But that wasn't important. He would go for a drink, sit in a bar and watch the screen, perhaps have something to eat there too. And then he would go home, sleep. Do it all over again.

It was like that for everyone, though, and in fact more so. For most people, the library part, work, would have been something they did to pay for everything else. Siegfried did everything else to keep himself coming back to the library. He had begun to scribble in a notebook he would later give to the author, as he read and pondered and gazed at the man-made clouds on the spiderless ceiling of the library, mostly thoughts about himself. He was no longer anything like a tourist or a bum. Objectively, he might have been described as a gentleman scholar. But it was no good describing him objectively, any more than it had been when he had been an insurance clerk. It was what he intended that distinguished him; the difference now was that it was also in some sense what he did, though not the circumstances in which he did it. This anonymous gentleman scholar was the pupa for the butterfly of Siegfried's ambition. He liked that: it meant that before, when he had felt like a louse, he had really been a larva. Or the ugly duckling? Siegfried was often distracted by such whimsies.

But in a sense, he felt, he had already succeeded in becoming his own thing, and already, he realized, that was better than being a gangster. Criminals, after all, are not known for transcending animal existence, but merely for transgressing transcendentals in furtherance of that existence. (That's from the notebook.) Most criminals spend their ill-gotten gains on stupid things. In buying gold watches and cars and spewing money in nightclubs, criminals simply act out their poverty, elevating it to an expensive lifestyle. A dealer or a pimp sitting in his BMW is like a child grudgingly awarded an ice-cream as a reward for a tantrum, and desperately licking it in an effort to taste the victory that somehow eludes him even in its apparent fulfilment. (That too.) 'I'm here to achieve greatness,' he wrote, and underlined twice. 'All the rest is light entertainment.'

To this end, Siegfried had suspended the need for sustenance, and put the question of sex, love, whatever, in abeyance. Free of such personal needs, he was at the service of something greater. When he resolved what that was he would be a beast no more. It was hard, but Siegfried did not have the consolation of despair. His thoughts were half-formed and contradictory, but they were not nothing. He had to persevere. When he awoke the next morning, the first thing he noticed was a black something on the ceiling. A spider. He laughed out loud.

Perhaps it was that same day that Siegfried first encountered the author, and I him. I was in the habit of visiting the library on Saturdays. There I was neither Nisha nor Claudette but simply a young woman experiencing the trouble with New York. Indeed, I had been staring into space until Siegfried got in the way. When his eyes flashed into mine across the crowded reading room, it was as if we were the only two people in the world. Perhaps we were; perhaps I was the only person there not just sharing the space with Siegfried, but occupying his world.

He was not particularly handsome, I considered. But there was something about him, this strange young man who came to the library every day wearing a business suit. A dark dissatisfaction, a mischievous vitality, a quiet passion, a scent of danger, a presentiment of greatness: I was in love with him. As for Siegfried, he could surely have seen in me no more than a blushing teenager, a girly curly brunette with a prettily awkward expression. But that was enough: he was in love with me. He even managed a smile.

Unbecoming a woman

We cannot help ourselves.
We live at home, quiet, confined, and our feelings prey upon us.

Imagine the preceding story as a film, ending on a moment of possibility and excitement, perhaps with the credits rolling to Van Morrison's 'Brown Eyed Girl.' Well after the credits, Siegfried and I were still there, left with the task of fulfilling that promise. And – though it took me a year – actually, this was where I came in by dropping my books at Siegfried's feet, where I made my own leap into the unknown in pursuit of the cool, older boyfriend and glamorous lifestyle that had been Claudette's birth right, and in pursuit of the more profound something I sensed lay in the same direction.

In approaching Siegfried as I did, and then throwing in my lot with him, I also took possession of his story. In time, having written that story so far to my own satisfaction, I began to inhabit it as an equal partner. It will be apparent from preceding chapters however, that even this was not immediately and unequivocally a Good Thing. Siegfried once described his flight from Glasgow as the result of a delayed adolescent crisis. In joining him I precipitated a crisis of my own, which centered on our relationship itself. More than worrying about colleges, or about what else I might do, or even the vexatious and rather terrifying question of what Siegfried would do next, I worried about us. And I worried indeed that this somewhat trivial question exercised me so much.

Our relationship was real, I felt, in a way that my relationship with the rest of the world was not. Being with Siegfried had made me think hard about the nature of relationships, and how personal relationships are inextricable from a social context, from society itself. And like Siegfried I had revolutionary adolescent ideas of my own about all this.

Sex is a strange thing, is it not? A 'bodily function' that requires social engagement. It is not possible to be only biologically human. An isolated human being is not humanity stripped down to an essence, but positively *inhuman*. Because to be human is to involve oneself in the concerns of others, and to be a sexual human being is to expose oneself to the perceptions and interpretations of other people. It is an unsettling prospect.

As a child I 'invented' oral sex (fellatio, that is; for some reason the other kind didn't occur to me till I was older). It was not something I would ever have committed to my diary, but just something I contemplated from time to time. When I later learned that it was an established thing, with a name, more than one, and worse, something that could be done well or badly, I felt robbed. Why was it called a *blow* job? And where had the idea come from that it was to be done for the benefit of the *boy*? In my mind it had been exciting in a funny dirty way. What I heard at school about 'blow jobs' was a terrible distortion of that. It seemed bound up with humiliation: rumors would spread that a girl had done it to a boy who then rejected her, and made a joke of her. But this new aspect, the possibility of shame, introduced a certain excitement. My thoughts became very complicated.

Later, there were stories about some 'stud' having agreed to sleep with a plain girl provided she wore a bag over her head so he could pretend she was somebody else. It was a gross story, and I doubt whether it was true, but it seemed to me that with or without bags over heads, everyone was always pretending everyone else was somebody else, nobody-in-particular in particular. That seemed to be the point of sex, to abandon particular identities in favor of a generic one, an eyes-shut, mouth-open, *grown-up* identity, that had nothing to do with either of the individuals involved, let alone being the unique product of their union. Not, 'I kiss you,' but 'We're doing kissing now.' So very far from being rebellious, teenage sexuality was extraordinarily conformist. And yet to reject it altogether was to reject the possibility of being fully human.

For all my considerable 'interest' in the physical side, and my desire for a boyfriend, I found the social reality of sex rather disgusting. Indeed, I could have been a poster girl for abstinence campaigners, except that I had no religious feeling whatever, and had a healthy disdain for such campaigns. (The girls at our school who did subscribe to the abstemious 'silver ring thing' were widely known to be more accommodating than they let on.) My own distaste for the activities of my peers seemed to me entirely of my own invention. I wasn't interested in signing up to some set of rules about sexual conduct, but nor was I interested in transgressing them for a cheap thrill. I wanted to be true to myself. It was precisely the annihilation of self that disturbed me: having sex seemed to be an expression of that same self-conscious grown-upness that I so disliked, with both parties subordinating themselves to a role familiar from films and TV. If there was a reason to resist sex, this was surely it, not rules obliging one to play a different part. And anyway, my thoughts went beyond resistance, as the thoughts of a true revolutionary will…

Excerpts from *Towards an Asexualist Manifesto*, by Claudette Dasgupta

…The division between the genders in modern society serves no useful purpose beyond the technical matter of procreation, and there is thus no reason for its prominence in culture. The division of labor along gender lines must be completely abolished in the home as well as the economy, in order to liberate individuals from gendered identities. Masculinity being the 'default' gender, free individuals of whichever 'sex' will tend to resemble men in dress and bearing, though not to the extent of styling themselves in overtly 'masculine' ways in sharp suits and 1980s hair and such. Conventional heterosexuality being a function of the division between the genders, sexual relations will be affected too. For a start,

there is no reason in principle to discriminate between the sexes in forming attachments. Instead of being the playing out of an archetype, sexual relationships, like all others, should each be unique, determined by the particular circumstances rather than abstract categories…

…A corollary of the above is that there is, in a sense, no such thing as sex. The use of common names for sex acts should be discouraged, tending as it does to diminish the significance of particular relationships as well as promoting vulgarity. Sex education should be limited to biology, so that young people are free to 'invent' sex as a cultural practice for themselves and in their own way…

…Prom, and other institutional forms of conventional sexuality, must be abolished, along with the expectation that teens will 'date' according to prescribed rituals, from the sentimentalized 'first kiss,' via the vulgar so-called 'bases,' to marriage and children. To the extent that the family codifies such expectations, it must be abolished too, liberating individuals to pursue their own ideas…

…Repression is supposed to mean the denial of genuine lustful feelings in favor of an artificial moral sense. The reverse is at least as true. Genuine 'moral' sentiment is often repressed in favor of an artificial sexual callousness. This phenomenon is not limited to the 'peer group,' but is affirmed by the culture in general. The prevailing cultural climate holds that young people should really be out 'partying.' This is despite messages to the contrary, which are increasingly empty and perfunctory, rules without purchase…

Unlike Ernest with his paper on crime, I had, perhaps foolishly, submitted my manifesto as schoolwork; Ms Kowalski chided me for my mannered precociousness. But when I showed it to Siegfried, he was very taken with what he called my theocratic tendencies, and congratulated me for my independence of mind.

But our relationship still vexed me, especially in relation to the wider world. Sometimes when I was intimate with Siegfried my thoughts wandered inappropriately. Other situations, other things. Yes, all right, other men. Or not so much 'other men' as men in general, a masculinity that exceeds Siegfried. In any case I felt guilty, and not just because I was being 'mentally unfaithful' to Siegfried. It seemed wrong to think about sex during sex, like humming a different tune at a concert, a lack of due attention, a failure to live the moment. Beyond that, though, you can't be held responsible for all the garbage that goes through your head. Sexual fantasies, in many respects, are like pop songs. They float around in the air, and you might catch yourself humming one now and again, but that hardly represents a personal commitment. I ought not to feel guilty, then, but I do: guilt joins the white noise, the worldly clutter of my consciousness. Delve inside the average mind and you'll find every sexual perversion in the book, all mixed up with advertising slogans, recipes, bloodlust, songs, love and hate, fear and loathing, jokes, jealousy, crackpot conspiracy theories, sentimentality and suspicion. And guilt.

But none of it has any more to do with the person in question than it does with anyone else. Whether you think of it as psychic pollution or the very stuff of humanity, it's just there. Deep down inside is where you find out the least about a person. Not least oneself. I resolved to stop examining myself as a patient and to stop thinking of my relationship with Siegfried in terms of what it said about me. If I was to be the author of my own destiny, I would have to start taking responsibility for my own feelings, not least about Siegfried. Instead of allowing my feelings to prey on me, I would go on the offensive by reaching beyond myself, and starting with the tiger in the room. It dawned on me that personal commitment is not about purity of sentiment or thought, but about determination. With determination the favored sentiment is never far away, surging back through the white noise to reassert itself with force again and again.

When I first told Siegfried I loved him, I pronounced the sentence literally, weighting the words evenly to convey the plain fact that I loved him. Siegfried pronounced the cliché, *'I love you,'* that I was resisting. And gradually I realized the meaning isn't in the words, but precisely in the cliché: the declaration is a kind of submission to that cliché, a deliberate sacrifice of originality for the sake of someone other than oneself, for the sake of something unique between the two of you, but not the property of either one. For a man who could not bring himself to say 'I'm fine,' I realized, '*I love you*' meant so much more than the words, and I hurled myself headlong into the cliché after him.

Jimmy the Chink is a dead man

L'audace, l'audace, toujours l'audace

Having once worried that my life was focused almost exclusively on Siegfried, I was now conscious that a new world was opening up through him. In befriending Ernest, he had not only reconnected with the original spirit of his flight from Glasgow, but also made a valuable contact, who had further connections of his own. It turned out that Ernest worked as an intern at a law clinic in lower Manhattan, which offered pro bono services to assorted small-time crooks as well as more deserving clients. Ernest had got to know this one young and coming wiseguy known as Jimmy the Chink. Jimmy was actually Italian-American, not Chinese, but he was a runner for a Chinese-American bookmaker named Mr Cheung. Mr Cheung was quite a character himself: he had an amazing goldfish collection, two wives and nine restaurants. Jimmy was fond of warning errant debtors about the dubious origins of the meat in Mr Cheung's chop suey. That was what Jimmy did. He ran around chasing up customers; taking bets, collecting debts and converting winnings into more bets. Mostly he was smart enough to stay out of trouble, but having used the clinic when he'd been pinched one time, he had taken a liking to Ernest and returned to ask him questions about the law and such. It was through Jimmy that Ernest had been able to get Siegfried a driver's license, which made life a lot easier. (Not that he could drive.)

Because of the circumstances of their meeting, Ernest was still under the impression that Siegfried too was some kind of gangster, an impression Siegfried had been in no hurry to correct. And so it was in this fictitious capacity, albeit implicitly, that Siegfried was introduced to Jimmy at a restaurant in the Upper West Side a few days after Ernest had been over for dinner.

'Claudette, Siegfried, I'd like you to meet my good friend Jimmy Colucci.'

'"Colucci"? Ernest tells me you're Sicilian?' Siegfried asked.

'Right.'

'So how come you're with a Chinese operation…'

'I'm Sicilian, but pretty deracinated, capisce?'

Siegfried capisced all right. He himself was as deracinated as you can get, after all. He laughed. 'You've read more than just Mario Puzo then?' It later transpired that Jimmy's late mother had been an avid consumer of popular sociology books, which Jimmy himself had devoured during long hours at her bedside when she was dying of cancer.

Siegfried knew better than anyone that Jimmy's disembeddedness wasn't just an ethnic thing, or post-ethnic or postmodern or whatever. There was more to it than deracination; it was more subjective. Siegfried saw instantly that Jimmy's equivocal attitude to his Sicilianness mirrored his own long refusal to recognize himself in others. And he had never fostered any illusion that this had anything to do with mere objective circumstances; the manifold ambivalences of 'Scottishness,' his unusual name, his family. No. It was about his own way of relating to the world, his own malcontented ambition. And it was only having embraced this that he could begin to recognize kindred spirits. That these were an Indian-American orphan, a Kentuckian Pip and now an off-Sicilian wiseguy, was of no significance.

In any case, Jimmy looked the part, in a dapper sports jacket and Tony Soprano-style patterned polo shirt (this was not exactly attractive, but he carried it off). Good shoes, too, if you notice that sort of thing. He invited us to come and sit down at his favorite table, where he was expecting his girlfriend Jeanie any minute. When she appeared at the door I knew instantly it was her: she was a stunning brunette, and standing in a long black dress and fitted black leather jacket, she looked for all the world like a human Coca-Cola bottle.

Jeanie was a writer for a lifestyle magazine, and since I was in the market for a career, the two of us talked about her work for a while. It was all very interesting, if not particularly inspiring, but Jeanie was unable to stick to the subject anyway. She couldn't seem to help talking about Jimmy, about how smart and cool he was. She liked Jimmy a lot, and seemed to regard him as a sort of edge that she had over her colleagues. Certainly she saw in Jimmy more than just some wiseguy; he represented those of her own aspirations that her career left for dead. What he saw in her was equally obvious. She was not only beautiful and charming; there was something menacing about her which I decided must be sex appeal. I surmised uncomfortably that this might have something to do with her independence.

Adjacent to this feminine diversion, Siegfried was struggling to understand how Jimmy and Ernest saw him, what they expected of him. They perhaps realized that he was more than a gangster, but not of course that he had come to the 'more than' without the trouble of being a gangster in the first place. Siegfried told me later that it had felt like a job interview, only he was the interviewer and nobody knew what the job was. Which, of course, was a reflection of our own situation. I was no longer the only one at Siegfried's disposal. For the first time, Siegfried was under pressure from other people. No longer merely free to pursue his own project, but compelled to.

For our part, Jeanie and I hit it off, and she convinced me to take more of an interest in the arts. She had just written a review of an art exhibit called 'Women I saw in the street and thought were You,' and she said I should go. The artist had taken pictures of women he'd mistaken for his ex-girlfriend, or at least that was the idea. Apparently he wouldn't say whether this was 'true' or just a concept, and it wasn't clear whether he'd really spotted the women like the title said, or whether he'd set it up somehow. I went along to see for myself. There were twenty-two pictures in all, eleven showing the women from a distance or behind just after the artist had 'mistaken' them for his ex, and eleven showing the same women from the front when he'd caught up with them. You could see the similarity: mainly that all but one had long dark hair (the other had a hat) and all were about the same height. Up close though, they were quite different, not even all the same color. Most were smiling, or kind of smiling, and three just looked bewildered; it looked like the artist had asked permission to take the second picture but not given them much of a chance to say no. Anyway, I wanted to believe the concept was true, and I fancied I could detect a certain quality all the women had in common. I found myself looking out for the real ex-girlfriend, the You, for several days after seeing the exhibit.

I emailed Jeanie to tell her I'd liked it, and how it had made me think about how we see and recognize people and what makes a person a person and how funny it is that even looking exactly like someone else doesn't make a person any closer to being that other person. Jeanie said in her review that the work took a movie cliché of romantic desperation and made it into something profound, and I agreed. It was this correspondence that led to our next outing, a night at the opera. Jeanie was something of a buff, and though Jimmy had taken her to the Met once or twice, she complained it had felt like an imposition. She thought it would be better if they went as part of a group rather than as a couple, and I thought it would be fun too.

Without conferring, we all dressed up for the occasion, and we must have looked like a pretty neat little scene. But it was after the opera, when we arrived in high spirits at a nearby bar, that the significance of Jimmy's designer suit came to me. Two young men approached him to exchange pleasantries. They were an unsightly pair, in tracksuits, evidently acquaintances from the betting business, but they had none of the glamor that Jimmy exuded, and they repeated in slow motion everything he said. When he finally got rid of them he shook his head: 'Don't ever let anyone tell you marijuana is harmless.'

Now I understood Jimmy's attraction to Siegfried. The world he inhabited was not cool and exciting; it was populated by losers. That world could not contain his ambition. Maybe Jimmy saw in Siegfried what Jeanie saw in Jimmy. All that remained for Jimmy was to perform his own equivalent of Siegfried's leap across the Atlantic, and it was to be Siegfried's hand in the maneuver that would justify Jimmy's faith. Reader, things are about to get all-action.

In the event, Jimmy felt like he didn't have much of a choice. A couple of days after the opera, he called Siegfried and asked to see him urgently. They met an hour later on a bench in Washington Square Park. Jimmy was wanted by his old neighborhood mob crew. There had been a dispute over some bets: Mr Cheung had accused the crew of messing with a fight, and was refusing to pay out. The crew held Jimmy responsible. They had never liked him even as a kid, when he had been an overzealous altar boy. It was bad enough for him to be working for a Chink bookie, but his inability to resolve this gambling dispute in their favor was the final straw. Things came to a head when three of the guys tried to rough him up. Unable to fight off all three assailants, Jimmy had concentrated his efforts on just one. A series of hard blows to the head, intended to intimidate the others, had killed the guy, the youngest brother of the crew's captain. Jimmy was a dead man.

Jimmy knew that Siegfried had helped Ernest. He had speculated that Siegfried was a sort of freelance fixer, like the Harvey Keitel character in *Pulp Fiction*. And now Jimmy was desperate and had nothing to lose, so he was asking for Siegfried's help. They talked for a long time; Siegfried wanted to absorb as much information as possible. Despite his lack of experience in the unlikely profession in which he was now cast, though, he quickly saw what Jimmy's first move should be. Time was of the essence, so he gave his 'client' immediate instructions and then came home to think about step two.

Siegfried stayed up till nearly dawn smoking and gazing at the night sky, and by the morning he knew he had to kill someone. He told me this without any great drama: 'I have to go and kill someone,' he said. I was aware of course that this was a big deal. And a voice in my head screamed that it was insane. 'What are you doing?! Get away from this lunatic,' it said. I simply shrugged it off. If Siegfried had to kill someone then so be it. I just hoped that he wouldn't get hurt, but I didn't really believe that was possible.

The soon-to-be-deceased was Frank Balbo, the mob captain who was after Jimmy. By all accounts he was as violent and unstable as a Joe Pesci character. Balbo was a psychotic thug who used the mob as insulation, living in a fantasy world and leaving others to smooth things over with reality. Only the other week he had broken a girl's nose in a restaurant. It had been the brother Jimmy later killed who paid off the girl and the restaurant manager. Whatever Balbo imagined, Greenwich Village was not in fact in the grip of the mob: as far as anyone else was concerned, he was just another asshole.

Jimmy had given Siegfried the beeper number of a gun guy. He paid five hundred dollars for a funny-looking snub-nosed .38 revolver, 'guaranteed' untraceable. The gun guy had said Siegfried could have half the money back if he returned the piece unused. That wasn't going to happen. Siegfried waited for his man in a diner in the Lower East Side. As soon as Balbo had sat down Siegfried walked over and pointed the gun straight at him and squeezed the trigger three times. Two in the body, one in the head, and he was dead under the table. Siegfried let his arm swing downwards, dropping the gun naturally with the same motion, just like Michael Corleone forgot to. Then he walked out the door.

The hit didn't exactly take the heat off Jimmy of course – since he would be the Mob's prime suspect (not to mention the cops) – but that hadn't been the point. Jimmy was ready to jettison himself in much the same way that Siegfried had done when he left Glasgow. His wiseguy persona, his position, his contacts, all the good faith that attached to Jimmy the Chink, had been compromised. He had left himself with no choice but to make a fresh start. And on Siegfried's advice, he took the opportunity to cash in his account literally as well as metaphorically. Simultaneously with Siegfried's intervention, Jimmy severed his links with Mr Cheung by absconding with a hundred thousand dollars.

In any sense that mattered, this much was white-collar crime. Accordingly, then, Jimmy took Jeanie skiing in Colorado for a couple of weeks to let things settle. In its own terms, Siegfried's hit had been an act of gratuitous audacity: even if Jimmy succeeded in transforming his identity, he would remain in danger when he returned to New York. But with Balbo gone the danger was of a different, less personal quality. Siegfried's intention had been to ease Jimmy's metamorphosis while making an impression of his own. What came next was both more considered and more audacious than the hit itself.

Siegfried visited a little Italian restaurant a couple of mornings after he killed Balbo. It was in Queens, and not at all like the place in Little Italy where he had sat on his first day in New York. Once he'd spotted the place from the street corner, he lit a cigar and turned the wrong way to begin a large spiral approach. Siegfried had made it known that he would be at the restaurant today to speak to Sonny Graziani, Balbo's godfather, who held court there from time to time. When he eventually went in, a young man told him the restaurant was closed. Siegfried introduced himself and said that he believed Don Graziani was expecting him. The young man announced him without taking his eyes off him, a tough-guy affectation that made Siegfried want to smile. Then a hoarse voice summoned him into the shadows toward the back of the restaurant. A fifty-year-old fat man was sitting alone at a little table in near darkness. Siegfried walked over and joined him, accepted an offer of coffee, and allowed the don to savor the silence. After two minutes, someone brought Siegfried an espresso. He sipped the espresso and replaced the cup in its saucer. Then Sonny Graziani broke the silence. 'You know something about Jimmy Colucci.'

'He's a friend of mine,' Siegfried said. 'I'm here to ask you a favor.'

I will spare you the rest of the details of that conversation: no doubt both protagonists took their cues from gangster films, and Siegfried said the effect would have been comical had there been anybody there to see it that way. The important thing, though, is that Siegfried looked into Sonny Graziani's eyes and spoke directly and honestly. He told him that he, not Jimmy, had killed Balbo, and that while he was sorry if this caused Graziani personal distress, he was sure that on reflection the don would agree he had done him a favor. Balbo had been a nut, making a fool of himself in Manhattan rather than taking care of business where he should have been, and a serious organization cannot afford to have a nut in a position of authority. Siegfried could see Graziani was impressed. Every instinct the mobster had was telling him to whack Siegfried there and then; Siegfried was sure of this because when he imagined himself in Graziani's soft, expensive, Italian shoes, that was exactly how he felt. But the don was deep in thought.

As a simple matter of fact, Siegfried was right that Balbo's removal had been in Graziani's own interests. Graziani had surely already had this thought, but it hadn't occurred to him till now that it might have consequences. Perhaps it was the realization that Siegfried had made him think, as much as the thought itself, that made Graziani not want to kill this man. My guess is that the don was at a stage in his life, or the mob was at a stage in its history, when the old rules seemed less rigid. Mafia lore seemed to be fading into a more prosaic, reasonable reality, and the don was ready to be reasonable too. He said that if he granted a favor Siegfried would still owe him; hitting Balbo didn't count. This was not fair, of course, but something told Siegfried to accept his terms, intuiting that it's better to owe the mob a favor than it is to have them owe you one. Mobsters of all ages love this favor business; it makes them feel like Marlon Brando. Owing someone else makes them uncomfortable, and that you don't want. Siegfried asked the don to forget about Jimmy, and he agreed.

As Siegfried sauntered out of the café into the sunshine, he reflected that this result was no more than he had expected. (It didn't occur to him that Graziani might come after both Jimmy and him anyway, and he did not, so there's no need for you to worry about that either.) In fact, Siegfried could not remember what he had expected. His own state of mind before the meeting was now a mystery. It was as if something in his brain had changed irreversibly; however he had felt, that feeling was no longer possible. What happens to faith when its object is proven? I think perhaps that Siegfried had been a little bit mad when he blundered into the restaurant, but even if his whole experience of New York before the meeting had been a psychotic episode, it had served its purpose. He was now someone else, someone for whom the old Siegfried's plans were not flights of fancy, just a little naïve. All things considered, the transition had been achieved remarkably smoothly.

Siegfried's bearing was far more purposeful after that. He said that when Jimmy returned from Colorado they would explore a couple of avenues together. He had an idea. He didn't want me involved in that, of course – the gangster life wasn't really an option anyway, for a teenage Indian-American girl – but he was confident that more suitable opportunities would arise. Meanwhile I read and thought and watched TV and was in love.

It was spring, and we took to spending time in the park. One day we strolled up after lunch and sat down in our usual spot to drink coffee and watch the squirrels. There had been some kind of event, and the park was strewn with litter the organizers had neglected to remove. Siegfried looked about in disgust, caught between despair and resolution. Finally he picked up a plastic bag and started filling it with the garbage in his immediate vicinity. I started to help, but was soon distracted by the sight of a woman fifty yards away following Siegfried's lead. It happened fast, as if she had been thinking about doing just this, and the sight of Siegfried had converted that thought into a decision. The woman also cajoled her son, who probably had been having no such thought, into helping. And perhaps others had been thinking the same, or perhaps our actions planted the thought in their minds; perhaps our actions gave confidence to would-be cleaner-uppers, or perhaps people simply felt pressured. In any case, before long everyone in our part of the park was engaged in the clean-up. Siegfried and I exchanged glances and laughed.

Six weeks after all the action, Jimmy returned without Jeanie; they broke up, he said. (I was devastated.) Officially, moreover, Jimmy remained in exile. While Graziani had come to an agreement with Siegfried, he could not be seen publicly to tolerate the assassination of one of his men. The word on the street was still that it was Jimmy himself who had shot Balbo, before disappearing with Mr Cheung's money. Jimmy was back in the city, then, but he was living in a different world, the same insubstantial world in fact that Siegfried had discovered when he had first arrived in New York. The difference, of course, was that if Jimmy stumbled upon either the Italians or the Chinese from his old world, they would try to kill him. He asked me with a wink if I knew any good Indian restaurants. I did, as it happened, but I had discovered these with Siegfried. I was even less rooted in any community than Jimmy: I didn't have anyone out to kill me.

Eventually someone from Jimmy's past did catch up with him, not to kill him but to ask for help. Laura Graziani, the Godfather's daughter, tracked him down. Perhaps only she could have done.

The two had been close as children, and Laura remembered his fondness for Laurel and Hardy movies: when a screening with live music came up at the Carnegie Hall, she appeared during the interval in the empty seat next to Jimmy, a blonde Italian beauty in a stylish silk scarf and dark glasses. He took her hand and kissed it, 'Princepessa.' She smiled with a sophistication that did not conceal her true affection for Jimmy. Siegfried and I were sitting next to him on the other side, but at the appearance of someone who obviously knew Jimmy, we had pretended not to know him, and he made the same pretense, wandering off with Laura to talk privately.

Jimmy later explained to Siegfried that he and Laura had been very close as children, but Jimmy had been unable to keep up with the precocious daughter of Don Graziani: by their mid-teens she had occupied a different world, or rather two, effortlessly combining the roles of Daddy's good girl and junior gangland socialite. They had seen each other only briefly and intermittently since then, but never without a charge in the air. Neither could forget the other. Now Laura realized that Jimmy's exile put him in a position to help her. Perhaps she reasoned that he could not be any deader than he already was. Of course that was not really true, but Jimmy was willing to indulge her.

Laura was secretly married, she told him, to a Russian gangster called Yuri Sokolov. Her father would never approve, and now her brother Enzo had found out and was trying to blackmail Sokolov. Jimmy had always hated Enzo, but he could not imagine Laura wanting him dead. She didn't seem to know what she wanted, except that she wanted the situation fixed. She wanted Jimmy to think of something, to help her, to take responsibility. Jimmy said he knew someone who might be able to help.

Siegfried was of course delighted to have a chance to aid the course of true love, and so arrangements were made for him to meet Sokolov at a card game at a social club in Queens. It was an unfortunate setting: Sokolov considered poker to be a test of character, and had told Laura he would decide after the game whether this 'fixer' was worth anything. Of course, Siegfried was lousy at cards, and not so stupid as to cheat with gangsters as he had with his friends back in Glasgow. It was a test he could only fail.

Having given up on the card game, Siegfried retired to the bar and struck up a conversation with another unsuccessful player, an older Hispanic man who had the air of someone for whom poker was a trivial pursuit. Siegfried warmed to that, having been chagrined by Sokolov's obvious contempt. The man's name was Paolo; he didn't give a last name, and Siegfried could hardly object to that. Paolo said he was in business with Sokolov: import/export. Siegfried returned that he was 'looking about him,' a phrase Paolo recognized from *Great Expectations*. He was a great admirer of Dickens, he said. They ordered more drinks.

Young man Ernest

Crime has a 'functional' role in the society, and the urban rackets – the illicit activity organized for continuing profit rather than individual illegal acts – is one of the queer ladders of social mobility in American life.

Ernest was exceptional among us in that he was fully embedded in the legitimate world. Whatever outlandish schemes and fantasies swirled around his head – and these were innumerable – he was a law student, a respectable member of society who could, as he put it, show his papers to the gendarmes without fear of arrest. No small thanks to Siegfried, his life still slotted into a readily identifiable script. He was a country boy making his way in the smoke, preparing for a career in a profession as conventional as they come. Ernest of course was anxious to assert his own authorship, but as Siegfried kept reminding him, his was a good script to have for now at least. It had been a near thing, of course: if not for the armed robbery, Ernest would have torn himself violently out of that script with his own reckless heist. As it was, however, unlike Siegfried and Jimmy – but in common with myself, I feared – Ernest would have to untangle his Gordian Knot.

It turned out that the rope was at least greasy, however. Siegfried had arranged to go with Paolo to a screening of the *Godfather* trilogy. Ernest went along, and immediately recognized Paolo as one of his professors. If Professor Cabrera-Hernandez was embarrassed by the collision of his two worlds, he did not show it. Perhaps he didn't even think of it like that. The professor recognized Ernest and even complimented him on an essay he had written.

After the film, punctuated by espresso and omelets, the three went to a nearby restaurant for spaghetti with clam sauce, and

Paolo Cabrera-Hernandez – having decided that he trusted Siegfried, perhaps because he saw something in him – divulged the story of his life. He had been born in a Central American capital city he would not name, to a wealthy industrialist of old Spanish stock and an Evita-like peasant-girl-made-good, who had instilled in him a certain ruthlessness. Following a brilliant school career he had trained for the priesthood until he was expelled from the seminary over theological differences. Then he had joined the army, which at that time was involved in the violent suppression of political dissent. He was sent to America to train and then returned home to do 'the Devil's work,' as he put it. After some years, he had an epiphany and left the army. He drove all the way to America in a red Corvette convertible, snarling at border guards with the absolute certainty that they would not stop him; that much at least the Devil had taught him. He had established an academic career in California and started a family. When his wife and children had been murdered two years ago, he had come to New York to start a new life, all the time cultivating criminal contacts in the hope that someday he would have his revenge.

All this was certainly a revelation to Ernest. Here in the midst of his own conventional world was this fantastic gargoyle, whose exaggerated features and cartoonish moustache now seemed to signify his other-worldliness, to carry his outlandish story with him for all to see. And there was no reason it should not be so. The conventional world did not exclude the fantastic; it merely failed to acknowledge it. Ernest resolved there and then, he later told me, that he would stop daydreaming about being someone else, and inhabit his own world wholeheartedly.

I had already grown very fond of Ernest, who, being closer to my own age than Siegfried, had become my particular friend. Occasionally, I would broach the subject of romance with Ernest, in that teasing way attached women have with single young men. Surely he had his eye on someone? His standard response was that he was too much of a workaholic to be bothered with all that, but on one occasion, after one or two drinks, he did mention admiring 'a gurl on the bus.' It probably goes without saying that he instantly regretted it.

It was embarrassing, and he was intensely aware of it, that a young man of Ernest's intelligence, wit, charm even, should be reduced to fantasizing about a stranger on a bus. It was not much different from developing crushes on people on TV, as I had as a young girl. There is, I had observed, a movement of sexual interest in adolescence from classmates to adult fantasy figures and back to classmates, transfigured in the mind as much as transformed in the flesh. But if this movement is not realized in actual relationships, interest drifts and it makes no difference whether it settles on classmates or celebrities or entirely fictional characters. Or composites, real people attributed with characteristics not their own. No doubt there are countless real relationships, real in the sense that people are at least having sex, which nonetheless are of precisely this nature. Ernest was incapable of such blatant self-deception, even had the opportunity presented itself, and so his self-deception – his belief in winning the gurl on the bus – remained private, contained, except for this one painfully touching slip.

If Ernest was tragically unworldly when it came to women, however, that same unworldliness worked to his advantage when it came to the law. He had a particular gift for legal theory, an ability to see through to the abstract principle even when the particular circumstances became complicated. He took the law seriously, not as a system of rules to be negotiated, but as something that was valuable in itself. Where the law was wrong he said so and explained the error in terms of the better nature of the law itself. He had none of the cynicism of his peers.

Ernest had been unsettled by the revelation about his favorite professor's past and present. It struck him that the professor did not live in two worlds, but made what seemed like two worlds one, without artifice or dissimulation. Time and again, Ernest's assumptions about life and the law were unsettled by the professor. On one occasion, they had been discussing the role of juries and Ernest had casually suggested that a defendant would want a jury to be disinterested. The professor had stopped him, 'Really? Doesn't that depend on the circumstances?' Ernest had hesitated, 'You mean if he's guilty, he might want a biased jury to help him get off?'

'You're assuming his guilt is a simple matter of fact. I can think of many cases in which someone might be guilty from the perspective of a disinterested observer – the judgement of the gods – and yet quite innocent in the eyes of a jury of his peers.'

Ernest made this and other thoughts his own. Gradually his idealism became sharpened, not more worldly in the sense of being *of* the world, but more precise and more resonant, more effective *in* the world. Ernest began to see how he could transcend convention not by serving as consigliore to some mob family as he had once vainly imagined, but simply by being faithful to the spirit of the law in all its human complexity and often radical implications. He began to see what it might mean to inhabit his own world wholeheartedly rather than leaving a dream. He now realized for the first time that he himself could bridge the divide between ought and is simply by acting in the world, the one true world. Nonetheless, Ernest maintained a healthy fascination with the criminal underworld and its unwritten rules. When Siegfried told him how he had met Paolo, Ernest wanted to know all about Sokolov and the secret marriage. He had Jimmy tell him the whole story.

What especially interested Ernest, and what he later explained to me at length, was that Enzo Graziani's objection to Laura's marriage did not rest on any moral code. In truth, he did not object to the marriage even on personal grounds, but merely saw it as an opportunity for blackmail. His father's objection, on which the blackmail was premised, was more complicated. First of all it was hypothetical: blackmail was only an option because the don did not know about the relationship. But Enzo was right to suppose that his father's ordinary paternal jealously would have been aggravated by a mafioso's ethnic-cum-professional disdain for the Russians. Then there was the don's desire – no less traditional, really – to go straight, to lift his family into respectable society and kick away the queer ladders he had climbed to get them there. He would not have his daughter consorting with Russian riffraff. Enzo underestimated his father's immutability on such matters, however. Naturally, Don Graziani loved his daughter, and for most of her life it had seemed natural to express his love in the manner befitting a man in his position, the Sicilian patriarch. But secretly perhaps he had always resented the distance this put between them. Perhaps as well as wanting to protect her, he wanted to know her, understand her. In his old age, perhaps he was beginning to realize that without such understanding, his protection merely kept her in the world he had wanted her to escape.

Enzo's blackmail was not as simple as he thought, then. Presented in the terms in which Enzo himself understood it, Laura's marriage was damning. But these were not the only terms available. Siegfried suspected that Don Graziani was weary of playing the Godfather, open – within reason – to other ideas. Laura's marriage was not only perfectly legitimate according to the state of New York – Sokolov already had a green card – it was the natural product of a healthy relationship according to the unwritten rules of modern society, which gave little weight to parental objections, least of all on ethnic grounds. Sokolov and Laura had a lot in common; he was good to her, and careful in his business dealings, not a liability like Balbo. Looked at from this point of view, it had been the weirdness of Laura's family situation, not the intrinsic unsuitability of her husband, that had forced her to marry secretly. It was the don's own fault. And just maybe it was not beyond the man to see things as any normal person would see them. After all, Siegfried had persuaded him to do just that over the matter of Balbo.

Of course Don Graziani was still a father, still capable of jealousy. Whomever his daughter had married, going behind Graziani's back was never going to endear him to his new son-in-law. Siegfried knew it was not Graziani who would have to be persuaded to be magnanimous this time, but Sokolov. But Sokolov and Graziani had more in common than either would have cared to admit. Both were in some sense 'men of honor,' and both therefore vulnerable to the exposure of their code of honor as hollow. The older man was more pointedly aware of this; Sokolov was still young and proud, and his situation was further complicated by the very different tradition to which he deferred.

Sokolov had arrived in New York from St Petersburg at almost exactly the same time as Siegfried had come from Glasgow. He was not in any credible sense a *vor v zahone* – a member of Russia's informal criminal brotherhood – never having been to prison and having had only limited contact with other criminals. But he was steeped in Russian criminal lore. Unlike many of his peers in the same boat, he had not gotten himself tattooed to look like a seasoned *vor*, precisely because he took such symbolism seriously; it would have been like buying medals at a flea market and passing himself off as a war hero. Even as he rejected the rules of respectable society, and felt genuine contempt for the conventional values of his adopted country, he clung to the notion that in doing so he lived by an alternative code; he 'had honor.'

Laura had liked Sokolov's attitude. It seemed a breath of fresh air, this brazenness, this deliberate, cool indifference, leaving behind the hypocritical family bullshit of the Italian mob. The Russians did not pretend to stick together; it was every man for himself, by any means necessary, and Sokolov made a virtue of it. Sokolov had told Laura he was the twice-bastard grandson of *homo sovieticus*, and she had fallen in love with him. In truth of course none of it made sense: Sokolov's code of honor was an eccentric mélange of gangster mythology, amateur theorizing and personal prejudice, held together only by the strength of his own personality. Ultimately, it was that strength that had attracted Laura to Sokolov, and it was fitting that it was his relationship with her that should provide the test of it.

The whole thing was painful for Jimmy, and that was partly why he had referred the matter to Siegfried. It was not, Ernest thought, that Jimmy still harbored hopes of being with Laura, but that he was hurt by her having asked him to do this thing. Ernest and I both agreed that it had been callous of her to take advantage of his affection by asking for his help in this of all things.

It was made worse by the fact that she didn't even know what she wanted him to do. It wasn't like he could grit his teeth and pull a trigger, or bribe someone or something like that; she wasn't asking him to move a sofa for her. Laura needed Jimmy to think, to immerse himself in her problem, to use all his creativity to figure out a solution, to help her find happiness with someone else. And yet, Ernest suspected that Jimmy had been touched by her very desperation; the fact that she had come to him was a kind of compliment, a recognition of his competence and decency.

Perhaps it would not have occurred to Laura that Jimmy would have been hurt; perhaps she thought him above that. Perhaps, then, he had been touched by her very callousness. And perhaps she was right about him. He had referred the matter to Siegfried not because he wanted to shirk it but because he wanted to do the right thing for Laura. In going to Siegfried, Jimmy was engaging his better self, putting aside his own hurt and resentment, and committing himself to approach the problem in a Siegfried-like way. And he had been sure that Siegfried would be able to help.

The failure of Siegfried's initial approach to the Russian

unsettled Jimmy, then. It made him see the whole affair through Sokolov's suspicious eyes. The flipside of Sokolov's peculiar individualism was an obsession with the threat of humiliation. He perceived every little thing as a slight and lived in constant fear of being insulted, ripped off, cuckolded, taken for a schmuck. If people asked him for the time he would snarl that they should buy their own fucking watch, because he wasn't their fucking servant. The twice-bastard grandson of *homo sovieticus* would have seen Laura's appeal to Jimmy as nothing but humiliation. If she admired this man's nobility so much why was she asking him to help her settle with someone else? Jimmy felt just this response rising up within himself, began to articulate it even, but refused to surrender to it. He would help Laura because he wanted to help her, because she needed his help. What others might think was of no importance.

Jimmy spoke to Siegfried at length after that failed approach – about the Grazianis, about the Russians, about what opportunities there might be among such people for free young men of courage and intelligence; about life, perhaps even love. Jimmy resolved to go directly and earnestly to Sokolov and persuade him to go to Graziani with uncharacteristic humility and tell him about the marriage. He would assure him that the don was a reasonable man, taking a big risk by confiding in Sokolov the truth about Balbo and the clemency Graziani had shown. Siegfried would set up a meeting, and mediate in any way that was necessary.

Ernest told me all this before Jimmy went to see Sokolov, so we were all, Siegfried included, anxious on Jimmy's behalf. The Russian would know that Jimmy was a childhood friend of Laura's, and would perhaps be less inclined to shoot him on the spot for that reason; he would also know that Jimmy was an 'outlaw' so to speak, and therefore not protected. It was a good thing Jimmy was a decent poker player. But if Sokolov snubbed him, Ernest suspected, Jimmy would kill him, Laura's happiness notwithstanding. It was a matter of honor that transcended the law, or any particular ethical tradition for that matter. The sort of thing Sokolov would have understood. But there was no need. Jimmy called Siegfried after the sit-down to announce that there had been no ugliness. Even better, Sokolov had agreed to Jimmy's request, having been persuaded that talking to his father-in-law man to man was his only chance of securing his marriage to Laura, though he doubted the meeting would end well. Siegfried called Graziani to set it up.

Paolo had the full story of what happened next from an associate of the Russian's, and related it to Siegfried. Graziani had ranted and raged, testing Sokolov, but the Russian had maintained a respectful attitude and the don eventually relented after interrogating him about his business. Graziani made the marriage his own by giving his son-in-law a restaurant as a wedding gift. The restaurant was a good, clean business – good quality Italian food. It wasn't that it was Italian that mattered, but that it was the real thing, the chef took pride in his work and only used the best produce; it wasn't some flashy place set up by someone looking to make a quick buck serving over-priced crap. The restaurant was part of a community. Sokolov got the message.

Amy Wong was not in the habit of writing gangland gossip. But when she got wind of developments in the Graziani crime family she contacted the city editor of her paper and asked if he'd consider a restaurant review…

At the table next to mine, an ethnically diverse group forms a picture of conviviality. An older Latino man and a young red-haired Southerner are dining with an Irishman and a younger Indian-American woman. Their conversation is loud and funny, bridging literature, history and politics. I mention the group because their presence seems to set the mood of the whole place. The two or three couples, a family group and perhaps business dinner party that sit

> *around the restaurant are perceptibly cheered by this central conflagration.*

When Siegfried and I returned to the restaurant alone a week or so later, the review was framed on the wall, and the maître d' made a point of showing us. 'Hey, it's the life and soul!' he said when we arrived. Siegfried would never forgive Amy Wong for mistaking him for Irish, but he thought this as good an opportunity as any to introduce himself. He emailed her the next day, explaining that he was the 'Irishman,' and said that he had an idea for a story. As a precaution, he gave her the name Art Vandeley, which he was still using with the bank and so on. The story concerned a harassment case Ernest was helping Paolo with, about which more later, but this was immediately overshadowed by what the journalist told Siegfried.

Having ascertained that Siegfried was Scottish rather than Irish (or Dutch), Amy Wong apologized profusely and got quite excited. 'You must be Siegfried,' she said.

The Devil made me do it

Alexander awoke with the proverbial hangover from Hell. It was made much worse, in fact, by his realisation that Satan himself was sitting on the armchair by his bed, and that he had tossed Alexander's newly pressed suit in a heap on the floor to make room for himself. It was 3.13am. Alexander rolled over, pulled his duvet aside and farted generously in the Devil's direction. This had the desired effect: Satan sighed with as much dignity as he could summon, and then rose and stormed out of the room. Alexander went back to sleep.

The Dark Prince had been visiting Alexander like this for some time; unannounced, uninvited and without any apparent reason. The visits thus forced Alexander to take stock of his life. Satan had first appeared soon after Alexander had separated from his wife and daughter; he was now living in a one-bedroom flat in Govan. He was in love with a schoolgirl, and despite the Devil's encouragement on his first appearance – the only time the Desolate One had spoken – Alexander harboured little hope that he could ever have her, even with all the inevitable complications that would bring. He was vaguely looking about for a more suitable paramour. And he was failing miserably to solve the biggest case of his life. It was six months since he'd inherited a child murder by exsanguination, which still had the public gripped by fear and horror. Even as he slept he was haemorrhaging time.

He woke again just after six, and immediately got up to go to the toilet, where he peed heavily and farted again. He felt better for the few hours of solid sleep he'd managed since the Evil One's departure, and this satisfying ritual seemed to purge his body. He almost felt good. It wasn't until he returned to his bedroom and bent to pick up his suit that the queasiness hit him again. It wasn't in fact physical; it was entirely psychological. Like all genuine hangovers, this one was less about chemical intoxication than the existential crisis caused by partial loss of memory.

He had been drunk last night, and it was possible that he might have behaved badly. He and DS Chalmers had been to a Rangers game and then to a pub on Paisley Road West where they met one of the new PCs and his mates, and they all sang inappropriate songs. That wasn't so bad, except that Alexander didn't particularly like Chalmers, and he worried what kind of impression he had made on the new boy.

Ordinarily Alexander was aloof from his colleagues, which suited him just fine. But he suffered from these periodic attacks of bonhomie, which he always regretted. Often, he would wake terrified that he'd revealed some secret, but fortunately Alexander's elocution tended to deteriorate as his candour increased. Typically, his confidant would have only a vague memory of Alexander mumbling with peculiar intensity. In any case, said confidant would invariably have been as drunk as Alexander. He avoided sober people when drinking, as if afraid that the condition might be catching. Indeed, it often is.

He shook down his suit and dressed. He paused at the door to fart once more, and then he was on his way.

DC Smith was running up the stairs towards him. 'Your phone isn't on!' she shouted when she saw him. 'What's happened?' he asked. She didn't have to answer. Another murder. As Smith drove Alexander to the scene, she kept looking at him nervously: 'Are you OK?'

'Fine. Do I not look OK?'

'You look… strange.' Hungover? Flustered? Like he'd seen the Devil in his bedroom? Who knew?

Smith didn't have any details of the murder, but after fumbling with his phone for a few minutes, Alexander succeeded in switching it on and got hold of his former boss DCI Kennedy, who was already at the scene. It was the same thing, another girl, seven this time, but otherwise the same: exsanguinated, the body found in the same position, everything the same. Different part of the city, though. The first body had been found by the Forth-Clyde canal in the north of the city; this one was in Knightswood, out to the west. As the depressing dirty-white, breezeblock-like houses characteristic of that part of the city appeared about the car, Alexander's stomach turned and the adrenalin came. 'The dance begins,' he might have thought, had he been capable of such whimsical reflection at a time like this. A fresh murder had been the last thing anyone wanted, but everyone knew it meant fresh hope, new evidence; the subtle differences between the two killings would say something about the killer. Alexander had secretly been wishing for this, for a fresh murder of his own, not like the cold dead corpse of a case he had inherited. He got out of the car before Smith had shut off the engine, and found DCI Kennedy with the pathologist. Eight hours, he reckoned.

It was Alexander's case, no doubt, but he had to assert himself. The unit had yet to win credibility, and Kennedy, who had led the initial investigation of the first murder, was eager to redeem himself, having been humiliated by his earlier failure. And he was here first. 'No fucking chance,' Alexander told him without even waiting for the suggestion. He knew he would have the backing of the brass, despite the miserable condition of his own subsequent investigation. Alexander was like a football manager who had taken over an Old Firm club mid-season with the league already all but lost: despite initial wild hopes, he was not really held responsible for his predecessor's failure, but he was expected to get a grip the next season. This was the real test, here, now. DC Smith appeared at his side with coffee, which made him look good. 'Thanks, Karen.' The coffeeless Kennedy yielded.

Alexander looked about him. He was always impressed by the way the police colonised a crime scene. The body had been found in a little park by a dog walker at around 6am. Two hours later there were more than twenty police on the scene: uniforms, detectives, scene-of-crime officers. Police tape was strewn around lamp-posts and now a tent was being erected, jammed uncomfortably between the swings and the roundabout in the pathetic concrete park where the dead little girl was. Alexander began to feel in charge. Imperceptibly the police presence went from being something impressive and alien to a slightly ramshackle little enterprise, and finally an extension of himself, a battery of resources at his disposal. He sipped his coffee, black, unsugared; Alexander varied his preference, but DC Smith had got the moment right without asking. Then he began to give orders, sending officers to canvass local houses, directing the photographer, briefing the press officer, and so on.

After that he spoke to the Chief Constable on the phone, reassuring him not by explaining how he would actually approach the investigation, but simply by saying the things he knew the old bastard wanted to hear. When the photographer was finished, Alexander stood in the tent with DCI Kennedy, looking at the body. Like the first one, this was no dump job. The girl had been killed in situ; she was probably local. She was naked, but probably had not been sexually assaulted; the first had not been. Not that this would be consolation to anyone. Exsanguination. What was that about?

The dead girl was identified: a distraught couple was in the makeshift incident room, having realised their daughter was missing only when the police canvassed their street. She had been taken from her room in the night. Alexander spoke to them after they'd made a positive identification. By now the media were arriving, and Alexander prepared to make a statement on camera. He didn't object in principle to this sort of thing, but he always wanted more time to get his story straight. He had made a point of recruiting a press officer to his unit because, as he had told her, he sort of believed in being accountable to the public, more so, certainly, than to the police hierarchy, though he didn't tell her that. He chose her in particular because she had warmed to this theme during her interview. (Her name was Morag, and she was a lesbian, so you can forget about her. DC Smith, on the other hand, smiled teasingly as Alexander adjusted himself in front of the camera.)

At lunchtime, Alexander called his core team together for a meeting at a local community centre the police had now taken over: Smith, Knox, McGrain, plus Morag, a couple of other detectives who'd be working the murder, and DCI Kennedy. Scene-of-crime officers were still sweeping the victim's house: the killer had broken in through the backdoor and simply walked in and taken her. She was similar enough to the first victim to suggest he'd picked her out carefully, and probably watched her for a while. Some of the neighbours had mentioned someone hanging around, but their descriptions didn't match one another's, and Alexander suspected they were just overkeen to help and more or less making it up; that wasn't unusual.

After the meeting, Kennedy and the other drafted-in detectives went off to follow up the best of the paltry leads they had (the rest would be investigated by regular detectives), Knox went off to assimilate the new details into her profile, and the rest stayed to finish off at the scene. Alexander wanted to linger for as long as possible. He sat down for the first time that day. DC Smith produced sandwiches from a plastic carrier bag. Alexander winced: carrier bags seemed mean to him; they symbolised grim practicality, disregard for quality of life, for joy. He wondered if Smith were that sort of woman. He accepted a perfectly good cheddar-cheese sandwich and they ate in silence as the last of the uniforms prepared to vacate the building.

Alexander thought of the Devil. It was strange to think that he had been in the Evil One's presence only a few hours before, and he found it hard to connect the two things in his mind: Satan sitting pensively by his bed in the dead of night, and this murder, work; sitting with Karen Smith on plastic chairs, daylight streaming in through the windows of this little community centre in Knightswood. Naturally it had occurred to him when the visits began that the Devil might be involved somehow in the first murder, in the occult, but that seemed faintly ridiculous; the Dark Prince didn't seem the type, funnily enough, or more than that, he had an aura of greatness that jarred with the awful pathos of murdered children. Instead, the Devil continued to be associated in Alexander's mind with Leanne. He missed Leanne, and had no reason ever to see her again.

The centre's caretaker appeared. 'Terrible, terrible,' he said; that sort of thing. He wanted to know how long the police would be. Not that he was anxious to be rid of them; he was clearly enjoying the excitement. Smith and Alexander exchanged looks, silently inquiring of each other whether this guy was on the suspect list, more out of annoyance than suspicion. 'If I can help, I know everybody around here,' the man continued. 'And they all know me.' He chortled. That would have been inappropriate for most people, but this guy had the air of someone who was always chortling, whatever the circumstances. He was short and lop-sided with red hair; he looked about forty-five but was probably younger. He had what people sometimes describe as a wicked grin.

'Aye, they all know me: you ask anyone.' He chortled again. Alexander didn't smile back at him, but he felt the smile within himself, a spontaneous reflection of the man's 'character,' a recognisable type represented here in a distinctly Scottish version, but surely more universal. Alexander heard a voice in his head, probably Billy Connolly's, describing the caretaker as 'a brilliant wee guy.' Such words arrived in Alexander's mind – 'he's a character, that one' – provided ready-formed by their object, and accompanied by an urge to cock his head knowingly to one side, and perhaps raise his elbows somehow. A-a-aye. How did this brilliant wee guy do that? Alexander was sure that the caretaker heard Billy Connolly too, like some people hear Jesus or the Devil. It was the last thought of this sort Alexander was to have for a couple of days. As he finished his cheese sandwich, the case took over, work thoughts came together in his mind, merging and colliding and finally succumbing to the discipline of procedure. He was off. DC Smith followed him like young Percival running on foot after the mounted knight.

Sixty hours later – in the middle of the night – Alexander arrested the murderer. The case was immaculate: the killer would go down. There was only one disappointment: this man was not responsible for the first murder; he was a copycat, a classic case according to Knox. He had taken the first murder as a sign, an order. In fact, he had actually told Knox: 'The Devil made me do it'. Alexander doubted it. The Devil had not visited him during the few hours he had spent in bed over the three days of the investigation, or perhaps had simply not bothered him; he wasn't sure. But he was sure that Satan had not spoken to the murderer: it was not a plausible mitigation. In any case, the first murder remained unsolved, its solution further than ever from Alexander's reach. Nonetheless, he had done what he needed to do. The unit was vindicated for the time being and his bosses were satisfied; two occult-tinged rape cases were to be referred to the unit next. A couple of nights after the arrest, he took the team out for a curry and actually enjoyed himself. They all looked up to him; they liked him. The evening was a warm blur.

Alexander's elation was short-lived. He was used to coming home to Laura after such triumphs. She would ask if he was drunk and shake her head disapprovingly, but really she would be delighted he was home and give him kisses and make him tea to sober him up ready for bed. Now he had only the Devil to come home to, assuming the Evil One was still interested. He walked home, losing cheer with every step. He should have sat next to Karen in the restaurant, he decided in retrospect, but he hadn't thought of it at the time, and as things had turned out he had barely spoken to her. He wasn't that sure anyway.

It was the weekend, he realised, and the streets were full of revellers, people who made a habit of enjoying themselves.

Sometimes, not just now, Alexander would catch the gaze of attractive women in the street. More often than he would have liked, they seemed to roll their eyes in response; an accusation and a put-down rolled into one. 'Stuck-up bitch!' he might think to himself. 'She's not even that good-looking; who does she think she is?' It sounds like the beginning of a terrible revelation, but it isn't. Alexander had been on all the courses and knew that deep down he was supposed to long to rape and humiliate women, but he did not. As a rule, men don't. 'Stuck-up bitch!' is not the sinister rumble of a beast within. It's an analgesic cliché. It was the easiest thing to do with his wounded pride. Rape is a different class of cliché. It's a general anaesthetic, contemptible almost as much for its life-denying quality for the rapist as for its brutalising effect on the victim. Such were Alexander's thoughts as he walked home, half-consciously anticipating his next cases.

The Devil appeared that night and at last they spoke at length, not about anything practical but about the nature of law and the place of reason. The conversation troubled Alexander's sleep for the rest of the night and he woke with a headache. He looked at his alarm clock but it was dead; the power was out. He had inherited a card-operated meter from the flat's previous, presumably less credit-worthy tenant, and Alexander was not in the habit of buying the cards. He took his phone from his pocket and checked the time on that – he had no time to waste. He dressed and had a glass of water and threw a towel at the base of the fridge and left for work.

Alexander's miserable mood gave way to agitation when he got to the station. Chalmers informed him that Leanne McGlone was in custody. She had been at a party where uniforms had gone to make an arrest. She had given them lip, Chalmers reported, and generally got in the way. She had spent the night in the cells and was now being charged with assaulting a female police officer, namely PC Judy McGovern, who was hardly a delicate flower. 'She's just being a cow,' Chalmers opined. 'I doubt anything'll come of it.'

Alexander arranged with the sergeant to have a word with her before she was released, and went upstairs to familiarise himself with the two rape cases.

'That woman is a fucking bitch,' Leanne said as soon as Alexander was alone with her. He raised his hands in a calming gesture that almost included a nod of agreement. 'Look, if it's what it sounds like you don't have to worry. You didn't actually hit her, did you?'

'Do you think I'm stupid?'

'No. Sorry. Look, I'm sure it'll blow over when everyone's had a chance to calm down... You're free to go now,' he added suddenly, realising he hadn't said.

'I know,' she said. 'They told me you wanted a word.'

'Yeah. I just wanted to check you're OK. I mean apart from this, is everything OK?'

She shrugged. 'Do you still not know anything about Adele?'

He suppressed his instinctive bureaucratic response, appreciating that it didn't matter to Leanne that it wasn't his case. And anyway, he hadn't lost interest. Far from it. 'You haven't heard anything?' he ventured tentatively.

She smiled, as if she'd known he would ask that. Her smile revealed her tongue and a piece of gum she was chewing. This seemed unbecoming to Alexander: he didn't like to think of Leanne as a vulgar person.

'I'm sure she's worried about you,' he said, 'I know you mean a lot to her.' It would have seemed inappropriate to suggest that Adele had killed Brown for Leanne's sake, sacrificing her own life so her sister would be free to make something of herself. Or that he was determined to see this act through, somehow.

Leanne shrugged again. 'Well, I can't help you,' she said. 'I've heard nothing.' She continued chewing her gum nonchalantly, provoking a surge of genuine irritation in Alexander. 'Open your mouth,' he said.

She opened her mouth. He reached in carefully with his forefinger and thumb, and removed her chewing gum. She blushed and then smirked. 'Is that for DNA evidence?'

'Yeah, that's right.' And though he hadn't thought of it before, he took a plastic evidence bag from his pocket and dropped it in.

A new case broke that afternoon, just as Alexander was reading the rape files. This one concerned African asylum seekers, and rumours of witchcraft. Worse, it involved children. A pair of eight-year-old twins had told their teacher that their aunt was a witch and was trying to harm them. One of them had burn marks on his forearms, but felt no pain; the other seemed unharmed but insisted he felt sore where the scars were on his twin. Naturally, there would be a rational explanation for this, but these days reason wasn't always given the benefit of the doubt.

Since its inception, the unit had been called in on cases involving a road-accident victim who'd been found to have frogspawn in her schoolbag, a domestic fight during which a man had been heard to call his wife a 'fucking vampire,' and a case of food-poisoning from an Indian restaurant where there was something that looked like a pentagram on the wall. These had all been resolved without attracting any media interest. It would have been too much effort to construct a compelling story around any of them, and in none of these cases did the professional who called the occult unit have a theory, or – except in the first case – anything as rigorous as a funny feeling; they were simply following procedure, covering their backs. It was only when these cases got to the unit that anyone would dare take it for granted that witches were *not* involved. Alexander felt as if he'd unwittingly been granted a monopoly on common sense.

As soon as he found some time, Alexander made further enquiries about Leanne. PC McGovern had been persuaded to let the charge go (he was relieved he wouldn't have to approach her himself), so it would be taken no further. And it transpired that the party had been with St Stephen's kids, not the likes of Darren Currie. The arrestee had been one Mark McDonald, possibly Leanne's new boyfriend judging from her determination to involve herself. He had been dealing drugs – some new amphetamine derivative – and the new drugs squad rapid response 'Night Watch' had traced a hospitalisation case back to McDonald and to the party. This was worrying, of course, but Alexander took some small consolation from the fact that Leanne hadn't asked him about McDonald. It was a relief not simply because Alexander was jealous that Leanne might have a boyfriend; he objected to this one in particular, even more than Darren Currie, who at least had the excuse of being a ned. This McDonald character was privileged, and therefore malicious in his delinquency; Alexander knew the type. He thought of Leanne's sister Adele, and enjoyed imagining her opinion of this posh wee cunt leading her little sister astray. It struck Alexander that the opportunity offered by St Stephen's was little more than an invitation to a better class of mediocrity, and one no less fraught with banal danger. If Leanne was to use her education truly to better herself, the spur would have to come from elsewhere.

He was more determined than ever to be that spur – and to bring Leanne into his own world; not the world of police or anything like that, but the world of his greater self, the world he inhabited when he thought of Leanne – and yet he felt no closer. He had always told himself that in his few fleeting encounters with Leanne they had connected somehow, there had been some kind of affinity, but now he doubted it.

He remembered seeing a documentary about John Lennon. Some poor kid had shown up at the Beatle's house in the States one day in the 1970s, convinced that all Lennon's lyrics had been addressed to him, and that he was expected. Lennon explained as pleasantly as he could that the kid was wrong, he'd made a mistake. And this kid was so gutted, so utterly thrown by the revelation, it was horrible. Alexander worried that his love for

Leanne was like that, the delusion of a stalker, without any foundation in reality. 'Have you eaten?' Lennon had asked the kid, trying to offer some crumb of comfort. As if food would have meant anything when his whole world had just fallen apart.

That evening, after feeding his electricity meter, Alexander lay on the sofa and took the bag with the chewing gum from his pocket. He opened the bag and smelled it – spearmint, not his own preference, but you can't have everything. He didn't know what to do with this token. If he chewed it, it would quickly lose its essence. One other possibility did suggest itself, but he would have felt ridiculous doing that. Eventually he bit a little piece off and chewed that, relishing the thought of Leanne's saliva mingling with his own.

What with might mean

A few days after finding Leanne in custody, Alexander went to see Father Barry. The rape cases were in hand – both seemed to involve hypnosis, which is why they had been referred to the unit – but Alexander needed a couple of hours on something else to clear his head. He told Father Barry he was worried about Leanne, and wanted to make sure she wasn't going off the rails after all that had happened. The priest knew about the arrests, of course, and thanked Alexander for anything he might have had to do with smoothing things over for the girl. Mark McDonald, Leanne's 'beau,' the priest called him, had been expelled, but was unlikely to get a custodial sentence, it seemed. Father Barry expressed some regret that the school was not a haven from such things as drugs, especially for a girl like Leanne, for whom school was so much more than an occupation. Alexander nodded, reflecting that the old Jesuit, the murderess Adele McGlone and himself were as one on this question.

Father Barry promised to keep Alexander informed about Leanne, and asked him to come back that Friday to speak to the sixth years at assembly, as he had done a couple of times before. Not about drugs, or careers or anything in particular, but about whatever he thought fit. 'Thoughts for life,' the priest called these assemblies. Alexander agreed; he had enjoyed it before, and besides, as Father Barry pointed out, that way he could see for himself how Leanne was getting on. They spoke briefly about a sermon the priest was about to give on Matthew 4; Father Barry recalled discussing the passage about the disciples with Alexander many years ago, and his then-pupil's fascination with the idea that they had chosen to follow Jesus without persuasion. 'Follow me,' had been enough. 'I think you were jealous of your Redeemer,' the priest said, and they both laughed.

That night, Alexander visited Laura to talk about Morgan,

who was now almost two. She asked if he was looking after himself and so on, and he insisted on increasing her share of his salary. Things were alright between them, but both were wounded, and now they were apart it was hard to understand why they had ever been together; it was obvious it had all been a mistake; except for Morgan.

Alexander tucked the child into bed before leaving. *There was an old woman who swallowed a bird. She swallowed the bird to swallow the spider that wriggled and wiggled and tickled inside her. She swallowed the spider to swallow the fly. I wonder why she swallowed a fly. Perhaps she'll die.*

'Alexander, it's late.'

'Aye, OK.'

Alexander went to the pub to meet Steph, then, and reported that Morgan and Laura were both well. Steph said he would go and see them soon. You perhaps imagined that Steph had forgone his interest in Laura after setting her up with Alexander, and maybe settled down with a nice tubby woman of his own, forming one of those comical sidekick couples you get in romantic comedies. But nobody can think of himself as a comical sidekick, even if everyone else does. Nobody with self-respect, at least, and Steph was no mug. He had yearned for Laura throughout her marriage to Alexander, and now he thought perhaps he had his chance. (Needless to say, Alexander was quite oblivious to this.)

The story of how Steph met Laura is actually funnier than the story of how Alexander did. It starts simply enough: Steph had to go to hospital for a tetanus jag after being bitten by a cat in the line of duty. Yes, a cat. He had been rescuing it from a hole (not important – just a hole), and it had bitten his hand, leaving a nasty puncture. After listening with great amusement to *that* story, Laura administered the jag, and Steph promptly fainted. While he was recovering with a glass of water, another patient went berserk in the waiting room, pushing over trolleys and throwing punches at anyone who went near him. Steph returned to himself and heroically subdued the lunatic. Laura was impressed, and teased him about his inconsistency. He asked her out. She agreed. By the time they met the following evening, though, Laura had cooled on the idea. Instead of going to a restaurant as planned, they got fish and chips and ate in the park. The beginning of a perfectly nice friendship – admittedly the last thing anyone ever wants, but in this case at least, better than nothing. You know the rest.

Alexander and Steph talked not about relationships, but about work, and Alexander's latest tough case. Two women had been raped on consecutive nights almost a week ago now. In each case, the victim had found herself walking in a state of confusion and dishevelment near her home at around midnight. The women had made it home and soon realised they had been raped. In one case a flatmate was on hand to take the victim to hospital; the other called her boyfriend. Both ended up in a specialist rape unit, where they were carefully examined: this would make it much easier for Alexander to build a case. No drugs were involved; in one case the victim had been drinking, though not nearly enough to explain her condition, and in the other not at all. There was mild bruising, suggestive of coercion, but not conclusive. The rapist, or rapists, had used condoms, but there were stray fibres on both victims' clothes that matched, supporting the supposition that the rapes were connected, and bits of grass and leaf, suggesting the women had been raped in a park or garden.

The hypnosis theory had come from a specialist at the rape unit. She had seen something similar down south a few years ago, she said. A man had approached his victim at a bus stop and asked her to come home with him, and for reasons she could not later explain, the victim had complied. He had raped her in a children's playground further along the road. In contrast to the current cases, he had left her there, asleep, where she was found a few hours later by a homeless man. The police had found the rapist, but failed to get a conviction. He had said she consented, and apart from the odd circumstances, there was no evidence to the contrary. The woman had been devastated, the specialist remembered, and it was only when she went into psychotherapy after the trial that the hypnosis theory had emerged, too late for the prosecution to use. On examining the second victim here and thinking of hypnosis, the specialist had immediately contacted the Procurator Fiscal, and been advised to refer the cases to the occult unit. Somebody there evidently thought this was a job for Alexander. He was of course sceptical, but he had used unusual theories successfully before, and was at least willing to consider it. He and DI Knox were to have a video conference at the weekend with one of the detectives in Manchester who had dealt with that case.

Alexander and DC Smith had already interviewed the victims, and found both to be distraught as much about the confusion surrounding their ordeal as the thing itself. Both had been on the underground, and remembered getting off at Kelvin Hall. The first had been going home after an evening with friends in the city centre, while the second had been on her way to work at the Western Infirmary; she was a nurse. Neither could remember anything beyond the immediate periphery of the station, however: the next thing they had known, they'd been walking near home. In the former case, this was very close to the station; in the latter, some distance away, on the other side of Kelvingrove Park.

Of course the loss of memory was new, but consistent in principle with the hypnosis theory – an improvement in the modus operandi even. They had no description of the rapist, but he must have approached the women near the underground station. Alexander had ordered a dramatic reconstruction in a bid to find witnesses. This was to be broadcast on tomorrow's evening news. The rapist evidently knew where his victims lived, had possibly been stalking them for some time before the attacks, but neither could think of anyone suspicious being around. Alexander told Steph he feared there was likely to be another attack before they got near the guy.

He didn't tell Steph that he had been discussing the case with Satan, who in any case had no supernatural clues, but was interested in the legal aspect of the cases. The Dark Lord appeared again, waiting at the kitchen table when Alexander got back from the pub. This was new. 'Tea? Or whisky?' Alexander asked, and then, before the Devil could answer, 'Let's have tea.' It didn't seem appropriate to ask the Lord of the Flies how he took his tea, so Alexander served it as he had his own, without milk or sugar. He also took a packet of shortbread from the cupboard and put it on the table; the Devil picked it up and immediately wolfed down its entire contents before sipping his tea as if that were perfectly normal behaviour. Alexander put the empty packet in the bin and sipped his own tea.

'You have a horror of persuasion,' the Devil told Alexander.

'Rape is not about persuasion,' Alexander replied.

'I'm not convinced this is rape.'

Alexander sighed wearily. 'These women have no memory of consenting. They were not in situations where that was even remotely likely. I don't know how it happened yet, but these women were raped.'

'The man approached them in the street, seduced them, if you will, and now they feel ashamed. Isn't that just as likely?'

'In the street? No. That just doesn't happen.'

'It's not that unusual, is it, for people to meet strangers and have sex? If it had happened in a nightclub you wouldn't think my version so strange.'

'Maybe not. But the unusual situation is relevant precisely because it supports the women's account of what happened. They say it was rape, and that makes more sense than your version.'

'*You* would say the same if it *had* been in a nightclub.' The

Devil smiled.

'Of course I would, if the women hadn't consented.'

'Others would have their doubts. He-said-she-said. No conclusive signs of coercion. Of course *you've* never picked up a woman like that, but that doesn't make it a crime.'

'Like *that?* No, you're quite right. I commend you on your perception, or your supernatural omniscience, or whatever. But *that's* not the point. Like *this*? This guy is not just some Casanova. He just goes up to strange women in the street, *in the street*, and what? He says, "Follow me," and...'

The Devil sat back in his chair and smiled.

'Jesus Christ did not fuck the disciples,' Alexander said, suddenly recognising his own unconscious reference.

'No,' Lucifer laughed, and then looked thoughtful. 'I was there, you know, on the shore of Galilee, when the little rabbi appeared and made the fishermen follow him. It was... creepy.' Alexander looked at the Devil nervously. He had never actually been frightened in the Evil One's presence hitherto, but this little vignette was unsettling. The Devil went on. 'People can be persuaded very easily. It's a cheap trick, really, to make someone follow you, if you know how. And there are none so persuadable as those who will not be pers...'

'So you don't dispute that the rapist *tricked* them?'

'I did say "seduced"; that's sort of the same, isn't it? But is that the issue?'

'The issue, in boring legal terms, is whether the women consented to sexual intercourse.'

'Oh. I don't know. Maybe you're right,' Satan said. 'Consent,' he repeated, making a show of grappling with the concept. The Devil shrugged.

Alexander wasn't ready to sleep when the Desolate One left. He felt now as often of late that he would not sleep soundly till he could lay his head on Leanne McGlone's lap and have her stroke his hair. He poured himself a whisky and lay on the sofa in front of the TV. *The Prime of Miss Jean Brodie* was on. Alexander had never seen it, but he remembered the novel from school. He couldn't at first remember the details of the plot: he hadn't felt the same sort of interest in schoolgirls then that he felt now. When it dawned on him that Sandy – not the obvious one but the clever one – was sleeping with the art teacher, he threw his whisky glass at the TV in a vicarious jealous rage. The screen exploded. The noise of the explosion startled him from his self-indulgence, and he raised his arms apologetically as if to pacify an invisible audience. He realised now that his face was wet with tears. He went next door and sat on his bed and picked up a stray vest to wipe away the tears. But instead he held it to his face and sobbed out loud for five solid minutes. When he was finished he pushed the vest under his duvet. He wondered what was on TV, cursed himself, and collapsed fully clothed into sleep.

Leanne was not at school when Alexander gave his talk that Friday. It went well enough anyway, but when he finished he excused himself from tea with Father Barry and went straight to the caravan park. Granny McGlone ushered him into Leanne's tiny room in the trailer; not strictly appropriate, but he wasn't going to say no. Leanne was surprised to see him, but not alarmed. She was quite pleasant, in fact, and apologised for missing his talk; she'd been stressing about some schoolwork, she said, and indeed there were books open on her little desk. She had not heard from Adele; neither had Alexander. That topic was quickly exhausted. Leanne was about to say something else when she realised Alexander was staring at the floor next to her bed. He couldn't take his eyes off a pair of knickers she had dropped there. Dirty knickers. She rode a blush by asking coolly, 'I suppose you want my pants for DNA evidence too?' Alexander was startled, and couldn't hide his own blush. 'You definitely can't take them,' he had to tell himself. The thought of Leanne's DNA on the pants inflamed him unbearably. He thought of the chewing gum, and his eyes rolled, only to find a crucifix on the wall. At this provocation he shouted under his breath, 'Do not mock me, Nazarene!' Now Leanne was startled, and took a moment before responding. 'Well if you're done shouting at the wee man, was there something else you wanted to ask me?'

Alexander recovered himself and apologised. 'I was just worried about you,' he said. 'I wanted to make sure you're not going off the rails,' he added, conscious that he was repeating the same cliché he'd used with Father Barry.

She pointed at her books and smiled reassuringly.

'Would you babysit for me?' he said suddenly. 'I have a daughter: she's two going on twelve. She's with me this weekend, but there's a meeting I really have to go to first thing tomorrow morning.'

'Babysit?' Leanne was surprised. 'Why are you asking me?'

'I don't know anyone else, and I don't want to advertise. You're from a good school… a good family,' he said. She smiled at his hesitation. 'You could study. And I'll pay you, of course. I mean, do you want a job?'

'Yes. All right, then.'

A little voice in Alexander's head had a lot to say about this as he left the caravan park, but technically it wasn't against any rule, or at least Alexander wasn't going to go out of his way to find out that it was. He had been planning simply to take Morgan into work with him in the morning; he didn't expect the video conference to take long. But this was better: Laura didn't like him taking Morgan to the station, and as long as he described Leanne as a protégé of Father Barry's rather than a wayward gypsy temptress, he supposed Laura would approve of this solution.

He spent the afternoon with his team, working through tips they had got in response to the dramatic reconstruction on the news. Mostly rubbish, but a couple of possible leads, and another possible victim. Alexander took Knox to interview the woman at home. This one remembered. She hadn't come forward before because she hadn't been attacked as such. She simply couldn't make sense of what had happened to her, she told them, in tears. But she had never 'decided' to have sex with the man; it had just 'happened.' They all knew this description was inadequate: it matched a million sexual encounters that were anything but rape. In objective terms, only the peculiar circumstances: the stranger's approach in the street immediately leading to intercourse in the park, marked the encounter as suspicious – and connected it with the other cases – and there was nothing intrinsically unlawful about those circumstances. 'Maybe if I can help you catch him, you can prove it was rape with the others,' the woman said. And that was indeed their best hope. The detectives took a detailed description, and as they left, Alexander asked Knox how many similar cases she thought there might be. 'God knows,' she said.

The description matched three of those given by callers who had seen a man hanging around by the underground station, and according to one of those he was the manager of a local internet café. It turned out this man had not been seen at home or at work since the day before the first rape. His description was not consistent with that of the alleged rapist in Manchester, however. The detective Knox and Alexander spoke to the next morning was now a high-profile national authority on drug-assisted rape; hence the video conference, his favoured means of communication. He remembered 'the hypnosis case' well, and with great regret. He believed the perpetrator was now in prison for unrelated offences, but he was surprised there had not been more cases like this. 'Hypnosis is a powerful tool,' he said. Indeed, he suggested using it to trigger the memories of the two victims, but Alexander had already ruled this out on the grounds that it would compromise their credibility in court. He preferred to pursue their one real lead, the missing internet-café man.

'Did you get much work done?' Alexander asked Leanne when he returned to the flat.

'Not really. Morgan says it's distracting to have someone reading in silence when she's trying to watch cartoons.'

'Sorry…'

'No, it's OK. She's great, uncanny.'

Alexander's heart swelled.

Leanne mentioned that there was a funny smell in the flat, like there had been a fire. Alexander told her not to worry – he had noticed it too of late and supposed it was the grill; he would replace the filter. It was either that or the sulphurous stink of the Devil, but he didn't mention this latter possibility.

'I like Leanne,' Morgan said when her sitter had left. 'Is she going to look after me again?'

'Maybe. Shall we have lunch and then go to the park?'

'OK.'

He looked in the fridge: good, honest tins of Tennent's Lager, not that bottled continental stuff that Laura had insisted on buying – 'a wee treat for you,' she had liked to say. And he had bought some square sausage, Morgan's forbidden favourite. 'Don't tell Mum,' he said as he took it out, and Morgan grinned and did a little dance, hopping from one foot to the other.

Alexander had to call Leanne again the next day when the internet-café man turned himself in at the station. He had been bullshitting when he told Laura he'd be able to look after Morgan for the whole weekend, but now it seemed he had got away with it and then some. He spoke to Leanne about the possibility of having her 'on call' for the odd weekend in the future. She said she'd be delighted, on the condition that she was guaranteed to see Morgan at least every so often! And there it was. Alexander had a relationship with Leanne. Not the one he had wanted, but something that kept her in his orbit. He told Steph about the arrangement, just to reassure himself how normal it was; Steph did not suggest otherwise.

Alexander and Knox interviewed the internet-café man, who acknowledged all three encounters and insisted they had been consensual. After twenty minutes the detectives left the man and conferred. Knox was convinced that he considered himself guilty but untouchable, and she feared he was right. Whatever part the women had had in what happened, he had set out to 'have' them, and not in a nice way. He was laughing at them. Knox shrugged. She knew that Alexander wanted to charge the man, but neither believed they could make the case. 'There's no law against being a shit,' Knox said.

'I still think it's more than that,' Alexander said emphatically, 'but we're not going to get anything else to come back at him with, are we?'

'I can't see it.'

'Fuck it – let's charge the prick now.'

Alexander charged the prick. A subsequent search of the man's flat brought up several books on hypnosis. It may have been the lamest theory Alexander had ever used, but he would give it everything he had.

The thing about babysitters, of course, is that the whole point of them is to be somewhere you are not. In those precious minutes when they did share the same space, when Leanne arrived to let Alexander go, and when he arrived back to do the same for her, they would speak quite seriously, not wasting time on chit-chat. About Morgan, about life, about the future. Leanne was frustrated at school, she told Alexander when he returned that second afternoon. She felt stuck, like she was just waiting around for her life to begin. She was to go on to the music academy to pursue her interest in music – composition, she said, blushing when she saw that Alexander was impressed. But even that felt like 'another bloody prelude,' she said. She complained that both she and her best friend, who was going to the art school, would both be within a couple of hundred yards of St Stephen's. Glasgow was too bloody small.

When had Alexander felt his life had really begun, she wanted to know? He resisted the obvious, 'I'll let you know,' and with greater difficulty the less obvious, 'Now. This instant. Standing in the kitchen, talking to you, my love, my life.' Instead he told her about becoming a detective, realising his youthful ambition and taking on responsibility, finally feeling like a grown-up. He laughed. It occurred to him later that there was something in this. He couldn't imagine being a father to Morgan were he not also a detective, and a senior one at that. But at that moment in the kitchen he remembered instead a line from Seneca: '*Non enim vivant, sed victuri sunt.*'

'That's very good,' she said, 'but shouldn't it be viv-unt?' She was right. He had misremembered the line all this time, and unlike Leanne's, his Latin was now inadequate to catch the error. He stood corrected. Taken in context, the line means something like, 'They are not living, merely preparing for life to begin.'

Later, when Leanne had gone, and Morgan too, Alexander brooded. He went to his computer and was probably about to waste his time when he changed his mind suddenly and looked up a book instead. He was pleasantly surprised to discover that his old Latin textbook, which had been ancient even when he was at school, was still available. He ordered it and then went back to brooding. He would have liked to think it was the Devil who distracted him from his work. But having met and conversed with Lucifer he now saw how self-serving was that way of thinking. The Evil One's interest in his work seemed more academic than invested. Unless that was just what he wanted Alexander to think...

That night Alexander discovered the light in his bathroom was broken, but went ahead and showered in the dark. As he washed, he was overcome by a sense of unease about the dark. About the Antichrist. And the dark. He was being visited by the Antichrist. His unease turned to fear and he panicked, bursting out of the shower and into the light of the hall. He caught his breath and felt ridiculous standing there naked and dripping, the water still running in his shower. Was he afraid of the dark now? He went back in and resumed washing, then just stood for a moment letting the hot water wash over him. Calm. What had he been afraid of? As soon as he asked himself the question, his fear returned and he burst out into the hall again. 'For fuck's sake!' he said out loud, and then, 'Wooh-ooh-ooh!,' mocking himself with a scary ghost gesture. Back into the shower, then. This time he turned out the light in the hall: he would prove to himself that he was not afraid. Still, he talked to himself as he climbed into the shower, just to hear a reassuring voice. As he resumed his shower again he reminded himself of his encounters with Satan, how unthreatening, or at least not threatening, the Devil had seemed. Except for that last time, the Galilee thing. Alexander's thoughts drifted for a moment, and he idly registered that he was not afraid. As soon as he thought it, though, and before he could claim victory, the unease returned. He felt a presence. It was not the Devil, but rather the kind of terrifying presence only the imagination can muster. Alexander felt as if he were sinking into Hell. He began panting, and began to moan, just to make a sound, as he fled a third time into the hall and desperately reached for the light switch. If anyone had been there to see it, it would have been fucking hilarious.

It was three weeks before Alexander had reason to call on Leanne again.

'Morgan's had her tea, but there's stew in the fridge if you want to eat.'

'Stew?' Leanne smiled teasingly.

'Yeah.' And he realised that stew represented something about him, a certain old-fashioned, meat-and-potatoes strangeness. He smiled back, deciding that this probably wasn't a bad thing.

'You don't smile much, do you?' she said, causing him to check his expression. Was this a tip? Alexander thought of the way he felt when Leanne smiled at him, and he wished he could make her feel like that, but he didn't know how. He was just not a smiler. (There were times when she made his heart swell and he adored her more than he could bear, but this feeling produced no more than an imperceptible tightening of his lips, and perhaps a sparkle in his eye that would have been observable only to a particularly observant ophthalmologist.) The thought of anyone else making her feel that way made him feel sick. As he reached the bottom of the stairs on his way out, he realised he was crying again. It was either sadness like this or blind rage: he didn't know which he preferred, which was better. And yet, despite his misery – no, because of it – it was quite true that Alexander felt not just grown-up, but alive for the first time in his life. His lovesickness seemed to serve the same function as the proverbial slap on a new-born baby's bum. He smarted, he was alive, he had a life. Even if it was a pathetic one.

'I know it's normal for babysitters to have their boyfriends with them sometimes, and I'm not saying you'd be negligent, but I'd just rather you didn't,' he said the next time Leanne sat for him.

'I wouldn't!' she protested, understanding that this had nothing to do with Morgan, and everything to do with Alexander's jealousy, and not minding that at all. Instead, she was offended that Alexander could think she'd be so thoughtless. Alexander was grateful for that, while feeling with a combination of guilt and satisfaction that there was something improper about her complicity with his jealousy.

He had always been jealous, though, even before Leanne. He'd been promiscuously jealous before marrying, and devotedly jealous after. There had been a time towards the end of their marriage when Laura had developed a peculiar appetite for fellatio. Whenever they had made love, she'd spent so much time with her head under the duvet that Alexander began to miss her kisses, and even grew jealous of his own penis. There was, after all, nothing special about his penis, and it annoyed him that she could be thinking about *anyone* down there. It annoyed him even more that this seemed to heighten rather than diminish his pleasure. At least, thank God, it wasn't like that with Leanne. Not anymore. Since she had grown into his life, there was nothing sexual in his jealousy. It was sheer, unerotic, agony.

He spoke to Leanne about Laura just once. It started with Morgan; Alexander tried to explain how a parent feels about a child, a love so fierce, so unilateral, so lacking in the contingency and prevarication that hover about even the best adult relationships. 'It's not even a feeling,' Alexander explained. 'It's a commitment, but deeper than marriage. It would be immoral to stop loving a child, so it just isn't an option.'

'But I suppose marriage used to be like that, when people didn't have a choice,' Leanne said.

'I suppose, except that an institution like marriage can't make you *love* someone the way parenthood can. Marriage might once have been a duty, but that's different. Look, I don't even think I've stopped loving Morgan's mother,' he went on recklessly. 'That's not duty either; if anything it's bloody-mindedness, my own vanity. Maybe I should never have married her, but I did, and I refuse to think of it as a mistake, even if Laura does.' He could see that Leanne was not convinced.

Listening to himself, he decided that there is no such thing as love as an abstract idea – not even parental love – only unique individuals and their manifold bonds, entered into more or less willingly, more or less consciously, and honoured with similar diversity.

Alexander thought about Leanne more than usual after that conversation, trying to decide what she was to him, he to her. He thought back to John Lennon and his stalker, wondering whether Lennon could have played along if he'd wanted to, could have pretended out of sympathy that he really had been speaking to this kid through his songs. Would that have satisfied the kid, or were there specific aspects to the fantasy that Lennon could not have known about? Maybe the kid's delusion was less important than his desire to be close to his hero any way that he could. Which was to ask, of course, whether Alexander wanted a real relationship with Leanne, on her terms as much as his, and with the risk – probability – of failure, or whether as the voices had once maintained, he was merely indulging a fantasy as part of a premature mid-life crisis.

He caught sight of himself in the mirror as he stepped out of the shower, the light repaired and brighter than ever. That beergut wasn't going anywhere. He sometimes thought about his body in relation to Leanne, but he knew that whatever attraction he might have for a young girl, it could only be precisely as a man, a grown-up, hairy, paunchy man with standing in the world. There was no point in wishing for a six-pack stomach like some wee poof in a boy band.

As for Leanne's appearance, he found it hard to picture her in her absence. He could see her short blonde hair, a few distinctive items of clothing, but not her face, not anything of the beauty that he saw when she was before him. She did not conform to any ideal; her features refused simile. Her mouth was perfectly hermouthlike, her eyes just that. Her breasts were not at all like clusters of grapes. I could hazard a description of her breasts, but that would communicate nothing of what Alexander saw. He saw very little, of course, but subtle contours and ripples in her clothing described her breasts just as soaring birds describe the wind. And when he closed his eyes all that remained was lifeless cotton. Her breasts were unbearable. Is that too much? It was too much for Alexander.

It occurred to him that he never really looked at anyone else, let alone anyone else's breasts, but simply at assemblages of similes. There is nothing erotic about similes, about types: the perfect smile, the perfect pair of breasts, such templates are anaesthetic. It is particularity that excites: the particular shape of the breasts, the colouring, the odd marks that distinguish this body from others, that distinguish a particular person with a real name and a life of her own. Such a body is a secret to be exposed, whether joyfully in an intimate encounter or callously in pornography.

He missed Laura, and he thought of Laura's body. All of it, even her elbows and the back of her head, stupid places like that, the parts of a woman you only kiss because you said you'd kiss every inch of her, and then you feel daft kissing, especially because there's not much in it for her either; it's best not to take these things literally. But he thought of Laura's body, every particular inch.

Some developments, revelations et cetera

First, the alarmingly precocious Morgan brought home a two-faced kitten. Literally two-faced, that is, not duplicitous. The little mutant had come from of one of her mother's neighbours, but neither the neighbour nor Laura could bear to have it in the house. Laura had told Morgan it was bound to die before long, but that if Alexander was willing to take it, then she could keep it. Alexander picked it up by the scruff of the neck and looked at it in fascination, its two mouths mewing in sequence. Neither face seemed to be dominant, or perhaps they were still fighting it out: each face was at the same slight angle to where the cat ought to have been looking.

'Can we? Can we? Can we?' pleaded Morgan.

'Aye, OK.'

Then the Procurator Fiscal got the rape conviction: the unit's hypnosis theory had convinced the jury. The internet-café man had used hypnosis to compel the women, and was therefore guilty of rape. It was an extraordinary verdict and Alexander wasn't even sure if he approved, but it gave a new credibility to the unit, which had supplied the Procurator Fiscal with more than evidence or even a theory; it had given the case a story, a wild, gothic story perfectly pitched for the market. All it was missing was a two-faced kitten.

The media had gone crazy on the case. In the case of the second child exsanguination Alexander liked to think he had reassured the public by demystifying a frightening murder and thus taming the imaginative excesses of the media. This time the unit's involvement had leant a more ghoulish aspect to what might otherwise have been seen as a banal series of dubious rapes. The defence advocate had facetiously coined the term 'speed date rape' in an effort to discredit and ridicule the case against his client, but the tinge of the occult put the case beyond such prosaic dispute. The prosecution won the case by making it more mysterious than it had seemed. The internet-café man had inevitably been nicknamed 'Svengali,' and to Alexander's great annoyance, the coverage had portrayed him as a devilishly clever seducer rather than the shitty chancer that Alexander saw.

Towards the end of the trial, Alexander had been approached by another 'victim.' This one had resisted. Svengali had approached her, chatted her up. She had found herself following him and then stopped, confused and angry with herself. He had laughed at her, making her angrier. She had felt she must say something; she couldn't just leave. But she was a stutterer, could not speak, and not for the first time in her life she had turned and fled instead. Alexander wondered if her speech impediment had saved her, if the others had been drawn into intercourse, unable to breach good manners by fleeing like the stutterer. Knox agreed: Svengali had succeeded in putting the burden of 'violence' on his victims, requiring them to get weird to get rid of him. Only this one woman who was used to doing the weird thing had been willing to take the only way out that he offered. The stutterer never appeared in court. She should have been a defence witness, if anything, but had no desire to testify, would not be compelled. Knox later used her unadmitted evidence in an academic paper.

Then another murder: a priest beaten to death in his own chapel with a plaster St Patrick. A few years earlier it might have been supposed a sectarian crime; now occult was all the rage. The unit found the culprit very fast using conventional police methods (DC Smith did most of the work): he was a mentally-disturbed kid, the son of a widowed parishioner. Nonetheless, no doubt flattered and emboldened by the attention of the occult unit, the church said he was possessed. Who was to say he wasn't? It didn't matter for the prosecution, at least; nobody was suggesting that the demon should be prosecuted in the boy's absence. But the media enjoyed it.

Alexander spoke to Father Barry, who was ashamed, embarrassed. Alexander's bosses, like Father Barry's, couldn't see a problem. The unit was doing what it was supposed to do, getting results. Of course, Alexander's intention had always been different. In his mind, cases were to come to him occult and be dispatched banal, not the other way round. The definition of an occult case was now a case dealt with by the occult unit; he wouldn't be able to collar a shoplifter without getting pixie dust on him. The Jesuit sympathised. People were coming to him demanding exorcisms, and they weren't buying his argument that the church was opposed to such superstition; they had seen it on TV now. 'God is not a ghostbuster,' he told them, but they had little other use for a deity. They were amazed by his objection.

Alexander would have liked to introduce Father Barry to Satan; he thought they would have got on. The Dark Prince was less sympathetic about Alexander's predicament, though no more frightening than he had been before Alexander's panic attack; he remained disarmingly personable. 'The road to Hell is paved with good intentions,' he said, with a rather smug grin. 'Why don't you resign, if you disapprove so much?' Alexander said he still thought he could do more good in charge of the unit than if he stood down. 'Oh, aye,' said the Devil.

Do you want an objective opinion? You humans are always making that mistake. I can't give you an Olympian view anyway. Quite the opposite. Let me introduce myself at last. I am the demon Andras, Grand Duke of Hell, Commander of twenty-nine Diabolical Legions, Grand Vizier to His Diabolical Majesty Beelzebub…

What? It could have been worse. I read a story once that turned out to have been narrated by a sofa. My perspective is neither Olympian nor human – I am not a character in this story – but at least I take an interest, and that's what you need in a narrator.

In any case, Alexander had his reasons for thinking as he did. One advantage of the unit's high profile and success was that Scottish CultWatch, the NGO that had been largely responsible for unit's inception, had been marginalised, and, especially having been surprised by the rape affair, had lost control of the agenda. But they had not disappeared, and Alexander was afraid that they would eventually take advantage of the new climate of institutionalised, albeit more sober, superstition, to push their agenda further. In particular, SCW had been wary thus far of talking about 'Satanic ritual abuse,' the focus of the notorious 'Satanic panic' of the 1980s, during which dozens of children had been taken from their parents following what turned out to be completely unfounded allegations of devil-worship, sexual abuse and 'that sort of thing.' (Only a lapsed Christian society could connect these things – all the fucked-upness, none of the faith.) But suspicion simmered, fuelled by vaguer anxieties. After all the first exsanguination murder remained unsolved more than a year on, the case all but abandoned. Once SCW had got to grips with the rape thing, they sent Alexander a briefing on 'sexual coercion in secondary schools.' There was no mention of devil-worship, but an insistent emphasis on cult-influenced or cult-like behaviour (the terms were used interchangeably).

Alexander was still sure, whatever his misgivings about the hypnotism theory, that those women had been raped; Svengali had done more than push his luck. But he now saw that the case had opened Pandora's box. SCW was presenting every horny schoolkid kid as a Svengali in the making. Alexander's team couldn't see it: they wanted to know what all this had to do with cults. But Alexander had been reading SCW's stuff all along; he knew they'd been talking about 'peer pressure' from the outset, and now this had gone from being their way of understanding the spread of cults to the essence of the problem itself. The Halloween mask was off: it didn't matter if kids were worshipping Satan, sacrificing gerbils or just groping in darkened rooms. What mattered was that they were meeting in secret, spreading rumours, 'negatively influencing' one another. It was Alexander who had transformed a difficult serial rape case into a sinister tale of barely understood psychological hocus pocus. If Scottish CultWatch had their way, the whole messy business of adolescent sexuality would be similarly recast. The distinction between rape, bullying and persuasion would be hopelessly blurred.

'Predatory sex is not "natural,"' the briefing said. 'It is an occult ideology, and one that must be challenged. For too long we have allowed our schools to serve as training camps for sex offenders, institutionalising the notion that sex is about conquest and submission. Through cult-like rituals, teenagers learn that coercion is normal. Young men conform by adopting the role of predator. Young women conform by acquiescing. Both are victims of a sinister ideology that must be confronted.' The Devil sucked his teeth. 'That's bold,' he said. 'Not so long ago it was hormones.'

'And the solution was discipline,' Alexander added.

'Discipline is cult-like,' Satan said.

Alexander smiled sarcastically at the Dark Prince. 'What's missing is agency,' he explained, relishing the opportunity to discuss this. 'What they're talking about is brainwashing, not ideology, and the premise of brainwashing theories is that people have no responsibility for the ideas they choose make their own. As cynical as I am, I don't believe that. And neither do you.'

Lucifer just looked at Alexander.

'Do you?'

'Never mind what I believe. Isn't that the whole premise of your work? That people are slaves to superstition and need to be shown the light of reason?'

'No. My job is to make people acknowledge the reality of their own responsibility.'

'Except when they're victims of persuasion?'

'This again? Persuasion implies agency on the part of whoever's being persuaded, and those women were not kidding themselves; they were just fucking had. It's just as wrong to attribute responsibility where there was none as it is to deny it where there was.'

The Devil was about to say something, but Alexander went on. 'You know what the trouble with sex is? Sex has become a practice without a theory. It goes on, but nobody knows why. And these clowns,' he brandished the SCW briefing, 'have come up with a theory that appeals to the worst in people.'

The theory was not just that but a worldview; it called for a different type of polis, not a polis of discipline, but one of containment. There were no criminals, no victims, just a world peopled by morally incompetent zombies. The occult unit was in danger of making itself redundant after all, not by exposing the banal reality of so-called occult crime, but by putting human wickedness beyond the remit of the criminal justice system. Scottish CultWatch and its acolytes would take over the shop, Alexander said. The Devil was fascinated.

For his part, Alexander might well have resigned, asked to work plain old murders for as long as they would let him, except for his new lease of life, except for Leanne. It had of course occurred to Alexander to imagine how Leanne might have responded to an approach from Svengali. He wanted to believe that she would have resisted, but this seemed an unfair burden. As much as he loved her, it was not because she was objectively so different from other women. What had she seen in Darren Currie, for God's sake, or in his upmarket equivalent Mark McDonald? Alexander had to forgive her her worldliness; she was a girl like other girls. And yet, he would not accept this diminished view as all that Leanne could be. If nothing else, what made her different was him, his love. He knew she valued their talks; he was her edge. This, after all, was what made Morgan special too: Alexander was determined Morgan would never succumb to low seduction. This being so, he could not abandon the occult unit. His entire being demanded that he stay and fight SCW's attempt to turn criminal responsibility, and moral agency, to mush. The Devil was fascinated.

'Are vampires real?' Alexander asked Satan suddenly during one of these discussions. The Evil One laughed at him. No, that was not what this was about, his being here; it was not an indication that 'it's all true,' the revelation you get in horror films. Alexander knew it really, even if he didn't understand what the Devil's visitations did mean. It was just that he'd been thinking about vampires in connection with Svengali. Vampires needed an invitation to enter someone's home, precisely the formal, explicit declaration of consent that the rapist had done without, that millions of non-rapists do without every day. Indeed, it seemed to Alexander that the whole notion of consent was better suited to the fictional world of vampires than the real world of human affairs, where 'consent' is hardly sufficient anyway ('And you're just going to lie there?'). If vampires were real, they'd be up in court every day while lawyers debated the legal status of disputed invitations. The law was only good for the minority of cases in real life where there was unequivocal violence or the clear threat of it, making the absence of consent explicit. As the Dark Prince knew very well, this left the great bulk of human affairs untouched. That was a good thing on balance, Alexander was sure, but it was the terrifying ambiguity of extra-legal morality that drove SCW to abandon altogether what they saw as the fictional world of legal agency, Alexander's world. The Devil did not express an opinion.

That's enough theorising to be getting on with. Alexander's thoughts were shaken up by news of Siegfried. Old news, in fact: Siegfried's embezzlement had finally been discovered. The fraud detectives who'd caught the case informed Alexander when they found his enquiries on file, but there was little they or Alexander could do as long as Siegfried was untraceable. Once again, though, Alexander found himself affected by Siegfried's mysterious actions. Apart from anything else, stealing money was so quaint: so straightforward, so downright reasonable. It was a world away from the weird and irrational crimes that exercised the unit. Siegfried had even heroically foiled a rape around the same time as taking the money. Alexander had no doubt that he had taken it for some specific purpose: it had been an instrumental crime. He was almost jealous of Siegfried's agency, and his apparent disregard for etiquette. And yet he recognised himself in Siegfried. He realised that his own devout defence of the law, his inner-directed struggle to bring criminals to account on his own terms, somehow bore an affinity with Siegfried's criminality. How was it that Alexander's orthodoxy felt so close to Siegfried's deviance?

Steph, meanwhile, failed again with Laura. She gently rebutted his advances, thereby affirming their silver-medal friendship. He felt awkward about telling Alexander about this, and so he took an interest in Alexander's own love life instead, voicing at last what had been on his mind since Alexander had told him about Leanne looking after Morgan.

'Alexander, you can tell me. Is there… Pardon my vulgarity, but are you shagging the babysitter?'

'No,' Alexander laughed genuinely at Steph's way with words before dealing with the question itself, which he'd been anticipating, 'Nothing like that. It's not even a vague possibility. But I won't say she's not important to me. She is. She's an extraordinary person, and I think we have some sort of connection.' He shrugged. The speech was not rehearsed, but the sentiment surely was. 'There's more than one way to love somebody,' he added quietly.

Steph nodded. They both knew that in other circumstances this last remark would have led to a joke about anal sex, but the thought passed through their minds without being offered so much as a cup of tea.

'So what about DC Smith?'

'What *about* DC Smith?'

Steph just frowned.

'Maybe,' Alexander said. He was about to say more, but suddenly he felt ridiculous, schoolgirlish. Steph had always liked this sort of conversation, considered it normal, but Alexander thought it effeminate, unbecoming, the fare of bad TV. 'I have great respect for DC Smith as a detective and a human being,' he said finally, and now Steph laughed at Alexander's way with words.

Alexander wasn't the only one to admire DC Smith as a detective; he had recommended her for promotion, she had passed the requisite exams, and following her part in the rape convictions she was made detective sergeant. She was to stay in the unit, of course: her promotion was a vindication of its work as much as her own abilities. Accordingly the whole team went out for a celebratory curry. This time Alexander sat next to Karen for the whole evening; she was his protégé after all, and he was proud of her. And there was something lingering between them when they parted at the end of the evening. Extended eye contact, perhaps, or a casual touch, or maybe it was just that Alexander's heart beat a little faster, but he was sure Karen's did too; there was something there.

Alexander resolved to strike while the iron was hot. The next day he suggested the two of them get together to discuss her role in the unit, her taking more responsibility and so on. But also it would just be good to have a proper chat about things. Not just work things. It might be nice even.

'We could go for a drink or something maybe. What do you think?'

'Are you asking me out?' She said it accusingly, teasingly.

'I think technically I was "sniffing around", but since you've forced the issue, yes, would you go out with me?' This was either gauche or attractively nonchalant; it was up to her to decide which.

'How could anyone resist such a charming offer?'

'Is that a yes?'

'Yes.' So they had a date, Alexander and DS Smith.

It went well; they got on, and even managed to talk productively about work. Not just work work. Karen was an enthusiastic polis, keen to learn from Alexander, and not just technique but philosophy. It had never occurred to Alexander that his philosophy of police work was something that could be communicated, something that anyone else would be interested in even – the Desolate One didn't count – but Karen was hungry for it. They discussed the unit, Alexander's misgivings about it, and the threat presented by Scottish CultWatch. Karen explained why she had volunteered for it in the first place, but seemed unhappy with her own answer. She wanted Alexander to explain even that; he put things better than she did. They spoke and thought and enjoyed each other's company, alternating profound conversation with trivial matters – their colleagues, personal anecdotes, likes and dislikes – all of which gave their minds time to reflect before returning to the passion that united them. And Karen wanted to know more about Alexander, what he was like, what he liked. The conversation came around to interviewing, one of Alexander's strengths, and then testifying, another. Karen said Alexander was persuasive, but he disagreed, and insisted on the point more generally, as a feature of his character.

'I don't like arguing; I'm no good at it.'

'But you're a star in court: everyone says so.'

'Aye,' said Alexander, forgetting to blush, 'but that's just assisting. It's the advocate that does the closing, and that's what I can't do. I'm no good at winning arguments, closing deals… clinching things.' On reflection that was a bit too true, so he tried to make it a joke. 'I cross from the wing and someone else has to knock it in.'

Karen laughed. 'You used to play, didn't you?'

'How did…?'

'I have my sources. Anyway, you must have scored goals when you were an actual footballer, no?'

He frowned.

'What, never?!'

'I was a defender… I did score once at school. But that was arguably offside…' He shrugged. She laughed louder, and then looked at Alexander and kissed him on the cheek. His heart quickened…

'Wait!' she said suddenly. 'Detective Chief Inspector Alexander, is this a *line*?'

'Well, if it is I guess I've blown it,' he said, looking at the floor.

'No. You haven't blown it.' She took his face and kissed him again, on the mouth this time. (So what was that, reader? A genuine score? Or just an unduly sympathetic goalkeeper? I shall leave judgements of that kind to you.)

'A kiss. Yes. My mouth remembers this,' Alexander thought to himself. It had been nearly a year, after all, since he had kissed his wife for the last time, and he hadn't known it at the time. You never do. Or, if you do, it doesn't count. (Nearly a year. Do you know how long it's been since I felt the hot breath of another? *Nine thousand, eight hundred and forty years.* She was a wood nymph: fucking heartbreakers all, I can tell you.) But it had been a year since Alexander had kissed Laura for the last time. Alexander and Karen kissed again. The same feeling, the same taste.

'My flat is just round the corner,' Karen said, with a smile that gave Alexander a rush of blood. Having been temporarily swept off his feet, however, he now took control of the situation: 'OK, let me walk you home.'

Karen looked perturbed, uncertain what this meant, but he smiled and kissed her again to reassure her. 'Early start tomorrow,' he added. It sounded lame and he'd have rather not have had to say it, but he wasn't sure what people expected in these situations. They walked to Karen's flat mostly in silence, but Alexander let his hand brush against hers and smiled at her several times. 'This was lovely,' he said at her door, 'Can we do it again?'

'Yes, please,' she smiled, surrendering to his way of doing things. They kissed again, not a goodnight kiss, but another kiss while there was still time, and Alexander squeezed her tight before parting. 'Sweet dreams,' he whispered.

Another rape.

'Rape? You're joking. You think I raped someone? That's crazy.'

Alexander said nothing; he just looked at the suspect.

'Seriously, this is a big mistake. I would never rape someone. I'm a nice guy,' he went on, trying to laugh.

'But women don't like nice guys, do they?' said Alexander, standing up. He stood leaning on the backrest of his chair and kept looking at the suspect, who shrugged.

'Seeing anyone?' Alexander asked.

'I'm divorced.'

'Me too.' Alexander let go of the chair and paced a bit. 'Well, separated. We haven't talked about divorce yet…'

'Look, spare me the disarming autobiographical chitchat. I've seen as many cop shows as you. Am I going to be charged with something or not?'

Alexander charged him with rape.

The duty solicitor was a woman, not always relevant in rape cases, but in this one it would work to Alexander's advantage. This guy wasn't stupid enough to submit to further questioning without a lawyer to fend Alexander off, but he would tell her nothing: this was a premeditated stranger rape, not a he-said-she-said, so he would stick to his denial all the way. He had been careful not to leave evidence, and he would try to brass the whole thing off. But it would be embarrassing for him to have a woman in the room, especially with the line of questioning Alexander intended to pursue.

So you're a nice guy. You might want to start thinking about character witnesses to attest to that. What about your ex? Was the divorce acrimonious? Third parties maybe? I know I'd have found that very hard to take. Have there been any women since your divorce? Do you find it difficult to talk to women? Men are from Mars, women are from Venus and all that. But you're not gay, are you? No. I think there are a lot of men like you. Hey, I'm no Casanova myself, believe it or not. Some guys have all the luck. And some guys don't. Are you unlucky in love?

'You don't have to answer that,' the solicitor said a dozen times, clearly hoping her client wouldn't, and not just for professional reasons. And for the most part he didn't, for all that he was squirming. Eventually the solicitor cracked, though, and demanded Alexander stop harassing her client.

He held up his hands and apologised and then handed her a file that had been sitting on the table all along. Her client had been careful, but the condom had leaked: Alexander had the evidence to take him to court and have him successfully prosecuted.

'So what was that charade in aid of?' the solicitor wanted to know. Alexander was looking at the rapist. 'There are others. Aren't there?'

'You don't have to answer that.'

'She wanted it. They all did, deep down.'

The solicitor sank back in her chair.

'How many?' Alexander asked.

'Four, including this one.' He said it boldly, more martyr than rapist.

'Nice guy, huh?'

'Like you said, women don't like nice guys. Women…'

Alexander had no desire to listen to the rest of this speech; he had listened to half a dozen versions, none very good. He could have put it better than any of them himself. Instead, he took details of the other rapes with great professional satisfaction.

The rest of the speech would have gone like this. 'Women are basically animals. More than men: men are rational and capable of self-control. Women are controlled by their bodies: what they really want is physical satisfaction, sheer animal sex. All the rest is bullshit. They say they want men to be sensitive, but they despise sensitive men; they laugh at them. A man like me could really love women, but that's not what they want. They play with men like me, they pretend to be interested, but what they really want, whether they admit it or not, is men who know what women are really like, men who'll treat them like whores. Well, fine, that's what I did. I cut the crap, gave up believing in romance and all the shit women are supposed to want, and I gave them what they wanted. What they deserve.' The shit that goes through human heads. And this guy had welcomed it, embraced it, turned his life to shit.

Alexander felt better for this case, better for how he had worked it. He was fighting the good fight, on more fronts than one, against a violent rapist and against those who would reduce his crime to something less than crime, and implicate everyone else. He had poached the case from sex crimes specifically because he had wanted a rape, as if only with a rape case could he close the portal he had opened to the parallel universe inhabited by Scottish CultWatch. The briefing on sexual coercion in secondary schools remained on Alexander's desk, 'unactioned.' To his surprise, nothing had appeared in the media about it; it dawned on him that SCW were waiting for him to give it credibility. If the unit would only take their theories seriously, give them 'the stamp of legitimacy' (the phrase was even used in the covering letter), the media would have to follow suit, and then government. Then there would be a national campaign; SCW would be allowed into schools; there might even be some sort of new 'cult-influenced sexual-coercion order.' (Don't laugh at the name; they always sounded like the opposite of what they were supposed to.)

Alexander had always assumed these people knew he hated them. Apparently not. Karen told him when he mentioned it that he had been a pin-up at Scottish CultWatch even before the hypnotism cases. Their press officer had told Morag how they had admired his treatment of the exsanguination case, regarding his emphasis on the copycat nature of the crime as more important than his assertion that the killer was a psychopath (they blamed Knox for that). Copycat behaviour was cult-like, in their argot. Alexander felt better for knowing SCW's opinion of him too: it gave him an advantage. And he had done them no favours with this last case, he told the Devil with some satisfaction when he appeared that evening. It had gone the way he had always intended the occult unit to work. Sex crimes had complained that it had nothing to do with the occult and Alexander had retorted that none of his cases did, and why should he sit about waiting for cases involving pentagrams when there were serious crimes to be investigated?

Satan asked Alexander if he had seen the local press coverage. 'Since when does the Prince of Darkness read the *Evening Times*?' Alexander asked, still on a high. The Devil shrugged, and handed him a copy: 'Serial rapist linked with occult.'

'For fuck's sake! Linked by what?'

The Evil One did an annoying little jig, ending with two fingers pointing at Alexander.

'Pixie dust,' he said.

Pixie dust stuck in his craw; the Devil repeating his own joke back to him like that. He had not thought things were really so bad that his own efforts could only work against his ends. Perhaps he had flattered himself. It was not enough to work cases as he had imagined, he now realised; he had to work the media. He flattered himself more deliberately that he could do that. He gathered Morag and the others for a team meeting. He told them he had seen nothing in any of their cases to suggest the existence of organised cult activity, let alone the actual supernatural phenomena that the media seemed increasingly to hint at. The others concurred. Alexander went on to warn that as long as such beliefs were indulged, the unit was in danger of creating public order problems that hadn't been there before. The others concurred, and DS Smith pointed out that the 'demonic possession' case had already led to a flurry of accusations, causing mayhem as self-styled exorcists were pitted against child services and ending in a small riot on at least one occasion. Exactly. Smith and McGrain had interviewed three of those arrested, each of whom had pressed the police to charge the others with occult offences. All had been charged instead with public order offences. Excellent policing, but you wouldn't have known it from the media coverage, which had been even-handed in its endorsement of every outlandish accusation going.

Henceforth the unit would pursue a careful and much more explicit media strategy. McGrain was to work with Morag monitoring and contributing to blogs and other online chatter to complement Morag's media releases and Alexander's briefings. Cases were to be seen as stories, with careful attention to the narrative arc: *Scooby-Doo*, not *X Files*. Each case began with a mystery, which was then solved, explained, de-occultified. If the media failed to notice this pattern, it was to be politely pointed out, highlighted, battered into their thick skulls. There would be no more dubious hypnotism theories, no muddying of the waters. Whatever cases it took on, the 'occult unit' would become synonymous with rational detection, a beacon of Enlightenment amid a storm of superstition. 'Henceforth,' Alexander told his team, 'we are writing the script.'

Alexander and Karen had been out a few times now, each rendezvous a success in its own terms – a nice meal, a film and a nice walk, an art gallery even – but things had not 'moved on' in the customary sense. Alexander had avoided situations in which the possibility was likely to arise, afraid of seeming to take advantage of Karen. By the time he suggested in his own subtle way that they spend the night together, this provoked consternation rather than enthusiasm.

'So I passed the test, then? I'm worthy of your attentions?'

'Would it have been better if I'd tried to bed you right away just because you're beautiful?'

She blushed.

'Maybe using a cheap line like that?' he added.

Her blush became a look of outrage. He kissed her, perhaps in the nick of time.

Alexander's thoughts were still occupied much of the time by Leanne. She was now helping with music lessons at Morgan's nursery; her own idea, but of course Alexander had then made it happen. And Leanne grew closer to the child with every meeting, at home or at school, their mutual affection cemented by Morgan's emerging love of music, which seemed to strengthen Leanne's vocation. The young girl and the young woman sang together and each in her own way filled the other with the joy and hope of youth. Morgan spoke to her father of nothing but the object of his own obsession, while Leanne was endlessly fascinated by the child. 'I think she only pretends to have an imaginary friend, you know,' Leanne told Alexander after one babysitting session. He had heard of no such entity anyway. 'I thought *you* were her imaginary friend,' he said laughing, and Leanne understood. They were always understanding one another like that.

On another occasion, Alexander returned from a police social function to find Leanne beaming. 'You won't believe what she called me,' she said, giggling, and then blushed as she waited for his guess.

Alexander smiled. 'Oh, God. Did she call you Mummy?'

'No,' Leanne giggled again. 'She called me Daddy.' They both cracked up.

As he reflected on this later, Alexander realised that he was bound to Leanne by Morgan in a way that he was not bound to Laura, though the child was hers. Laura's and his shared custodianship of their daughter was a practical thing. With Leanne it was different. Leanne was much more than a babysitter to Morgan, and the child had evidently realised that what she got from this young woman was in some sense the same thing she got from her father. Alexander wanted not just a better life for Morgan but a better world. Leanne was seeking such a world, not merely moving from her unprivileged roots to the middle-class world of music, but reaching beyond that to a world where she could truly be herself, and so could Morgan.

Having finally determined Leanne's place in his life, Alexander came to another resolution so gently that he barely noticed it. He loved Karen.

Second marriage

Vogue la galère!

There are two reasons commonly given for the breakup of a relationship. The first is that people change. They grow apart. You're not the person I fell in love with. The second is that they don't change. They get stuck in a rut. I'm sick of the person I fell in love with. Both have the air of finality, which is all that is fundamentally required of a reason. Relationships end. Coming to terms with that is part of growing up. Except, of course, fuck that.

Since his days of dissatisfaction in Glasgow, an unspoken component of Siegfried's rebellion against Reality had been an aggressively romantic outlook, his doubts about the actual business of love and romance notwithstanding. Through our thing, our own invincible romance, which seemed to vindicate this against the cynicism of the world around him, he felt that he had cheated Reality once more. By now, though, I was no longer the goofy kid Siegfried had fallen in love with. I was becoming a formidable woman, not easily impressed by big words and flashing eyes. I loved Siegfried no less, but he sensed that if he were to have his triumph over Reality, he would have to win me properly. He worried that he had not changed enough, that he had not become the man he had promised to become. Given the ease with which he had won me in the first place, it was inevitable that there would come a point later when outstanding issues would have to be resolved. Boy meets girl, *boy loses girl*, boy gets girl – it's the law. Siegfried of course had no regard for the letter of the law, but he knew he would have to reckon with its spirit, and overcome adversity somehow.

Siegfried was not the only influence on me, and he recognized early on that he would have to fight if he was to win me and keep me. Even if I had no parents, or any friends to speak of, I was a part of the world. A young person is an impressionable creature, and one given to conformity, whether conventional or otherwise. Siegfried was perfectly aware that even my attraction to him had been scripted before his appearance, although he was so charmed by my early perception that he was a cross between James Dean and Jesus Christ that he was tempted to run with it. He would not, of course, which was the greater part of his appeal. There was little danger of us becoming a clichéd dysfunctional couple – delusional sociopath and teenage moll or whatever – any more than of me dragging Siegfried off to the suburbs for a life of lawn-mowing and mall drops. But my very eagerness to do things his way, truly a new and meaningful way, meant that he was in a rush to determine what that way was. Siegfried's struggle to win me, then, was always intimately bound up with his struggle to establish himself in New York.

We had friends now, a milieu even. Siegfried had made some moves, widened his influence and flexed his muscles, but I still wanted to know what it meant. While Siegfried had been able to involve Ernest and Jimmy in the things that occupied him, he had not found work for me, and so I was not able to lose myself in that. Having finished writing the story of Siegfried's first existential leap, I spent my days as he had when he first arrived in New York: reading, walking, brooding. The difference was that I had Siegfried, both as a companion and an object for contemplation.

Just as Siegfried was conscious that he could not take me for granted, I was increasingly unsure of what he saw in me. Siegfried realized now that his initial attraction to me had been very immature – he had simply fallen for a pretty girl who flattered him with her attention. Like I said, I was a rather more formidable woman by now, but I'd better not overdo it. The question was what that formidable woman had to do with Siegfried, what she meant to him and why he should love her.

This question was no less pressing for me than the question of how to keep hold of me was for Siegfried. In fact my question was rather better, as well it should have been considering the amount of time I had to think about such things.

At issue for both of us was that I was a real person with particular qualities and ideas; I was unpredictable. For all that I was enthralled by the world Siegfried had begun to imagine for us, I did not, could not inhabit it completely, any more than I could be a simple creature of American culture. As a matter of fact, nobody can. The script that leads to white picket fences is a fantasy, one that is ultimately rejected by even the most conventional girls. Undoubtedly, though, I had been more conscious of this than most, more determined, however faultingly, to live a life that made sense to me rather than simply accepting the way things are done. This was part of what made me attractive to Siegfried, but it also meant there was no question of replacing one script with another, even if Siegfried had possessed such a thing. Whatever role I played in Siegfried's life, Siegfried's world, had to be of my own invention, which meant that I had to understand that world, to be complicit in it. I couldn't be content to take it on trust, even if I recognized that Siegfried didn't fully understand it himself.

I was aware that my determination to resist convention or co-option might make me not the easiest girlfriend for a guy to get along with. That had always been true and probably still is. By the time I'd reconciled myself to the fact that I didn't have a boyfriend in high school, I'd genuinely convinced myself I didn't want one anyway. I did want Siegfried when he came along. I didn't want him as a boyfriend, or a husband, or a friend, or a mentor, or as anything else, and I didn't want to be anything like that to him. I wanted Siegfried and I wanted him to want me, to have me.

Our romance had begun so conventionally as to be less believable for it, eyes meeting across a crowded room and all that. And yes, I had been 'seduced' by Siegfried's chivalry, and his gallant violence, both physical and existential. But the seduction had been accidental. Siegfried had never tried to be the man, to make me the woman. He loved me and, in his own way, wooed me, but there had never been any question of conquest. By conventional standards he was soft, even; the ridiculousness of this characterization only exposed the inadequacy of conventional standards. This put me in a much more interesting position. Having drifted into our relationship, I found myself, still after more than a year, unburdened by a fixed role. Siegfried had not set the terms of our relationship in my absence, as it were. After all, he continued to be exercised by the world beyond us. Our relationship was something he cherished rather than owned, something that remained open for either of us, both of us, to define and develop. Having allowed things to drift without pressure from each other, we both now felt ready to do that together. Siegfried welcomed my proposal: we married.

Such an apparently conventional thing, but it was meant defiantly. Marriage is a strange thing, simultaneously accepted as part of a normal life and also considered to be unworkable. Nobody seems to believe in marriage. And there are endless statistics that people enjoy reciting to show how naïve it is to marry, how people inevitably split up, how the only thing on the rise is remarriage, which is even less reliable. I called ours a second marriage as a private joke, recognizing Siegfried's anxiety about the narrative structure of our romance. But now it stopped being about Siegfried. It was no longer Siegfried who was triumphing over Reality by snatching a nubile maiden from the midst of Americana, but two young people deciding at least one aspect of their own future in defiance of fickle fate. There was plenty in the world that we could not be sure of, but why let that uncertainty dictate what we might determine for ourselves? We put an end to the absurdity of two people in love worrying about what the other is thinking or might think in the future. We made a promise to one another. Siegfried being a doubly illegal alien, it was impossible for us to marry officially. But then being married in the eyes of New York State was not the point at all. We decided to arrange a small party to celebrate, but that personal promise, rather than any bureaucratic tie, was the foundation of our marriage, and indeed the form of our wedding. We promised to love one another for ever.

Yes, to love one another. Of course you can't promise to feel a certain way, but as I've already explained, love isn't just about feelings. If you felt sure that you would always feel passionately in love with your partner then there would be no point in getting married. Our decision to marry was not purely emotional: we each made a rational decision to privilege our affectionate feelings and loyalty to one another over any doubts or resentments we might happen to feel in the future, in the knowledge that, like a self-fulfilling prophecy, this decision would itself shape the way we experienced those things. After all, most of a relationship is mental – it happens in your head, because most of the time the two of you are not physically together: so it is about belief and expectation rather than literal experience. And I had come to realize that being a person is about more than being a bundle of feelings – it is about giving shape to experience as a first step in shaping life itself. Siegfried was pleased with that way of putting it.

For his part, of course Siegfried wasn't worried about succumbing to Siren voices in any conventional way. He had never been much of a strayer even before he found true love. But his instinct when he ran into trouble with other people was always that they were not worth the effort: 'Fuck 'em,' as he still liked to say from time to time. While there are some advantages to this kind of self-reliance, he appreciated that there were also difficulties. The ability to kill without losing sleep is a useful one, but killing is rarely an appropriate course of action. And a bloody-minded resistance to compromise in less dramatic circumstances can result in life becoming much harder than is necessary. The light-headed frenzy that had characterized Siegfried's bachelor days was significantly reduced by our marriage. He even put on a little weight. He became a man of substance in many ways. He was less troubled by the feeling of illegitimacy that had haunted him for so long. And he began to see something of himself not only in me, but also in others like Jimmy and Ernest. He was no longer simply a daydreamer in an oblivious world.

But I'm getting ahead of the story, and I haven't finished telling you about Siegfried's meeting with Amy Wong yet; I'll get to that presently. You see, everything happened at once. Before I saw Siegfried and we made our promise and I got that story myself, I had a meeting of my own. The day before, I had gotten an email from Jeanie, Jimmy's ex. She was back in town and wanted to meet up for lunch or drinks, preferably drinks. I was happy to accede.

After she and Jimmy had broken up on vacation in Colorado, Jeanie had gone to Los Angeles for an extended work assignment. Now she was back in New York she was researching a piece on the human interest side of the black economy, and especially the lives of illegal immigrants in the city. She wondered if Siegfried would be willing to talk to her; I said I didn't see why not, though I didn't think he was very typical. 'Typical is boring,' she said. We talked a little about Jeanie's other more interesting angles, and then, after a couple of glasses of wine, she finally asked me about Jimmy.

Jimmy had said nothing about the break-up other than that it had happened, not even to Ernest. Jeanie explained that they had only been together a few weeks when Jimmy had been forced to flee New York, and that while she had enjoyed the romance of it, and they'd had fun skiing for a few days, it had all been a bit insane. Suddenly they had both realized that they didn't know each other very well. They had argued over stupid things, and begun to suspect one another's motives. She had been willing to persevere, but Jimmy had been increasingly distant and reluctant to talk about things. Jeanie said it was as if he'd realized she wasn't who he'd thought she was, and had simply lost interest. He had told her he loved her only once, and Jeanie said it didn't count because it had been part of a longer sentence. 'I guess I didn't match up to his Sicilian mamma,' she said, with an ironic look that disavowed the cliché. For the most part, I could see that Jeanie took pride in her dignified response to the affair, and her ability to bear the pain. Who would have denied her that consolation?

I told her that Jimmy was OK, but single as far as I knew and certainly not radiating happiness. Just as Siegfried had, he was struggling with his new anonymity, but at least he had Siegfried and the rest of us for company, and would surely carve a niche for himself. I wasn't sure at first whether to tell Jeanie about the business with Laura and Sokolov. I was wary of seeming gossipy or of presuming to counsel Jeanie. But I felt I had to tell her, because it might help her understand things. Perhaps it was true that Jimmy had mistaken Jeanie for someone else, as it were. For Laura? I hoped Jimmy was not that naïve.

Having seen them together briefly, and from talking to Ernest, who had stumbled through an awkward discussion with Jimmy, I think I came up with a good idea of the relationship between Jimmy and Laura. It was unique and strange, but I was beginning to realize that this is true of all relationships, not least Siegfried's and mine. There is no such thing as a generic relationship. You can't simply have relationship X with person Y. A relationship is no more or less than what two people mean to one another. And Laura had fallen in love with Jimmy's own unrequited love for her. Even having acknowledged to herself how she felt, she could not reciprocate openly without destroying the very things she loved about him: his selfless devotion to her, his noble resignation to not having her. She admired these things in Jimmy as one might admire them in a character in a book or a movie. Her love was no less genuine for that: what we love is never anything so simple and so unworldly as a real, whole person. It was at least *Jimmy's* devotion, *Jimmy's* resignation that she loved; not some ideal that she'd projected onto him.

But it didn't do Jimmy much good. He was doomed to suffer just as surely as if Laura had despised him. Except that she didn't, and he too learned to love something other than Laura in her impossible entirety. He loved her very unapproachability, not in a masochistic way, but because he recognized her unapproachability as the form of her love for him. It was not the form he would have chosen, but like Laura, he preferred real, imperfect love to a perfect fantasy. He admitted to Ernest that he liked his own way of loving Laura: unilateral, without condition, without reason, without expectation of reciprocation. It made him feel like God. And as with Christ on the cross, there was a defiance in the condition itself that did not require Jimmy to feel it. Much of the time he felt sorry for himself, but even that was defiant. It was love and it was real. How strange, but how like life, that the reality of the inner life was opposed to the illusion of immanent happiness in the 'real' world.

I can't say whether it had been Jimmy's devotion to Laura that kept him from establishing a proper relationship with Jeanie, or whether he had been trying to reproduce something of that relationship with Jeanie. But I knew that what Jeanie had seen in Jimmy had been the promise of a more exciting life, and perhaps this had felt like a burden to Jimmy, especially at a time when his life was changing so dramatically. They both wanted new lives, and ideally that should have brought them together, but – you know – life is complicated. The third reason for the break-up of a relationship is that two people carry conflicting ideas of what the relationship is, and this conflict is revealed over time. How people deal with that depends on how prepared they are for it.

The more I thought about that, the more I wanted to be sure of

Siegfried, to be sure that even if we had each other wrong we would persist. I thought about it as I walked home, and we made our mutual promise before Siegfried had time to tell me about his meeting with Amy Wong.

Queer snakes, queer ladders

Jacta alea est.

So, Amy Wong had recognized Siegfried on realizing his accent was Scottish, because he had been described to her by John Paul Gizzi. Siegfried's old friend had been in New York for six weeks, and contacted Amy after reading a story she'd written about a bank robber who had delivered the baby of a customer shocked into labor during a raid. This had nothing to do with Siegfried, in fact, but John Paul had been right to make the connection: it was just the sort of thing Siegfried would have done. He told Amy he was making a documentary, and explained that he had followed his friend from Glasgow in the belief that he would be an ideal subject. He wondered if she had come across him. She had not, of course, but the two promised to contact one another should either find Siegfried. So, Amy gave Siegfried a number for John Paul and then he told her about this harassment case involving the professor, which I'll get to shortly.

Siegfried and I met John Paul the following afternoon in a bar near the library. John Paul was intensely curious about me, Siegfried's *wife*, but polite enough not to interrogate me. I had heard much more about him, of course, and almost felt like I knew him, except that his being here was at odds with his character as described by Siegfried. Anyway, Siegfried had told him about Ernest's and the professor's harassment case, and they had agreed that this would be a good thing for John Paul to have in his documentary. Siegfried had been embarrassed by John Paul's suggestion that he should feature, and had fudged the issue by agreeing to advise John Paul on ideas for the time being.

Professor Cabrera Hernandez stood accused of harassing a female graduate student. This was bubbling into a major campus controversy on which everyone had to have an opinion. The undisputed facts of the case were that the professor had raised his voice with a student following a disagreement over the direction of her work, and that she had subsequently fled from his office. Some said he had assaulted her, or worse, made sexual advances. Others insisted that he had merely voiced his opinion forcefully. These positions were quickly taken up by a campus women's group and a student Latino group respectively. The professor was suspended pending a university inquiry, and the police were said to be considering action. Rumors began to circulate to the effect that Professor Cabrera Hernandez had a prior rape conviction in California, and conversely that the student who was accusing him of harassment belonged to an organization called the Lesbian Avengers. Neither of these rumors was true, but both were about to make it into the press.

Pre-empting this, Ernest wrote a letter in defense of Paolo, arguing that he had done nothing wrong, and his detractors and even some of his defenders were motivated by other concerns that threatened to compromise justice. He sent it to the student newspaper and the *New York Times*, and it was published in both, alongside other letters on both sides, on the day the story broke outside campus. The following day, an article by Amy Wong appeared, based on an interview with the student at the center of the case. It was an exclusive Amy had got by ignoring the campus circus and approaching the young woman's parents to persuade them that their daughter needed to put her case plainly, away from the overheated university. The mother had come in from Connecticut and the three had met in a hotel lobby. The student was angry about having been shouted at, and insisted on calling it an assault, but she did not go any further than that; there was no suggestion that Professor Cabrera Hernandez had touched her in any way. The words she used were 'intimidated,' 'belittled,' 'humiliated'; the professor was 'arrogant,' 'macho,' 'mean.' Undoubtedly the student was being manipulated by friends who wanted to make more of the case as Ernest suggested, but she was driven primarily by a genuine sense of grievance. Her mother was supportive, if bewildered, and felt that the professor should apologize. The police quietly dropped their interest in the case, while the university issued an awkwardly worded statement to the effect that the inquiry was ongoing.

Meanwhile, John Paul was enjoying himself on campus, filming the furor. Though the professor was still suspended, protestors were nonetheless 'boycotting' his classes on the grounds that the assistant professor who was filling in had refused to condemn him. The campaign was led by three or four hyperactive students, but there did seem to be a wider resonance for the sentiments underlying their protests. John Paul did dozens of vox pops, and there was an overwhelming consensus that the professor should apologize, with several of his students testifying that he had an intimidating manner. Some of the professor's defenders put this down to Hispanic culture. The assistant professor was also Latino, though his moustache was less intimidating than Professor Cabrera Herndandez's, one student joked to John Paul. But even those who saw the funny side tended to assume that the professor had done something wrong.

Increasingly, it didn't seem to matter that nobody knew exactly what the professor had done wrong: there was the incident itself, whatever that had been, there was his general manner, his 'machismo,' which seemed to signify a more general problem with the relationship between professors and their students, particularly when male and female respectively, and then there was the content of his classes; more particularly there was something wrong with the law itself. As Ernest had argued in his letter, the case had become a lightning rod for discontent about just about anything. And, of course, since there was no evidence of wrongdoing, it was the law itself that insulated the professor from any more dramatic consequences of this discontent, 'his own precious Law' as someone had described it on a leaflet, and so the law itself increasingly became the focus of discussion. Ernest understood that at root the hostility to the law was about frustration with the fact that it would not resolve the other issues. It was too rigid, implacably and inscrutably 'objective,' whatever that meant. What good was the law if it could not express what was wrong here? If it could not make the professor apologize?

That there was no credible legal case against the professor was precisely the problem. More than one student told John Paul they feared if the case went to court, *it would be like her being raped all over again*. This was not a misunderstanding: nobody thought the student had literally been raped. But somehow the analogy seemed apt. The professor had done something wrong, victimized his student, and yet the law took his side, diminishing the significance of his crime, making her seem ridiculous for complaining. To approach the matter in narrow legal terms would be to perpetuate the crime. There were still those who wanted to see the professor sued, but the student had no appetite for that, and preferred to seek an apology through the university, or failing that, by shaming the professor in the media.

There was an impromptu strategy meeting in Paolo's luxurious, university-owned apartment in Greenwich Village, with Ernest, Jimmy, Siegfried, myself and John Paul, who was filming, though he had to turn the camera off for some of the discussion. The professor was considering suing the university to make them reinstate him. It was the obvious thing to do now, but he had misgivings; he didn't like the media attention for obvious reasons. Media attention was all the university administration cared about; they just wanted the whole thing to go away, and would have fired the professor by now if not for his renowned 'legal powers,' which had taken on an almost supernatural quality in the campus imagination.

Siegfried argued that it would be a mistake to sue. The goal was to have the professor reinstated without compromising his privacy: the university administration would have to be persuaded that they could reinstate him without losing face. The media, not the courts, would have to be persuaded that this was a just outcome. Ernest reluctantly concurred; and he thought he might be able to have an op-ed piece published in the *New York Times,* as his letter had provoked several responses. But he regretted that the truth mattered less than appearances. Siegfried disagreed with this assessment, arguing that winning public opinion was a good fight, a noble enterprise, not something to be entered into cynically. This sparked a lively discussion about the nature of truth. I won't reproduce that in detail, because I don't remember the nuances, but suffice it to say that it was mostly a dialogue between Siegfried and Ernest, with occasional interjections from me. Paulo sat quietly taking everything in, John Paul filmed the discussion and also took notes, while Jimmy seemed distracted and sad, as he usually did at that time.

Eventually Paolo brought the meeting to a close by announcing he had prepared food for us. He duly disappeared into the kitchen and returned with several dishes of home-made sushi; it was a hobby of his, he explained. We ate heartily, then, and after a few cups of sake, John Paul was persuaded by the others to tell us a little about Siegfried's past in Glasgow. He chose to tell us about the time he had decided to take Siegfried and their other friends to a lap-dancing club.

No-one else had wanted to go, but it was only Siegfried who had actually refused. The others would have allowed themselves to be dragged along in the same way that philistines with cultural pretensions force themselves to go to the opera, ready to tolerate a torturous evening in order to affirm a set of values. When Siegfried had voiced his resistance, Tommy and Jamsie had tried to hide behind him for a while, arguing that if Siegfried didn't want to go they should do something else instead, but John Paul had soon dismissed such bleating. (Siegfried interrupted to explain that John Paul had instilled in their group a kind of ravenous hedonism which ultimately made it impossible for the others to turn down anything that might be called an 'experience.') Siegfried's own ethic was far too vague to convince anyone else, and so simple refusal had been his only recourse.

Siegfried had not wanted to go and so Siegfried had not gone. What he had not known till now was that the others had not gone either. 'We didn't see the point of going without you,' John Paul said. Siegfried now realized that even though he had lost the argument, he had influenced, even dictated, his friends' behavior, or at least freed the others from John Paul's malign influence. By voicing his own resistance, he had legitimized their own reluctance. A small achievement, and indeed not one he had noticed at the time, but this revelation touched Siegfried. He explained later when we were alone that it revealed not only the person he had once been, but the person he still was, even as he saw the possibility of changing.

The next day I met Ernest at the university library to have lunch, and we went for a walk so he could tell me about the op-ed piece he had started to write. He had come across two recent *Times* articles in which Professor Cabrera-Hernandez had been cited as a legal authority, and he was disturbed by how quickly that authority had been undermined by this absurd harassment case. The professor's undiminished intellect and academic achievements had now become sinister 'legal powers,' and no journalist would dream of deferring to his judgement. And yet, if he were to be reinstated according to plan, with good grace and no hard feelings, those things would count again, and he would win back the fickle respect of the media. Authority was a terrifyingly relative thing, Ernest had realized, terrifyingly dependent on the assent of others. What was all the more worrying was that Paolo's very legitimacy was now at stake. If his history, or the identities of some of his current acquaintances – not least Siegfried – were to be exposed, there would be no way back. Unlike authority, legitimacy was binary rather than relative, and once lost, even less easily regained.

It caused Ernest to reflect on his own legitimacy. He had come so close to abandoning it; only Siegfried's intervention had kept him from embarking on a life of crime. Like Siegfried, he had wanted to live by his own sense of morality without regard for what the rest of the ant heap thought. The ant heap was wrong about the professor, after all. But Paolo Cabrera Hernandez (if that were really his name) needed the ant heap's assent in order to *be* the professor. Ernest could still aspire to be a professor someday, or a judge or even the president for that matter. The likes of Siegfried and Jimmy could not, regardless of their abilities. Or at least, like Paolo they would have to invest themselves in new lives, submitting themselves to the authority of the ant heap before they could earn any authority of their own. And even then their illegitimacy could be exposed, bringing the whole thing down: embezzlement, illegal entry, racketeering, murder. No number of night classes could wipe those things away. Ernest stopped walking and turned to me: 'Siegfried must be insane.'

I laughed a little, and started us walking again. 'He thinks he *was*, but he's all right now.'

Ernest had never fully understood what he had been about to do when his gas-station heist was foiled – what Siegfried and Jimmy had done, and what it meant. 'You're free in so many ways, but you lose so many options. It's not really freedom, is it? As free as a bird. Who wants to be a bird?'

'It would be nice to be able to change into a bird sometimes, and then change back.'

We both laughed.

'Like a witchdoctor,' Ernest said. 'Yes, I suppose that's what *that's* all about.'

Andante: life and work go on

'What do you want for your tea?' Alexander asked Morgan.

'Toasted cheese!' she said. 'I've had a wee notion for toasted cheese all day.'

'Have you been at your gran's again?' he asked, amused by her granlike turn of phrase. And she gave him her special smile, her lips pressed together with a faintly audible hum of contentment. Before making the toasted cheese, Alexander gave Morgan a saucer of milk for her two-faced cat, and she gave him a running commentary on how the creature was lapping up 'the precious liquid' with both tongues. He was secretly pleased with her eccentric vocabulary.

Morgan had just been dropped off by Laura for the rest of a long weekend with her father, and the girl's parents had discussed her schooling while she watched cartoons. Morgan was four now, a proper little person. They were both immensely proud of her, and had agreed easily about things, and all was well. Laura had begun a new relationship with a doctor at the hospital. 'I know it may suggest a certain lack of imagination,' she had conceded, but then Alexander too was involved with a colleague, DS Smith. A consequence of having busy lives, they had decided, rather than a lack of imagination. Morgan had been on outings with both colleague-partners, been shamelessly spoilt by all concerned, and was quite content with her domestic situation in general, though as she only saw her father for a couple of days a fortnight, he was her secret favourite.

Shortly after toasted cheese, Auntie Leanne came over. Alexander was not going out, but she sometimes visited now just to see Morgan, and talk to Alexander over tea. The two sat in the kitchen chatting while Morgan watched yet more cartoons in the living room. Leanne was studying at the music academy now, and enjoying it while experiencing the same frustration as always that life moved so slowly. It was the sort of thing she felt she could only discuss with Alexander; not that she didn't have a surfeit of friends, but they didn't think like her, like Alexander. They wouldn't have understood. 'It's good to be ambitious, isn't it?' she asked Alexander, knowing he would understand the term in all its complication.

He told her that he had always thought of himself as ambitious, but that it had been a point of contention between Laura and him that he lacked ruthlessness. It was not the idea of a successful career that motivated him, so much as a desire to impose himself on the world in his own way. So while it was true that he was disdainful of conventional careerism, to Laura's great frustration, if anything his ambition was more self-centred, more driven by vanity.

'Is that a bad thing?'

Alexander supposed it depended on the results. The good thing was that he was not distracted by other people's perceptions of his achievements, and did not seek position for its own sake. But making his mark on the real world meant getting a grip on reality in a way a careerist does not have to. It was not about meeting targets but about achieving what was supposed to be measured by targets. And for Alexander, that meant detecting and preventing actual crime, rather than going through the motions to create a bureaucratic simulacrum of successful police work, which is what he and his colleagues were actually paid to do. He wanted to be able to claim credit for cultivating civilisation, forging a gentler and more humane society populated by responsible adults and well-behaved children. Alexander smiled. He had to admit that in those terms, he was doing no more than winning occasional battles in a war he seemed doomed to lose.

'Isn't that pretty much the definition of policing?' Leanne asked.

He could not have been more taken aback if it had been Morgan asking the same question. Leanne's expression was playful, but her tone suggested she was merely reminding him of an obvious piece of wisdom. It was as if she were suddenly channelling DI Knox or Father Barry.

'I hadn't thought of it like that,' he said after a moment's pause.

Leanne began to apologise for making light of his work, but he shrugged it off. 'I did say my ambition was vain,' he said by way of recovery, before seguing cheesily: 'But enough about me, let's talk about you.'

Leanne's ambition was no less out of tune with its institutional confines. She would finish her course at the music academy, cultivate relationships with orchestras, funding bodies and so on, and if she got lucky she'd have some work commissioned. But she found that side of her prospective career depressingly unromantic. She could not imagine herself being 'ruthless' in pursuit of advancement. But the course at least allowed her to take one day at a time. It gave structure to her musical life. She hoped it was less like a conveyor belt than like stabilisers on a child's bike, to be cast aside when she'd mastered the technique. Only it wasn't like that, because really there's only one way to ride a bike. She wanted to find her own way to be a composer. Her immediate goal was graduating, then getting a first commission, maybe a residency of some kind. But these goals were only vaguely related to her real ambition: to write the greatest music the world had ever heard, and of course have it performed.

Alexander said he understood. Then he explained how he approached new cases at work. He started with the facts as they appear, then entertained various theories to explain those facts, inevitably favouring one theory and running with it for a while. But very often the theory had to change in the light of new facts, or because he realised he'd had the initial facts wrong. Because a fact is always a theory in disguise. The worst thing you could do was dig yourself in to a dead-end theory.

'I think life is the same,' he said. 'You have a rough idea of the script you're living by, but you can't let that script dictate your life.'

The spiel had been perfected for Karen, but Leanne got its new meaning for her. 'And goals are like facts? Scripts in disguise?'

'You're quite clever, aren't you?'

Leanne shrugged in a way that said precisely, '*bien sûr*.' 'Does that go for marriage too?'

Alexander hesitated and Leanne almost withdrew the question, embarrassed. 'If it had been up to me, I'd still be married. I think I always wanted to be married.' The thought flashed through his mind that he had wanted marriage more than he had wanted his wife, that Laura had merely served the purpose and perhaps that had been the problem. But he did not pursue this thought. Instead, he told Leanne there was nothing wrong with committing to something, or someone, but that it was important to do it consciously, deliberately, rather than getting stuck with something for want of a better idea.

'Like you and music, I suppose. I mean you've made a decision about music, haven't you? That's good; you need to make decisions in life. All I'm saying is that decision doesn't now commit you to a particular career path. Your ambition doesn't have to mean, I don't know, getting a first-class degree and a commission to write for Scottish Opera.'

Leanne laughed. 'I was thinking New York.'

'Well there you go, but I'm not going to hold you to that if you decide ten years down the line to write TV theme songs instead.' They laughed, both quietly thrilled by Alexander's casually deliberate assumption that they would still be in one another's lives in ten years.

'God, I'd rather not be held to stuff I said two weeks ago, let alone ten years,' Leanne said.

Alexander smiled at the thought of Leanne ten years ago, a child, but he did not say anything about that thought. 'I was thinking something similar the other day. But it's different at my age. There comes a time in your life when you can no longer expect to look back on yourself with embarrassment. It's not that you stop learning, but that you realise your mistakes are just that, not the result of inexperience or immaturity. You won't look back with amused detachment someday. And there's nobody to patronise you anymore, nobody you secretly know has your number. You realise that older people have their own endearingly naïve enthusiasms, their own childish pride in whatever sophistication they've achieved, clever-sounding words and expressions they enjoy overusing. But all that's some way off for you.'

'I think you've got my number.'

Their discussion was brought to an end by the sound of Karen's key in the door. 'I'll leave you to it,' Leanne said when she appeared in the kitchen.

'You don't have to. Stay for a glass of wine,' said Karen.

'No, really, I've got to be going. I'll just say goodnight to Morgan and the mutant cat.'

Alexander would have liked to think that Karen and Leanne hated each other, but in fact they seemed to get on fine.

With Leanne gone, Karen unloaded some shopping into the fridge – she was cooking tonight – and put a couple of bottles of wine on the work surface, with a wink at Alexander. He enjoyed drinking with Karen. She was a hearty drinker, not like Laura, who had been too temperate for him, sometimes even making him wish he'd been alone so he could drink properly. He drank less with Karen than he would have done alone, but it was enough. It was good; he felt like a civilised person, a domesticated person. 'I'll get your dinner on then, dear,' Karen said wryly. 'Why don't you go and have some quality time with the wee one before her bedtime? I'll come and join you once I've got this started.' Alexander happily complied, and even enjoyed Morgan's short-lived howls of protest when he changed the channel on the TV.

When he returned to work a couple of days later, Alexander felt good. The unit's new media strategy was holding up. While the papers still had a taste for the gothic, the unit refused to give credibility to any but the most prosaic accounts of the various cases that interested them; and thankfully they were clearing them well. Inevitably, though, the unit's good run was threatened by a new case: occult pornography.

'Jesus,' Alexander said when DS McGrain filled him in, feeling himself sink back into the fraught routine of work. 'What's the crime? Tell me it's not kids,' he said, more from professional weariness than sentiment.

'Not kids. Disputed consent.'

'Shit. And was that enough to send it our way? Or are there costumes?'

McGrain laughed. 'You have to see it really.'

Cloaked figures stood around a church altar. One of them stepped naked from its cloak and lay on the altar, a young woman, but not too young. Attractive. One of the others stepped forward, still cloaked but evidently male, and appeared to penetrate her briefly. Then he stepped back and another did the same. Alexander was reluctantly aroused, until during the third turn the young woman coughed. Suddenly the whole situation seemed ridiculous, the spell broken. The ritual went on regardless, five men in all, but Alexander saw only the absurdity of it. The cloaks were purple silk, or something like it. He took note of the varying heights of the five men. It would be possible to identify the church; it was Catholic, nineteenth-century.

The woman was a student; the video had been sent to her family. She claimed she had been duped into taking part in the film, and had provided names and addresses of two of the men responsible for it. One of them was a caretaker at the church, which was in the West End. At least the church itself was not implicated, just a few perverts with access to the keys most likely. The bad news was that the family had already been to Scottish

CultWatch. A representative of the group had requested a meeting. Alexander asked McGrain to get them in within the next couple of days: better that than have them running loose. This case was manna from Heaven for them. Before that, Alexander wanted to interview the victim. He and DS Smith went to see her at her parents' house in Bearsden.

Ailsa Cairns was twenty years old, and studying chemistry at Glasgow University. Her parents were well-off and respectable; her father a businessman and her mother a housewife and stalwart of the local Episcopalian church. The three sat together on the sofa in the family's front room, presenting a united front as if to a press conference. Ailsa was embarrassed, understandably: everyone in the room had seen the film. She seemed normal enough, neither weird and gothic nor sinisterly conventional. She seemed nice, a typical Scottish student.

Having ascertained that the parents did not know the accused, Alexander said that DS Smith would have to speak to Ailsa alone, and the parents consented without acrimony, suggesting the two ladies step into the garden, this being the first nice day for some time. Alexander sat down and asked Mr and Mrs Cairns who they thought had sent the video. They had no idea, supposed it was someone trying to shame Ailsa rather than alert them.

Alexander asked how Scottish CultWatch had got involved. Mr and Mrs Cairns had known about the organisation through its media profile rather than anything more organic – Alexander had wondered whether there might have been a connection with the church – and had simply got in touch by phone shortly after receiving the video. It turned out that Ailsa had been somewhat estranged from her parents, and after leaving a series of messages for her without reply they had decided to call in a 'cult-buster' to get her back from whatever cult she was involved with. (It was not a service Scottish CultWatch actually provided, but it had seemed like the sort of thing an organisation like that might do.) Ailsa had summoned the courage to turn up at her parents' before SCW had responded, but they had then offered her counselling and promised to help with any prosecution.

Ailsa made it clear to DS Smith that she had not been raped. She regretted taking part in the ceremony, but it had not been rape. But she had not known about the camera, and had never consented to be filmed. 'Surely that must be a crime?' she asked. It was not a crime comparable with rape. 'I was told it might be covered by new legislation,' she went on. SCW had obviously fed her that.

There was indeed new legislation that the team had just been looking at, but it was not that it made a serious crime of filming without consent; rather, it allowed such deception, or anything cult-related, to diminish and transfer agency. The main purpose had been to allow prosecutors to go after 'cult leaders' rather than particular offenders – this following a series of cases in which gangs of youths had rampaged through the streets robbing shoppers, apparently under the direction of older 'Svengalis' (the term was more popular than ever). In this case, it would render void Ailsa's consent to sex, thus making the hooded men guilty of rape.

Karen reported this to Alexander as they drove back to the station. He was not surprised, of course, but frustrated that despite the unit's success so far in marginalising SCW, they were able to take advantage of wider developments; they had the wind in their sails. He phoned Morag, who had been talking to SCW. They had agreed not to release the story until an arrest was made, provided there was an arrest within twenty-four hours. They looked forward to an update when they came in for the meeting.

The ringleader of the hooded men was one Seth Wilson. Ailsa knew him from the students' union, where he hung out despite no longer being a student. In fact, he was a 'mature drop-out,' having enlisted for a philosophy degree at the age of thirty, and given it up a year later. Two years on he was still an 'ex-student,' making his living by working part-time in a bookshop. 'Seth' was an affectation: he had renamed himself after the evil Egyptian god. He was obsessed with the occult, and conformed to most of the associated stereotypes. Superficially it was not at all clear what the attraction had been for someone like Ailsa. But he was not her boyfriend, or even a friend. Ailsa's own circle, like most of the students who frequented the union bar, considered Wilson to be something of a joke. He had a couple of younger acolytes, who were similarly disdained. Ailsa had told DC Smith that she 'wouldn't have been seen dead talking to any of them.' Yes, I know. Talking?

Karen explained to Alexander. 'She told me she'd fantasised about something like this long before she knew Wilson. It was an "idle fantasy," she said, not something she ever expected to happen, and she allowed herself to put Wilson and his friends in the fantasy only because she was sure it could never happen. So when he suggested it she was taken by surprise, "overcome by a feeling of inevitability" she said, that just carried her along.'

'How exactly did he suggest it?' Alexander asked, bewildered. It turned out that Wilson had emailed Ailsa a short story describing ritual sex. She had sent a suitably disgusted and dismissive reply, but when he had responded to that with nothing but the name of the church and a time, she had grown curious. She had told herself she would just walk by on the other side of the road and have a look, but then she'd been drawn in against her every rational instinct. 'This again? Well, let's go and pick him up,' Alexander told DC Smith. 'I'll decide what to do once I've interrogated the pervert.'

The pervert was unrepentant. He said that the film was evidence that everything had been consensual: he had recorded the ritual for that very purpose. Alexander asked why he'd sent it to Ailsa's parents then. He said he hadn't; one of the others must have done it, but it wasn't a crime anyway, so it was none of the police's business. Alexander was not angered by this. His disposition was properly forensic. He simply noted Wilson's responses to his various questions and then released him. He wanted to get Knox's psychological opinion before deciding how to proceed.

After the interview, Alexander went for a walk – instead of lunch, which he could not face – down through Townhead towards the river. He stopped on a motorway overpass and surveyed the cityscape thoughtfully, till his gaze was met by a CCTV camera perched on a pole below so that it was level with his own head. 'What you lookin' at?' he growled. The camera did not respond. He thought of Karen. She had seemed funny with him earlier; he didn't know how exactly, but it was bothering him.

They had been together for some months now, and things had developed differently from how Alexander had expected. It was not so much that he was disappointed, as unsettled, discombobulated by the transformation of their relationship. And not entirely in a bad way. The first thing that had happened was that Karen had seemed to get smaller. Alexander had noticed this before, with Laura. It's a perspective thing: when women are at a distance, men tend to 'correct' their size mentally. Unless a woman is especially small or big, a man registers her simply as a 'person' of normal proportions. Up close, measured against a man's own body, this is no longer possible. This particular woman's actual physicality supplants the generic person and impresses with its littleness. Fortunately, most men find this quite attractive, and enjoy protectively cuddling the little creature. But a particular woman's deviations from imaginary type are never all charming.

Not least of these in Karen's case were her annoying friends and family. 'The ideal woman is an orphan with no friends,' Alexander told himself. 'And one you can switch off and keep under the bed when you're not using?' the thought continued. All right, better a real person than not. But did it have to be such hard work? Alexander had started by thinking of Karen as an adjunct to his own life, which, he realised, had always been unrealistic, and not even all that desirable. But until you know a person, how can you imagine anything else?

He realised he still had Karen's bracelet in his pocket; he had meant to return it to her. She had left it in his bedroom a couple of nights before. It was a rigid jade thing, nice, and it had made him realise how much he missed the trinkets and paraphernalia of Laura, her jewellery, makeup, pager even, the things he had seen again and again, in public and in private, and which had felt almost like extensions of herself, himself. Leanne never left anything lying around, and he supposed that was probably deliberate – and just as well after the chewing-gum thing. Maybe Karen in contrast had left the bracelet deliberately or semi-deliberately as a sign that she felt at home with Alexander; maybe Alexander had subconsciously recognised this and forgotten to return it because he was afraid of hurting her feelings. Whether it would have done or not, perhaps he felt guilty that the bracelet had made him nostalgic for Laura. After all he could have left it where it was; there was nothing improper about it being in his room. All this might account for his sense that Karen had been funny with *him*. Unconsciously he had now put her bracelet in his mouth, like a teething ring. Christ, what would Dr Knox make of that? He resolved not to find out, and put the bracelet back in his pocket.

Steph had once or twice insisted that DI Knox was the sexiest woman in the world, in an intimidating older woman kind of way. Alexander had never thought about it. To him, Knox was a formidable colleague, a resource, or maybe a guru in some ways. He'd never thought of her having a personal life.

The story of Theresa Knox's first love

Theresa Knox's first love was a fellow student at Glasgow University. For the first six months of their courtship they barely spoke. It was 1974; everyone else was having sex. They would meet in the same café every week or so and glower suspiciously at one another over 'frothy coffee.' Then they would part, each wordlessly accusing the other of wanting out of the relationship. Sometimes he tried to kiss her; she allowed it, no more, and he withdrew, infuriated. But there were letters too, and the letters were better than the meetings.

As students of psychology, both were skilful at reading 'body language.' Unfortunately neither was very good at speaking it. Consequently each took the other to be hesitant and unaffectionate, while in fact harbouring the opposite feelings. Harbouring, yes, arguably that was the problem. It was not that they didn't express these feelings in writing – they did, abundantly – but somehow that was not enough. They both found it hard to reconcile the easy familiarity of their letters with the awkwardness of these face-to-face encounters. It was as if they only existed for one another at a distance.

Fittingly, it was a problem they were able to discuss in the letters, but not in person. And in the letters it was not a problem: it was something they could laugh about, dismiss in the certainty that it would pass. When they met they were confronted with the possibility that it would not, and they didn't dare raise it for fear of destroying all hope.

They went camping together then, by Loch Lomond in August. Moonlight tempered the awkwardness. After that things were better, more confidential. They agreed to marry after graduating the next year.

But shortly into the new university term Theresa's lover became ill. The first manifestation of it was a return of the distance between them: he said he needed time to study and could not see her more than once a week as before. But it soon became clear that he was not attending classes either. Then he refused to see her at all. She wrote to his sister, the only relative she knew, to ask if he had been in touch, only provoking him to send a short, angry note telling her to stay away from his family. It soon became clear that was as distant from his friends and family as he was from Theresa. Then he killed himself.

The story of their relationship was transformed retrospectively, or would have been, except that Theresa refused to let go of the relationship as she had lived it. What Theresa had seen as the tender awkwardness of first love now seemed to anyone else to have been an early indication of her lover's mental illness. But she refused to relinquish her ownership of that awkwardness; it had come from her us much as him, from the two of them, and she was not mad. Everyone told her there was nothing she could have done. She would not accept that either. She had no desire to blame herself, but felt unable to abandon the hope represented, even now, by that trip to Loch Lomond. She refused to see that as a mere blip, the promise of happiness it had held out as no more than an illusion. She suffered more than she might have done, then, but felt she had no choice.

Perhaps this had been one of the experiences that contributed to Knox's wisdom. That was the quality Alexander did associate with her. It wouldn't have occurred to him to ask her advice about his own personal life any more than to enquire about hers, but if he'd bothered to think about it – if asking advice about personal matters had been the sort of thing he did – he'd probably have concluded that she would be a better person than most. She was wise, and wisdom was better than expertise. She had plenty of the latter when it came to criminal psychology, and who knew what else, but Alexander valued her for more than that.

Knox's expression gave little away as she watched the video of Alexander interviewing Seth Wilson. She watched it three times, not taking notes, but simply noticing different things each time. She was not the type of forensic psychologist who spat out diagnoses at the drop of a symptom. She rarely used technical jargon at all, and thus did not have to switch between registers. It was not, she had once explained to Alexander, that she was a polis first and a psychologist second, but rather that she was a total polis. Her scientific discipline was her way of being a polis: thus she did not think in terms of diagnoses but in terms of cases.

Knox said it was likely Wilson had approached other girls in the same way with as much success as you'd expect; he had just got 'lucky' with this one. Alexander thought of Satan's jibe about people being 'victims of persuasion.' He didn't believe that

Wilson had done anything comparable to the hypnotist-rapist. It was not rape. But nor in fact had he 'persuaded' the girl, seduced her. She had walked into it, seduced herself. Maybe seduction was always like that, though. Alexander and Knox agreed to arrest Wilson and level a minor indecency charge. If SCW made trouble, they'd just have to respond with a statement about the rule of law. Fight the fight.

Laura asked Alexander for a divorce. She was sorry to bring it up suddenly, but supposed it was always like that. Anyway, she didn't mean it aggressively, but she wanted to marry her new partner. Alexander consented of course, but this business made him think again about the oddness of the law. Their marriage had been over for some time, but still legally valid. A divorce would officially cancel their union, rendering it a thing of the past. In one sense – the one that mattered to Laura – it would be as if it had never happened. And yet in another, the marriage would always be part of who each of them was, indelibly. It made him think of criminal convictions: ideally at least, a convict serves his sentence and returns to society to start again. There was something of divine forgiveness in the idea. Divine forgetfulness. And yet that was an inhuman perspective, impossible for mortals to maintain. A convict might be forgiven by God and formally reconciled with society, but for all the rightness of treating him as an innocent man, or trying to, his crime would always be with him, part of him. He would know that, and to a greater or lesser extent, so would those around him. Marriage, love, were surely the same.

Alexander and Karen went for a meal that evening. She was in a better mood than him, though she soon cheered him up, and became quite amorous over coffee, to the extent that he blushed and shifted awkwardly away from her.

'Don't you want to kiss me?' she teased.

'I don't want to kiss you *here,*' he said.

'Where *do* you want to kiss me?' she demanded.

He smiled. She had walked into that one, and now blushed furiously as Alexander's little thought invaded her own mind. 'Let's go,' she whispered.

Karen was deep asleep when Alexander woke in the morning. He farted long and loud, as if purging his body of all the sins of the world. Do you think I've overdone the farting in this narrative, by the way? In fact, it had often occurred to Alexander that an alien observer might overlook the finer details of law enforcement and society in general, and regard him as a farting machine. Which is to say that he had felt that way himself sometimes, so it's not just my demonic indifference to properly human concerns. Lately, however, Karen had given Alexander a properly human perspective on farting. When he had been with Laura, Alexander would get out of bed and go to the bathroom to fart when he woke in the morning, before returning for any kind of conjugal discourse. Laura would certainly not have been amused by laddish pride in farting, and he couldn't have imagined any other way to excuse himself. When they had first slept together, he had risen like this in the spirit of self-conscious chivalry, imagining that as they grew closer and more intimate, it would seem unnecessary. Somehow it never did.

At first Alexander followed the same procedure with Karen, but then one morning she farted loudly herself. She was embarrassed about it, but only a little: 'Oops, here comes the morning chorus,' she said, and Alexander was delighted. She didn't in fact fart as much as Alexander, but when she did, Karen farted fulsomely and joyfully. It was not childish, but sexy, and not in a weird way. She farted with the same unaffected enthusiasm with which she stretched and yawned before rising. It was natural, but more than natural. It was almost spiritual.

Karen changed the way Alexander thought about his own body. He felt physically alive and well in a way he hadn't felt since he had played football. He was more aware of his body and its functions, not only as an encumbrance but as an expression of his being. He became fascinated by the relationship between his physical condition and his mental state – in both directions. Rather than just noting that he had a headache, he would think about how it was the result of a work problem, and conversely how after physical exertions he felt more powerful and able to take on other problems. He also noticed that his temperature rose when he was annoyed or under pressure. What had seemed metaphors were quite real. Once Karen asked him if his indigestion also was brought on by stress.

'No. Too much coffee,' he told her, shaking his head. He quite liked talking about himself with Karen: she seemed sufficiently interested that it didn't feel self-indulgent. 'You know, sometimes I think I can't be trusted to make the most basic decisions about what to eat and drink.'

She patted his stomach sympathetically.

'And sometimes I feel like I should be the supreme commander of the universe.'

They kissed.

Still, despite the relative success of their relationship so far, Alexander and Karen were still regularly misunderstanding and confounding one another, and it was mostly his fault. Early on he had explained that if he seemed ill-at-ease with Karen it was because he hadn't expected to get so far with her so fast. This seemed reasonable to Alexander, but somehow Karen felt it was unflattering. He certainly did seem ill-at-ease much of the time, though. When Karen was flirty or coquettish with him – her way of being nice; and she was *very* nice to him – he just got impatient. On one occasion, when she was weighing up whether she was free for a drink or was in fact planning to wash her hair, Alexander blurted: 'Make up your mind, woman.' Things came to a head one evening when Karen hinted that she would require some persuasion to stay the night.

'If you're looking for seduction, you've come to the wrong guy.'

'Where do you get these lines?' she said in exasperation. '*The Big Book of Things Never, Ever to Say to a Woman*?' That had made them both laugh, and dispelled the hostility between them.

He told her he loved her.

'I know,' she said.

He kissed her, supposing 'I know' was an alright response. After all, 'I love you too' is such a pat response it's almost cold, 'Yeah, yeah.' She might as well have said, 'Fuck you' as 'I love you too.'

But he also thought it would be nice if she would reciprocate freely within twenty-four hours, say. Find an opportunity to tell him that she loved him, preferably in a natural way, but actually an inarticulate declaration towards the deadline might be quite nice.

Karen blurted as Alexander was about to leave for work the next day, 'I love you!'

He nodded coolly. 'I know.'

Why does anyone do anything?

Alexander had been determined that Leanne would be part of his life, and now that he was with Karen, this meant Leanne was part of *their* life, since Alexander had neither the time nor the inclination for a third life beyond work and home. Karen recognised in Leanne part of what she loved about Alexander, and Leanne saw not the least part of what Alexander saw in Karen. The three got on well, then. When Leanne returned from a weekend whisky tour of the highlands with some friends from the music academy, and brought Alexander a bottle of something special, he suggested the three of them try it together.

Morgan was staying and had just gone to bed, but appeared as soon as the grown-ups had settled in the living room, and announced that she had spilled paint on her duvet, having carefully placed her watercolour set at the foot of her bed before getting in.

'Why did you do that?' Alexander asked, exasperated.

'Why does anyone do anything?' Morgan replied, throwing up her arms.

'Have you been watching *Seinfeld* again?' Alexander demanded. Leanne suppressed a smile; she had brought over a boxed set of videos to make a change from cartoons while she was minding Morgan. Everyone had got up to investigate the mess, but Karen told the others to sit back down, and went through to Morgan's room to sort it out.

Leanne took advantage of this to bring up something she'd been nervous about mentioning. The last time Leanne had looked after her, Morgan had broached the subject of her parents' separation. Leanne explained that Morgan had seemed to float the idea that it was her fault. But she didn't believe the child really believed it. It had been more like a performance, no doubt inspired by something she'd seen on TV: the child blames herself for her parents' divorce, and a trusted adult tells her that's nonsense. Cue reassuring hug and peace restored. Leanne had followed the script, but been more charmed than disturbed by Morgan's performance. She hoped Alexander would feel the same.

After pondering the matter for a moment, he did. He told Leanne he had seen something similar in interviewees, that 'performance,' an appeal to an imagined audience if not to the detective himself. An appeal to the imaginary viewers at home who would surely see the sense of the suspect's point, vindicate his righteous indignation – 'quite right, can't that stupid detective see?' The suspect's exaggerated consternation – perhaps, like Morgan's faux guilt, learned from TV – became a symbol, in the suspect's own mind, of wisdom, maturity, understanding. Alexander had never thought of this as childish before, but now he saw that it was similar to the way children and halfwits imitate the angry tutting of admired adults or authority figures, in the apparent hope that such tutting is the source of authority (sometimes it works).

He didn't like to think of Morgan this way, but she was only four, and if anything her grasp of the form was precocious. Childishness, after all, was appropriate enough in children: the point was to get past it, and that was where his interviewees had failed. Because whereas Leanne, *in loco parentis* (Alexander smiled at this thought), had been obliged to play along with Morgan, and had done so with love, Alexander stood in no such position to his interviewees. Their performances were worse than childish, because there was no parent figure to appeal to. Indeed they were a direct appeal against the only authority figure in the room.

There was more to Alexander's authority than his position as a senior policeman. It was his refusal to accept a suspect's performance of bad faith; not just his refusal to believe it, but his refusal to *have* it. It was his ability to stand and hold his gaze as a suspect flailed. His adultness in a world of children. And there was no cynicism in his steeliness. Alexander believed in the rule of law – if that short phrase will suffice to describe what it is that he fought for every day – in a way that might have been considered embarrassing had he raised it explicitly with other colleagues.

Few of Alexander's fellow officers were without a glimmer of idealism. At the very least, they were proud to be polis. But there was a bravado in that pride that galvanised their idealism against the world. It allowed the job to be a job, and lent its adherents to the worldly pragmatism of bureaucracy. In contrast, being a polis as Alexander understood it was not just about working cases as instructed, nor even upholding the law for its own sake. In the course of a working day, the ungalvanised Alexander was often accused of idealism, or being unrealistic. But while he had once or twice been labelled a dinosaur on account of his quaint beliefs, he sensed that his thinking belonged to the future rather than the past. The notion of law that he held dear – depending on a certain existential responsibility that was almost unimaginable in a universe of cults, psychic manipulation and other sinister influences – was not 'outmoded' as his superiors had argued. Rather it was a presentiment of a world to come. Alexander did not hold forth on such things at work, but they were in his bearing. The same quality that unnerved his childish suspects discomfited his career-minded colleagues.

Undoubtedly, though, it was Alexander's unworldly adultness that made him attractive to Karen, and not just because he exuded the reassuring sense of somebody who believes in something, anything. More profoundly it was because DS Smith was able to share his beliefs and thus to share Alexander's professional life as well as his personal life.

Karen returned from Morgan's room to report that all was well. She had replaced the duvet cover, and the paint would come out in the wash. Sensing the end of a previous conversation, Karen asked Leanne how her music was going. The young maestro shrugged, and repeated some of what she'd said before to Alexander. Creativity was a struggle, she said, not because she didn't have ideas, but because she didn't know what any of it was for. Karen was impressed to learn she'd had some of her compositions performed – having not really thought of her as a 'real' composer till now – but Leanne explained that she still felt the same. She felt she had been admitted into music as an institution in the same way she'd been admitted into music school: 'The whole structure feels artificial. Beyond my course, there's competitions, young composer projects, some of my classmates are doing a stupid reality TV thing even, but it's all so institutional. Sometimes I wish I believed in God. I wish I could believe there was some cosmic connection between the music I want to write and the world around me.'

'You wish you could write church music, like Bach?' Alexander said smiling.

'Yeah, Bach had it easy.'

After Leanne left, Alexander told Karen the girl gave him hope. Leanne was unquestionably a creature of *this* world, and yet she was something more. She was shaped by the world around her without being bound by it: she was serious about her freedom, and determined to live it fully. Doubtless it was his faith in Leanne as a harbinger of the future (as well as his lingering sexual jealousy) that had made Alexander so anxious about how she might have responded to the Svengali, but for obvious reasons he didn't mention this to Karen. Instead he joked that Leanne's ethnicity marked her out as a child of the future.

'What ethnicity?'

'Exactly!' Alexander explained that Leanne was multiply deracinated, first in that as an individual she was disembedded from her gypsy background, second in that the gypsy identity, like others, was increasingly dubious as a meaningful social grouping, and finally in that the gypsy identity is classically rootless anyway. And despite all that she seemed more at home in the world than anyone else he knew.

Karen was bemused by this foray into sociology, though she kind of saw Alexander's point. It was true, Alexander reflected later, that this thought had not been exactly right for Karen. Even leaving aside what he still considered the awkwardness surrounding his feelings about Leanne, it was too – what? – not exactly intellectual, but perhaps too theoretical. Alexander was given to theorising, and this was not a trait Karen shared. And neither did Leanne, again, even disregarding awkwardness. Steph? No. The only person with whom Alexander could imagine having a satisfactory discussion about this was the Devil himself.

Satan appeared now for the first time in weeks. And for the first time he appeared somewhere other than Alexander's flat, which was now much more of a home that it had been when the Desolate One had first visited, and perhaps less inviting for that even when Alexander was alone, which was still most of the time. But he was at work now, the last member of the unit still working at nearly midnight, and alone apart from night staff in other parts of the building. He offered Lucifer a glass of whisky, perhaps just to show off that he was indeed the sort of detective who kept a bottle in his desk drawer. The Devil did not say no.

Alexander took the opportunity to ask Satan about a report he was writing on the African twins who had accused their aunt of witchcraft. The case was now caught awkwardly between the registers of conventional abuse and the trauma of war.

'What is conventional abuse?' Satan wanted to know.

'When people hurt others just for badness,' Alexander told him. 'With no extenuating circumstances beyond human evil. Aren't you supposed to know something about that?'

'*Human* evil? No. What do I know about that? It's your area, surely.'

Alexander shrugged.

'You don't believe in evil, anyway,' the Wicked One continued. 'Do you?'

'Not really, no.' Alexander shrugged again. 'What does it mean? Selfishness, laziness, stupidity: these things I understand. But to hurt for the sake of it, that's not man's fallen nature; that's "fucked up," and it's not the same thing.'

'So you're going with trauma?'

Alexander shrugged a third time.

'You should give yourself a break,' Satan told him. 'You think too much.'

'It matters,' he insisted. 'There's an *appetite* for evil, and *that's* just old-fashioned human weakness. Sometimes I think it would be better to abolish the unit and just let cases take care of themselves untainted by this stuff. But you can't even ignore a problem if you don't acknowledge at least to yourself that it's there. And if I don't ignore it, no-one else will.' Alexander sipped his whisky and sighed. Here he was discussing his work with the Prince of Darkness as if he were a reliable if slightly jaded Enlightenment humanist. 'You must know a bit about witchcraft,' he said at last. 'Tell me something interesting.'

'I don't believe in witches,' the Devil said.

'They believe in you. And that, apparently, makes them a menace to society.'

Lucifer looked thoughtful for a moment. 'Witchcraft is all about secrets,' he said. 'Witches don't want to know why or how it works. "God knows why and the Devil knows how," they like to say. It's the way humans always think, as far as I can tell.'

Alexander got home at 2am and picked up his Bible, the same copy he had kept since school. He looked up the various passages describing Jesus calling the disciples, but was distracted by the part of the story that comes just before: Jesus in the wilderness resisting the persuasions of the Devil. Alexander's head reeled as he connected his knowledge of the scriptures with his personal acquaintance with the Desolate One. Never mind that Satan had been a spectator by the shore of Galilee – not long before he had been centre-stage with a speaking part in the Greatest Story Ever

Told, this creature who now appeared to Alexander just as he had appeared to Jesus Christ, and not to offer helpful advice. This *mythical* personification of Evil. What had seemed somehow normal, acceptable, for over a year, was suddenly terrifying. In the morning, Alexander made an appointment with the doctor. If he felt the same when he went into the surgery, he would tell, have himself referred to a psychiatrist.

Dr Ramzan was a young woman who looked about sixteen and wore a headscarf. Alexander wondered idly if Muslims believed in the Devil these days, but it was her youth that made him decide right away not to tell. It would have seemed irresponsible. He asked her about his stomach problems instead.

Despite his perspective-altering appreciation of the way Karen farted, Alexander still sometimes suspected that his own excessive flatulence was God's way of mocking his atheism, by reducing him to a beast. It was either that or something to do with drinking too much beer, but the latter sounded too much like something a doctor would say without much encouragement; he was not about to give the woman a slam-dunk diagnosis, so he lied in response to the inevitable question. He was 'practically teetotal.' Anyway, he did have another theory to suggest. Alexander's ill-fitting teeth made him an inefficient chewer, causing him to gulp his food rather than chewing it properly. This caused his indigestion, and the acid reflux that attacked his teeth during the night, making the whole problem worse.

'It's an elegant theory; I'll give you that,' said Dr Ramzan, suddenly seeming a bit older than sixteen. She suggested he see a dentist about his teeth. As for his gut troubles, she would have him tested for helicobacter pylori; failing that, it was probably 'irritable bowel syndrome' (she made air quote marks) and there wasn't honestly much she could do about that.

Alexander admired Dr Ramzan's candour: part of respect for science is recognition of its limits, after all. A witchdoctor would have sent him off with a concoction of some sort. He decided that psychiatry was probably not yet sophisticated enough to deal with his problem either, so he should probably just soldier on. He was determined to have it out with Satan next time, though, and establish once and for all what these visits were all about.

The opportunity came about a week later. Alexander went to a Rangers bar to watch a European away game, and found himself in a mild stupor after a painfully narrow defeat. The pub was still busy but quiet, even melancholy, after the frenzy of the game. A small ensemble of Orange bandsmen had played at halftime, and they were still drinking in one corner, a couple of them gently tapping their drumsticks on the table; a flutist played casually, almost conversationally. The Devil appeared. 'A half and a half before closing?' he suggested. Alexander nodded and went to the bar, returning with two half-pints and two whiskies.

'What do you want, then?' he asked the Devil.

'That's not a very friendly question. What do *you* want?'

'Forgive me if I seem unfriendly. But have you been visiting me just for the pleasure of my company?'

'Why else?'

'You don't want my soul or something? That's traditional, isn't it?'

'Can I have your soul?'

'No.'

'Well, that's that, then. I don't know why you brought it up.'

'The first time you visited me, you told me…'

'Yes, the girl. I'm glad you took my advice.'

'I didn't… Oh, well, I suppose it depends what you meant.'

'As always. I know I have a bad reputation, but it's not my intention to help you do bad things, or good things for that matter. Is it so hard to believe that I simply enjoy our talks? Sometimes I don't know who else I'd talk to.'

'I find your presence unsettling.'

The Unsettling One laughed and poured his whisky into his beer.

'What did you do that for?' Alexander asked.

'Why does anyone do anything?'

'Why did you rebel against God?'

'Buy me a smoked sausage supper and I'll tell you.'

They finished their drinks and went to the chip shop a few doors along from the pub. They ate as they walked towards Alexander's flat, and the former Prince of Heaven talked about his Fall. Alexander looked at Satan as probingly as he dared, wondering whether this was still a sore point. The Insolent One did not betray any emotion, though he did reveal that it had been no more than a knee injury sustained when he fell from Heaven that had robbed him of his once graceful bearing, transforming him from an angel to a beast. Alexander felt sympathy for the Devil on account of his own youthful cruciate ligament injury, which still gave him occasional gyp. Perhaps if you'd looked closely you'd have detected slight hobbles in the gaits of both figures ambling along the Paisley Road West with their suppers.

Why did Satan rebel? Why did *I* rebel? For the Hell of it. There is no other answer. Why does anyone do anything? It's a good question, not just for fallen angels. Why do men and women keep going? Why do good? Why do evil? What's the point of any of it? Never mind who made God. The Creation happens every day, and you make it happen: that queer but unmistakeable something out of nothing. And you can do it without thinking, because the world makes it easy just to follow a script. Or you can stop and ask yourself why, and how. And then what?

For his part, Lucifer went on the offensive. 'What was the last thing God did here on Earth? I'll tell you in case you've forgotten: he showed up. He made himself one of you. Ha! And I bet he had *no idea* how hard it would be. *No fucking idea!'* The Devil was genuinely angry now. 'Why did Christ perform miracles? Was that really the most productive thing for a Messiah to be doing?

Of course not. Signs and wonders, my Satanic arse: it was make-work. *He didn't know what else to do.* He didn't know what it means to be a Messiah. So he walked about telling stories and doing stupid stunts. Walking on water? More like treading water.'

'Until he was crucified. He died for our… my sins.'

'You think that was *his* idea? Even when he saw it coming there was no way out. It would have been embarrassing. Martyrdom, redemption, "penal substitution"? Fuck off! …And *you* don't believe it anyway!'

'*You* brought it up.'

'It's been getting to me for two thousand years.'

'Fair enough. But it's not the life of Christ himself that matters anyway, is it? But the meaning that's layered onto it: Paul's epistles, the church, art even. And anyway, we make our own stories now.'

'And are you satisfied with that? Stories?'

'No. I suppose not… That was a bad choice of words. It's just how we tend to think of things at the moment. But the Christian story is nothing special if it's not actually, historically true; I realise that. And no story means anything if it's just culture, just entertainment.'

'So what else is there?' They had reached Alexander's tenement, and hovered outside.

'Real life?' ventured Alexander.

'Maybe you're right,' the Devil said. He nodded farewell and wandered off. He would not trouble Alexander again.

Our thing

Men are only powerless when they declare themselves to be so.

Falling out of a plane without the aid of a parachute is one of those things people mistakenly associate with certain death. In fact, if the original altitude is not excessive, if conditions are favorable and one's landing both fortuitous and well-executed, it is possible to survive such a fall with only minor injuries. Siegfried had an inkling of this as he tumbled through the troposphere, but his overall assessment was that things were not going well. 'So this is it,' he thought to himself, and was still reflective enough to be disappointed by the banality of the observation. He thought of me instead, and I told him to make more of an effort to survive, so he struggled to assume the position taken by skydivers – arms and legs extended with the joints bent – and finally settled into it as the Earth seemed to accelerate towards him. Suddenly he landed on a grassy hillside, his fall happily transforming into a fast roll before he finally came to a stop in a ditch, where his head glanced off a rock, granting Nature a token blood sacrifice. But he had made it. He stood up, composed himself as best he could, and limped out of the ditch towards a road that appeared in the distance.

Siegfried's brush with death was both utterly surreal and rather too real. A reminder that brute reality can defy the artificial logic of our lives. Things can happen for no reason, or no reason that has anything to do with us. Siegfried's abduction by unknown parties, and subsequent ejection from the plane, were not accidents, but they had a strangely unreal, even ridiculous, quality. These were things that were *done to* Siegfried for obscure reasons rather than things he *did* for reasons of his own, and thus they threatened to make a mockery of his self-authorship.

That Siegfried did survive and even in time triumph over his assailants – that's a whole other story – seemed to me in retrospect to have been inevitable, but I knew that this was a false impression, a comforting story to tell myself. In reality, even the most heroic of us can be sunk by stupid misfortune, and the unlikelihood of being struck by lightning is no consolation when it happens. It is a sickening defeat for our sense of ourselves as autonomous beings in control of our lives. Jimmy once said something similar about being arrested. He described the horrible, creeping realization that no amount of guile or even brute force can get you out of this: you are literally in the grip of the police. The time you take for granted in normal life – to think, to negotiate – is not granted. I suppose it's the same as being violently attacked or raped. You can tell yourself it won't happen, it can't happen, it isn't happening, but it is happening *now*.

Somewhere between sheer individual self-mastery and the slings and arrows of *outrageous* fortune is, or ought to be, real life. That is, the human world of possibilities and constraints that *make sense* because even if we are not individually responsible for them, we are in some sense connected to them, complicit in them. There ought to be a big difference between being mugged and being arrested, between being struck by lightning and thrown from a plane. But that depends how connected you are to the law, to other people, how complicit you are in how society as a whole functions. And anyway, an ideal society would abolish random violence and control lightning too. Isn't the point of society to diminish contingency, or at least to render it human? To make us all, collectively if not individually, the authors of our own destiny?

While Siegfried was having his adventure, I was visiting Jeanie's new place to catch up some more. Jeanie revealed that she was now writing a history of the New York Yankees. Thanks to an insightful contact at the magazine she wrote for, she had been commissioned by an independent publisher with the idea of producing a book of general interest rather than something just for either baseball fans or cultural historians. The premise was that sports history is one of the few connections people have with history in the absence of more political histories of particular communities or social movements.

This seemed very true to me, or, at least, whether or not sports clubs connected people with history, it seemed to me that very little else did. Every day I studiously read the *New York Times*, but often I wondered why I needed to know this stuff. Reading about the world somehow made me feel less rather than more connected to it. American politics always left me cold, so I preferred the international news, about battles and skirmishes here and there, diplomatic initiatives and stand-offs; there was always a crisis somewhere. Sometimes I read the business news, and became idly fascinated with 'international capital flows,' which always seemed terribly important, but Siegfried made a face whenever I tried to talk to him about that stuff and I couldn't really blame him.

I did sort of adopt a company called Mithras Industries, because it had a good story: it had been founded by a young Indian who'd started out as a scrap dealer in Mumbai and then bought factories in Russia and made it really big. Now he was trying to buy a big American steel company and it was all very controversial, first because some people considered him no better than a gangster, and then because a Christian lobby group said he was in league with the Devil, and of course everybody made fun of that, at least everybody respectable, but it added a certain glamor to the whole story. Still, it didn't feel like *any more* than a story.

I was conscious, of course, that my sense of being uninvolved in the world – a mere spectator – may have been a reflection of my true position. I was still outside society, as it were, having no job or recognized position. But it seemed to me that nobody could possibly *inhabit* the world of the *New York Times*, or indeed of any other newspaper or TV show, except perhaps in a narrow professional sense. It was too vast and too superficial. At the same time, my immediate life, my life with Siegfried and the others close to us, felt more and more real and vital in a way that the impersonal worlds of politics and business did not.

When Siegfried returned from his unworldly tumble, we spent several hours together without talking much. Then we got round to discussing our wedding party at last, and remembered those others close to us. Siegfried asked what the news was. I announced that it looked like Jeanie and Jimmy might be back together. He smiled and seemed pleased, but then I realized he had probably meant news about Professor Cabrera Hernandez: the university administration had been meeting to discuss his case while Siegfried was away. I told Siegfried that Ernest had called to report that the administration had agreed with the professor that he would leave with the university's blessing to take up an offer to head a new center being established by a think tank with ties to the university. It was a face-saving compromise; the offer had been engineered for the purpose, but it suited Paolo. The center would allow him to pursue a long-standing interest in the relationship between law and religion. As part of the deal, he also got to keep his university-owned apartment for five more years. And he would make no phony apology.

Ernest, meanwhile, had become something of a figure on campus. His op-ed had been widely read and cited, he had taken part in student radio and TV discussions and been invited to speak at a public debate on the whole business of campus speech codes. I was actually quite jealous of Ernest, who while securely ensconced in university life was beginning to find a way to be himself in the wider world, by making vital connections of his own, not least with and through Siegfried and co. You see, it isn't that 'real life' means only private life or personal relationships, that the wider world is too complex to be real. It's very real in the brute sense that we are all prey to stock-market crashes and the like. But it is possible to be more than a victim, or indeed a beneficiary, of that world.

In his own rather prosaic way, Ernest was not only writing his own life story, but taking responsibility for something greater. Inspired by Siegfried's insane example, he was finally getting a grip on reality. And his academic work now shed light on this very idea. He was now writing a book about how the law reflected and shaped changing ideas about individual responsibility and agency, taking as a case study some new developments in Scotland.

Ernest discussed his dissertation with John Paul, whose brother was a policeman in Scotland, and who had some good second-hand stories. For his part, John Paul had found temporary work as a gopher on a documentary film about roaches in New York restaurants, but was keen to make progress with his own film, and finally confronted Siegfried shortly after the plane thing. For the first time he told Siegfried how angry he'd been about his disappearance, and Siegfried conceded that he should have said something, but just hadn't known what to say. 'So do you know what to say *now*?' John Paul demanded. 'Can you tell me what the fuck my film is about?'

Siegfried sat in Professor Cabrera-Hernandez's apartment, with an impressive view of Manhattan in the background (the view he had promised himself in Glasgow). He smoked slowly and spoke directly into the camera, his gaze defying documentary convention, and seeming to penetrate straight through to the viewer's eye. He described his fall from the plane, not the backstory but just the experience itself, how he had felt, what it had meant. He had thought hard about this, and spoke carefully. Siegfried disdained the idea that one should speak one's mind, or 'speak as I find,' as he later said affecting a Yorkshire accent (or so he assured me). 'I speak as I want others to find,' he said. 'That's the point of speaking.' This was not meant cynically. He simply insisted on maintaining distance between his own thoughts and the words he meant for others.

This was no less true with his friends and even with me, though there was much more that could be taken for granted with us, which meant it was easier to talk sense. In any case, the blurted impressions other people divulged were not authentic reflections of reality, but merely undigested thoughts. It was a kind of solipsism to talk that way, something people like us had to get past.

When Siegfried finished talking to the camera, John Paul was already excited about reproducing the event visually. Maybe he would use animation, he suggested: a cartoon Siegfried being hurled towards the Earth. It would be cut with Siegfried's narration, and perhaps set to the dramatic final movement of Mahler's first symphony. This was a start.

It transpired that John Paul had dropped out of a documentary filmmaking course, having excelled at the technical aspects, but been frustrated by the conventionality of the supposedly creative side of the course. John Paul was pleased with Siegfried's direct register, as he'd gotten sick of being told 'show, don't tell': he said it was epistemologically naïve and ultimately mendacious, which sounded great in his strong Glasgow accent. 'There's another irritating slogan,' he went on: '"speak truth to power." What bullshit. Why should I speak truth to… and what is this "speak truth" crap anyway? Who *talks* like that? But why tell anything to people in power? Not my job. My film is for people like us.' People like us. That's who the film was for, and that's what the film would be about.

Siegfried was heartened by this, having felt uncomfortable about being the 'hero' of John Paul's film. He liked the idea that the audience would not be mere spectators, judging him according to his entertainment value, or even his ability to inspire. He had stuff to say to people who wanted to hear it, people who would make a connection with their own lives. People who had enough faith in themselves to give Siegfried the benefit of the doubt. People with his kind of ambition. The rest could make their own entertainment.

In rejecting the assumptions and constraints of the social world in which he had found himself in Glasgow, Siegfried had not abandoned the idea of society altogether. Rather he had dared himself to make himself accountable in terms that made sense to him, not to the whole world – who does that? – but to anyone who would get it. Unlike Raskolnikov's, Siegfried's new life had not been and would not be given to him, and nor was it a case of simply making it for himself. But Siegfried at last now found himself somewhere that felt like home.

Along with Jimmy, Siegfried was now pursuing a new idea, a 'consultancy for people who can't go to consultants,' to offer advice and encouragement to others with ideas beyond their station in life. The consultancy was proving an intriguing enterprise, and a natural extension of the sorts of thing Siegfried and Jimmy were already doing. Paolo asked them to help a former student who had immigration problems, and they were working on a system that would help other illegals to settle in the US. This was pro bono, though they figured it wouldn't do any harm to have hard-working multitudes owe them a favor.

That turned out to be the way of things. Money was not urgent since both men still had small hoards from their previous lives, but in any case they found that in the course of things there were opportunities for bounty, and so they were able to operate on an informal rather than strictly business model. For example, Jimmy gave advice on dealing with the mob to a construction firm in which Graziani (of all people) had a private interest, and he soon figured out ways to help them with the city authorities too, for an occasional fee. And when Sokolov introduced the consultants to a British entrepreneur and card player who had just lost a fortune trying to market beads as pure commodities whose only function was to have been their desirability, Siegfried convinced him to write a book about the experience. Then he helped him to conceptualize it and wrote some draft chapters, taking an option on any film adaptation as payment.

Jimmy and Siegfried were now talking to Amy Wong about involving her in the consultancy, making use of her contacts and imagination, and giving her a chance to act in the world. The three met to firm up the arrangement and realized they needed someone to coordinate and organize their work. Someone to lift the whole enterprise beyond the level of individual hustling. If Siegfried had learned anything, it was that it is harder for an individual to make a decision, to make up his mind, alone. Because an individual is unfocused, many-minded. Only organization with others creates the singlemindedness in individuals that really makes a difference in the world. And they wanted someone to help make that happen. Someone who would get it. So once again, this was where I came in, not as an adventurous schoolgirl, but a woman of the world. At last I had a job. But that too is a whole other story.

To celebrate this, and belatedly our wedding, a gang of us went to a concert at the Lincoln Center, the world premiere of an unconventional oratorio by the young Scottish composer Leanne McGlone. It was wonderful, and filled us all with a renewed sense of possibility and excitement. When the piece was over, the audience erupted in applause, and a little blonde girl in the front row turned around in shock. Uncharacteristically, I could not help winking at her. After the adulation had died down the musicians and singers left the stage and a piano was put in place. McGlone, who had been conducting, reappeared and performed a selection of preludes and fugues by JS Bach. It was electrifying. Though I had heard the pieces before I had never seen them performed, and certainly not like this. McGlone brought an elegance, a grace, that I had never seen, and yet which I experienced as an extension of myself.

The next day Siegfried and I went over to New Jersey for a kind of honeymoon. And as we sat on a concrete beach on the Hudson, talking gently and enjoying the last of the sun, Siegfried lit a cigar and took a moment to look across the river at New York. *His* city, *our* city, populated by our people in their millions. And cut.

So that's it. End of story. Roll credits. 'Brown Eyed Girl.' Only this time it isn't just me left with a promise to fulfill, a story to complete. Our thing is not just our thing, but *our* thing, yours too. You are more than just my imaginary friend after all. You inhabit the real world, or could do. So look at it another way. End of Prologue. To be continued. Unresolved chord? The world is yours.

Epilogue

Tell me, when did you first realise you were different, special? And what spurious form did that take in your mind? An ethnic quirk, a talent or disability? A sexual proclivity, a distaste for this or that social norm? Mistaken parentage, extra-terrestrial origins, a mission from God? How *did* you account for your failure to fit in? And when did you start to doubt whether that was it at all? To sense that something more fundamental was amiss. Do you ever find yourself behaving in ways you don't like for reasons you don't understand? Do you have a pulse?

Are you a happy person? I don't care. I envy you your painful corporeality, your vexed subjectivity, your fucking reality. But there is more to the last than the sum of the first two, and I'm not interested in boring, generic humanity: it's this particular story, after all, that interests me. There is, after all, something special about it.

Yes, as you probably guessed, the little girl Koshka winked at was none other than Morgan Alexander. Her father took Karen and Morgan to witness Leanne's debut in New York. And was Adele McGlone there too, to see her little sister's moment of triumph? I don't know, but I'd like to think so. And maybe she found Siegfried too, and joined the gang. She could be a love interest for John Paul. Or even Ernest – there's a thought! But Alexander didn't bump into Siegfried or any of the others in New York. He did later have a brief correspondence with Ernest, in fact, about the cult legislation and the work of the unit. He enjoyed the opportunity to discuss it with a legal scholar, but neither he nor Ernest realised their other connection, and Alexander never did hear about the strange New York 'consultancy' doing interesting things on the fringes of respectable society. Maybe one day he'll see John Paul's film and understand everything.

And Alexander never did find that first child-killer. And nor did he win his battle with Scottish CultWatch. Last I heard that was still raging, but it's only a small part of a bigger war whose sides are ill-defined and mutually confused. But Alexander went on working cases and solving crimes: holding people to account. His daughter was justly proud of him. And Morgan herself – was she a special child? Not like that, no. No Messiah, no Golden Child. Which is to say she was free, to make her own story, to negotiate her own reality.

The one unequivocal success story I have for you is Leanne's. Under the unconscious tutorship (though not quite following the example) of Alexander, she had learned that commitments and obligations can give shape to a life, allowing it to fit imperfectly but effectively into the space one has to live it in. Leanne's was a disciplined creativity that involved others around her as well as her own pulsing being. Indeed, those others looked to her for inspiration. Still, it was only when a professor referred to the group around her as Leanne's 'coterie' that she realised it existed. That was an odd moment. And strangely not. Her influence over her friends was a natural consequence of their shared vocation. They looked to Leanne because she had found a way to work, and a style of composition of her own. And the better ones learned from her and developed ideas of their own as well as borrowing hers. More general than that, what is there to learn or to teach?

Before the concert in New York, Leanne had told Morgan about how she'd got interested in music, and what it meant to her. She explained that when she'd been younger, music had made her very aware of physical discomfort. Anticipating a particularly beautiful passage, she would wriggle frantically to make herself comfortable, making last-minute efforts to suppress a lingering itch, or adjusting her clothes to eliminate a troublesome tug or crease. The instinct was to render herself more susceptible to spiritual movement by freeing herself from her physicality. It didn't work. Finally she realised that the music itself did the work, and to listen attentively was to let the music take over rather than worrying about one's own reception.

In New York, Leanne played with such energy that beads of sweat formed on her brow and dropped onto the keyboard. Splash, splash. And she smiled and breathed deeply and played on.

Zero Books

CULTURE, SOCIETY & POLITICS

Contemporary culture has eliminated the concept and public figure of the intellectual. A cretinous anti-intellectualism presides, cheer-led by hacks in the pay of multinational corporations who reassure their bored readers that there is no need to rouse themselves from their stupor. Zer0 Books knows that another kind of discourse – intellectual without being academic, popular without being populist – is not only possible: it is already flourishing. Zer0 is convinced that in the unthinking, blandly consensual culture in which we live, critical and engaged theoretical reflection is more important than ever before. If you have enjoyed this book, why not tell other readers by posting a review on your preferred book site. Recent bestsellers from Zero Books are:

In the Dust of This Planet
Horror of Philosophy vol. 1
Eugene Thacker
In the first of a series of three books on the Horror of Philosophy, *In the Dust of This Planet* offers the genre of horror as a way of thinking about the unthinkable.
Paperback: 978-1-84694-676-9 ebook: 978-1-78099-010-1

Capitalist Realism
Is there no alternative?
Mark Fisher
An analysis of the ways in which capitalism has presented itself as the only realistic political-economic system.
Paperback: 978-1-84694-317-1 ebook: 978-1-78099-734-6

Rebel Rebel

Chris O'Leary

David Bowie: every single song. Everything you want to know, everything you didn't know.

Paperback: 978-1-78099-244-0 ebook: 978-1-78099-713-1

Cartographies of the Absolute

Alberto Toscano, Jeff Kinkle

An aesthetics of the economy for the twenty-first century.

Paperback: 978-1-78099-275-4 ebook: 978-1-78279-973-3

Malign Velocities

Accelerationism and Capitalism

Benjamin Noys

Long listed for the Bread and Roses Prize 2015, *Malign Velocities* argues against the need for speed, tracking acceleration as the symptom of the on-going crises of capitalism.

Paperback: 978-1-78279-300-7 ebook: 978-1-78279-299-4

Meat Market

Female flesh under Capitalism

Laurie Penny

A feminist dissection of women's bodies as the fleshy fulcrum of capitalist cannibalism, whereby women are both consumers and consumed.

Paperback: 978-1-84694-521-2 ebook: 978-1-84694-782-7

Poor but Sexy

Culture Clashes in Europe East and West

Agata Pyzik

How the East stayed East and the West stayed West.

Paperback: 978-1-78099-394-2 ebook: 978-1-78099-395-9

Romeo and Juliet in Palestine

Teaching Under Occupation

Tom Sperlinger

Life in the West Bank, the nature of pedagogy and the role of a university under occupation.

Paperback: 978-1-78279-637-4 ebook: 978-1-78279-636-7

Sweetening the Pill

or How we Got Hooked on Hormonal Birth Control

Holly Grigg-Spall

Has contraception liberated or oppressed women? *Sweetening the Pill* breaks the silence on the dark side of hormonal contraception.

Paperback: 978-1-78099-607-3 ebook: 978-1-78099-608-0

Why Are We The Good Guys?

Reclaiming your Mind from the Delusions of Propaganda

David Cromwell

A provocative challenge to the standard ideology that Western power is a benevolent force in the world.

Paperback: 978-1-78099-365-2 ebook: 978-1-78099-366-9

Readers of ebooks can buy or view any of these bestsellers by clicking on the live link in the title. Most titles are published in paperback and as an ebook. Paperbacks are available in traditional bookshops. Both print and ebook formats are available online.

Find more titles and sign up to our readers' newsletter at http://www.johnhuntpublishing.com/culture-and-politics. Follow us on Facebook at https://www.facebook.com/ZeroBooks and Twitter at https://twitter.com/Zer0Books.